LOOKING FOR LEO

J.A. BAKER

Copyright © 2021 J.A. Baker

The right of J.A. Baker to be identified as the Author of the Work has been asserted by her in accordance to the Copyright, Designs and Patents Act 1988.

First published in 2021 by Bloodhound Books

Apart from any use permitted under UK copyright law, this publication may only be reproduced, stored, or transmitted, in any form, or by any means, with prior permission in writing of the publisher or, in the case of reprographic production, in accordance with the terms of licences issued by the Copyright Licensing Agency.

All characters in this publication are fictitious and any resemblance to real persons, living or dead, is purely coincidental.

www.bloodhoundbooks.com

Print ISBN 978-1-913942-19-9

ALSO BY J.A. BAKER

Undercurrent

The Cleansing

The Retreat

The Other Mother

Finding Eva

The Uninvited

The Woman at Number 19

The Girl I Used To Be

In The Dying Minutes

To Laurie and Patrick.
My wonderful, beautiful boys.

Love all. Trust a few.
William Shakespeare

1

NOW

They cut a sorry sight, the two figures, as they stumble down the road, their shadowy outlines incongruous against the backdrop of the sinking sun; one small silhouette, one larger person, bent almost double, clutching hands as they attempt to break into a run, only to falter and fall by the roadside, landing in an ungainly heap together. Their cries fill the air, drowning out the birdsong from the nearby treetops and hedgerows.

A car approaches, the roar of its engine growing closer. It rounds the bend, metal and sunlight colliding in a sudden eye-watering flash. The couple stand up, cry out, wave their arms frantically. The vehicle drives past them then slows down, grinding to a sudden halt, the gravelly sound of rubber against tarmac filling the silence. It begins to reverse, the high-pitched whine of the engine a howling screech.

The driver's door opens, a man steps out, his expression pained and bewildered, turning soon to panic as he stares first at the child then back at the person huddled by their side.

'Please,' the adult says, holding their head, blood oozing

through their trembling fingers. 'Please help us. You have to do something.'

The child begins to cry; an ear-splitting howl that could shatter glass. The adult tries to comfort the youngster but is too unsteady, too broken and damaged to console them properly. Tears mingle with snot as they sob uncontrollably.

'I'll help you,' the man says as he opens the passenger door and pushes the child inside. Before the bleeding adult can protest, the man grabs their arm and pushes them against the back door of the car. 'I know who you are. I fucking know you and I know what you did.'

In a flurry of terror and blind panic, the adult cries out as they are bundled into the back seat. They hear the sharp slam of the door and the click of the lock, realisation dawning that they are trapped. They pull at the handle, cry out, claw at the seat as the driver climbs back in and starts the engine, pulling off at speed.

The child is suddenly silent, slumped in their seat, limbs frozen, face ashen, stricken with terror.

'You,' the driver says, staring through the rear-view mirror to the person behind them. 'It's you. Don't move and don't speak.' His voice is low, laced with menace and intent. The adult begins to object, their shouts reverberating around the confined space only to be met with a hand that connects with them as the driver swings around, fist clenched, and smashes it into their face, silencing them before turning back to grip the steering wheel.

'I said, don't speak, okay? Don't say a single word. I know exactly who you are. I've heard about this on the television, read about it in the paper. You're a fucking psychopath. People like you should be hanged. You're nothing but scum.'

Momentarily dazed, the bleeding adult slumps back into the seat, more blood pumping through their fingers, saturating their clothes; sticky warm blood oozing out of the wound in great waves, coating their skin, their clothes, the upholstery of the vehicle.

'I hope they arrest you,' the driver says, the words loaded with vitriol and venom as he spits them out and stares in the rear-view mirror, 'and throw away the fucking key.'

2

BEFORE

The likeness is uncanny. It catches me off guard. His face sends me into a near swoon as he steps away from the heaving throng, his features suddenly coming into sharp focus, hitting me in my solar plexus and turning my blood to sand. Despite the rare sweep of heat from the late afternoon sun, I feel a chill on my flesh as a shard of ice penetrates me, digging into my bones and rippling over my skin. The hairs on the back of my neck stand to attention. My scalp tightens and prickles. As hard as I try to look away, my eyes are drawn to him; to the shape of his face, to his gait, to the sound of his laughter as it sails through the late afternoon air like the delicate tinkling of fine china. Everything about him resonates with me. I can hardly breathe, oxygen seeping out of my lungs in short erratic bursts. He is here. After all this time, he is here. So many years of emptiness and yearning coupled with an acute sense of loss, and now I have found him.

By the time the crowd has cleared and almost everyone has departed for home, I feel as if my world has shrunk to the size of a pinhole. My head pounds, my throat is dry. The most basic of bodily functions – breathing, blinking – feel laboured and onerous.

I continue to watch as a small car pulls up and an exasperated woman leaps out and runs over to the boy, leaning down and speaking to him. Her face is flushed as she grabs at his schoolbag, holding it tightly while she ushers him back towards the car. He is the last child to be picked up. After the 3 o'clock pandemonium as the school gates opened and a small army of children spilled out, the road is now deserted. He is the last boy standing.

Trying to regulate my breathing and put my thoughts in order, I slip the key into the ignition of my car and start the engine. Using an inordinate amount of strength and focus, I am able to drive home, concentrating on staying the right side of the white line and keeping within the speed limit. Skills that had become reflexes seem to require a whole new level of attention as I remain alert and rigid, my eyes glued to the road, every nerve ending in my body screaming, every sinew stretched and taut with agitation and excitement. An intoxicating combination of terror and trepidation pulses through my veins.

I take a deep breath, tell myself to calm down, but it's pointless. Everything feels like such an effort. My mind is in a spin as I picture his face – my boy's face – and think about his voice, the soft rush of his breath as he leans in to give me a kiss goodnight. Everything about him was as familiar to me as my own features. It's him. There's no doubt about it. It's my boy.

Trees, buildings, pedestrians, they are all a smear in my peripheral vision as I sail past them, eyes fixed ahead. Nobody else matters anymore. Nobody and nothing is important. They are meaningless now that I have seen him, now that I've been near him and sensed how lost he is, how abandoned he feels. He needs me. We need each other.

We are meant to be together.

Once home, I slam the door behind me, close the curtains and curl up on the sofa where I remain for the rest of the evening, tears blinding me as I fight off the memories, those wicked memories of what I lost. Those wicked memories that remind me of how I was left on my own. But not for much longer. I have a chance to make everything better, to go back to how things used to be before I lost him. Before I lost everything that ever mattered to me.

I sleep fitfully, waking at regular intervals, my skin hot and cold simultaneously. The following day, I arise and dress, choosing my outfit with care and precision, knowing that I'm ready for this. I know what it is that I must do. My mind is made up. I'm ready for him.

3

THE ABDUCTOR

A bubble of air catches in my throat, my chest contracts. The trapped oxygen concertinas, making me wheeze as I spot him again, a solitary figure, small and helpless in contrast to the milieu of school with its swathe of dark brickwork and ugly green spiked gates. Once again, he is standing unaccompanied. Another late pick-up. Abandoned once more and left to fend for himself.

I take my chance and step out of my car, the squeak of my training shoes on the pavement a thunderous roar in my ears as I approach him and give him a warm smile. He is truly alone. Everybody has gone, disappeared, leaving just the two of us. No teachers waiting around to watch over him, no other parents or pupils. Just the two of us. Me and my boy and the soft whispering of the wind as it passes through the treetops, a reassuring susurration as I walk towards him and lean down to speak. 'Hi,' I say as casually as I can. 'How are you doing?'

He eyes me cautiously, a furrow wrinkling his small brow as he gives me a small courteous nod.

'Your mum asked me to come along and see if you're okay. She's been held up again.'

I see his shoulders sink a little then feel relieved as he lets out a sigh and straightens up, narrowing his eyes while surreptitiously assessing me. He's wary. That's as it should be. Such a good boy. Such a careful intelligent boy. Then a smile from him, as he grasps my words. 'Is she stuck at work again?'

'I'm afraid she is.' I suddenly realise I don't even know his name. Not his everyday name, the one she gave him, his so-called mother. I need to know it if I am to make a connection with him. I glance down at his bag and reach out to take it. Without missing a beat, he holds it up for me. A small white piece of card is slotted into a plastic pocket bearing his name and class. I glance at it furtively then afford him a quickly friendly wink.

'Well, Leo,' I say casually, 'she asked me to pick you up and said that she's going to come and collect you as soon as she can get away.' I keep my voice light, a sing-song timbre to it as I give him a broad smile, making sure my eyes crease at the corner to signify sincerity. I have to get this right. Failing isn't an option.

He brightens, a sudden recognition striking him. 'You must be the person she talked about. She said she was going to get some help to look after me. A childminder or somebody like that. She even mentioned getting somebody from the youth club to help out.'

My heart soars, a comforting rhythmic thump beneath my breastbone. 'Yup, that's me. I'm the new helper. My car is just over there.' I point at my vehicle, the one I keep garaged up and use only on special occasions. I'm hoping it will tempt him, appeal to his boyish nature. It's my special weapon, my treasured prize. I use it rarely and now it's about to serve me well. Better than I ever hoped.

His eyes widen as he spots it. 'A two-seater Mazda? That's your car?' He lets out a small giggle and covers his mouth with his hand. I stare at his fingers, at those long slim perfectly shaped nails and am overwhelmed with a desire to pick him up and hold him close, to feel the weight of him, the solidity of his body as it presses against mine. It's been so long. Too long. I can barely breathe.

I place his bag under my arm and walk towards the road where I am parked, praying he follows me without question. Like a dream, he breaks into a run to keep up, his grin so wide I want to dance and clap my hands with joy. It worked. I still have the ability to climb inside the heads of children, to know what stokes their interests and makes them tick. Already, we have a connection, a tie that binds us together. Unadulterated bliss blooms within me.

'Right,' I say a little too sharply, aware that time is against us. Aware that his mother could turn up any second and steal my moment, this tenuous link to my past, to all I hold dear. She could take it all, the only thing I have ever wanted, snatched away from me in a heartbeat. 'Hop in, Leo.' I hold up my mobile and give him a warm grin. 'Once we get going, I'll ring your mum, let her know I've got you and that she can pop round mine once she's out of work.'

He hesitates, his face impassive, his limbs locked rigid in a stance of uncertainty.

'Oh, that's yours as well.' I say nonchalantly as I point to a bottle of Coca-Cola in the centre console. I pretend I haven't seen his reticence and let out a silent breath of relief when I see him relax, his eyes lighting up with boyish delight. 'A special treat for you.'

Without hesitation, he slips into the passenger seat and grabs at the bottle, holding it aloft and staring at it as if it is made of solid gold. 'This is ace,' he says as he pulls on his seat belt. 'Mum doesn't let me have Coke. She always says it'll rot my teeth.'

'Ah well, she asked me to give it to you as an apology for being late and not introducing me to you properly.'

He is nodding now. I can see him out of the corner of my eye. I can see his smile, sense his easiness in my presence. Our relationship is already growing, strengthening, becoming stronger with every word and action that passes between us. I'm trying really hard here and it seems to be working. 'Drink up,' I say encouragingly.

'In your car?' His is suddenly cagey, a distinct uneasiness in his voice.

'Why not?' I swing out of the narrow side street and onto the main road. 'I trust you to not spill it all over the seat. And if you do, then so what? I clean it up afterwards. No big deal.'

He waits a second and I hold my breath, praying he isn't so fastidious that he refuses, then relax, warm air passing through my pursed lips as he twists the lid and takes a long greedy glug of the fizzy liquid, suppressing a sudden burp by holding his fist over his mouth.

'May as well drink it all,' I say, forced conviviality in my words that he thankfully doesn't seem to pick up on. 'There's plenty more where that came from.'

I grip the steering wheel tightly and sink down in the seat, my muscles unknotting as in my peripheral vision, I watch him drain every last drop. Relief floods through me, waves of it slipping over my cool skin, warming me through. I put my foot down and take him home.

It doesn't take too long for the effects to kick in. The bottle hangs limply in his hand as I pull up on the driveway and press the remote on my key fob to open the garage door. My temper begins to unravel, my heart thudding in my chest while I count the seconds; the interminably long seconds that it takes for the door to open fully. How slowly everything seems to move when time is of the essence.

Only when we are finally inside the garage, our bodies hidden in the gloom, do I turn and take a good look at him, at the soft line of his jaw, the feathery cut of his blond hair and the slow droop of his eyelids after drinking the Cola that I laced with sleeping tablets.

His mouth drops a little, his tiny tongue lolling to one side. I lean over, touch his jaw and close it with my knuckle then smooth down his hair, thinking how fortunate I am to have this boy with me. I can hardly believe it's happened. And yet it has.

Leo. Little Leo. He is here. I've done it. I've got him. But not Leo. Not anymore. He is Timothy. My Timothy. I've finally got him back. My little Timmy is here after all these years. Back home where he belongs.

4

EMILY

S tanding close by his bed and watching him as he sleeps has become her guilty pleasure. From the slightly downward turn of his mouth to his dark fluttering lashes, everything about him makes her glad to be alive, sending a flush of adoration through her, gliding beneath her skin and warming her body through to its very core.

She is not usually an overly tactile person nor is she the type of gushy woman who likes nothing better than to talk about her children to others, insisting they are riding high above everybody else's offspring with their special talents and abilities, but after listening to the news over the last couple of days, seeing her young son tucked up in his bed, knowing he is warm and safe, she is unable to stop herself. Just standing here gazing at him sends a ripple of delight through her veins. Not delight. That's the wrong word. Relief is more fitting. She is relieved to have him here, in their house, where she can take care of him and know that he is happy and free from harm.

The world, for all its positives and beauty, can also be a cruel violent place, proven by the recent news that has infiltrated every home. She is torn between being repulsed by the coverage of the missing boy and feeling compelled to watch it over and over, gleaning what she can from every new piece of information, filtering out the dross and storing the important stuff, keeping it in her mind so she can apply it to her life and keep her son safe. She has taken to watching every repeat of the reports until she is unable to think straight and is able to replicate the news correspondents' script off by heart.

She slips out of the room, leaving the door slightly ajar. A crack of light spills onto the carpet from the landing, highlighting the small mound under the bed sheets that is Joel's body. His hair is mussed up, his skin like porcelain, smooth and unblemished. She thanks whichever God may be listening for gifting her this boy, this wonderful clever human being who never fails to bring her joy even when he is tired and grumpy and backchats and refuses to do his homework. Even then, she is eternally grateful that he is hers and hers alone.

She pads down the stairs, careful to avoid the creak of the third step which is as familiar to her as her own skin. She could sidestep it blindfolded having lived here for over ten years. She made many trips up and down here in the dead of night when Joel was a screaming baby, her body at its lowest ebb after giving birth and suffering from sleep deprivation for months on end, and then being abandoned by a man who decided that fatherhood wasn't for him after all. A stab of annoyance still darts through her at the thought of Samuel and his lack of compassion and wafer-thin veneer of resilience that broke after only a few weeks of being subjected to an exhausted wife and a crying baby. It should have waned after all these years, that sentiment, that anxious fretful feeling, but it is still there, sharp and angular in her mind, as if it was only yesterday when he walked out of the door never to return.

The bottle of Malbec in the kitchen tugs at her. She tries to resist but it's so hard. It's midweek and she has an early start in the morning. Her boss is out dealing with customers for the next few days, leaving her in charge of a busy office with their recently trained assistant who is still acquiring the essential skill required to deal with irate engineers faced with broken machinery and thousands of hours lost. She will have to open up the office and man the phones. It's the end of the month and she needs to process any outstanding orders and make sure all the invoices are paid. A clear head is a necessity. She bites at her lip. She also needs to de-stress and prepare for a difficult day and what better way than a glass of the good stuff? Just one. That's all it will take to help her unwind. Just the one.

~

So often, thinks Emily, *the idea of doing something is far more appealing and satisfying than actually doing it.* The wine leaves a bitter taste in her mouth, coating it with a residual oily tang, making her feel marginally nauseous. She places the glass down on the coffee table, her mind raking back over the disappearance of little Leo and how it has lodged in her consciousness. The more she tries to dismiss such thoughts, the more they creep in, slithering into her brain, soiling and tainting her little world, her tightly protected family unit. She takes another swig of the wine despite feeling ever so slightly sick. She needs it to blur her growing feelings of disquietude, to stop her thinking about how it could have been Joel.

Leo Fairland's bed is currently empty, his sheets taut and cold. She lets that image linger for a while before she turns her thoughts to his family, to his parents and possible siblings, wondering how they are coping. She would be a wreck, unable to hold herself together. She knows this for certain. Just the thought of it makes her dizzy with fear and dread. No number of drugs designed to calm and sedate her would stop the screams from escaping. She would be inconsolable, a trembling quivering hollowed out version of herself. There would be no way of climbing out of that yawning abyss.

Her palate gradually acclimatises to the sour yet now appealing tang of the wine. She takes another long slug, hoping it will dull her thoughts, stop her from torturing herself over something that may never happen. Atenby is the village next to Middleham, where she and Joel live. So close. Close enough to make her feel permanently on edge. Things like this don't happen around here. They shouldn't. Not in their neck of the woods. They are a close-knit community here in Middleham. They have a small library, a quaint post office and a village school. She tells herself that these things, these quintessentially middle-class things, will protect her and her boy from such an atrocity, but then reminds herself that Atenby also has a quaint post office and a village school as well as a tiny little church and a village green complete with pond and ducks. It's a slightly bigger village with a larger school, but still...

Before she knows it, panic has gripped her and she is already convinced that Joel is next. She visualises a stranger waiting outside the school gates, a sinister individual, somebody in a raincoat who will scoop up her boy and take him away to do God knows what to him before dumping his body in a dirty alley somewhere, miles away from home.

She is shivering and her glass is suddenly empty. The need to refill it is overwhelming; an itch she needs to scratch. She knows that she shouldn't, but a long and weary night stretches ahead of her. *Just one more*, she tells herself as she stands up and shuffles her way into the kitchen to pour another. *Just the one.* She drops back down on the sofa, her body bone-achingly tired, her mind clogged up with dread, and savours the taste as it slips down her throat. *No more after this.* She has a busy day ahead of her tomorrow. A really busy day.

~

Her mouth is gaping open, her tongue gritty, her throat dry as sand. Her eyes flicker open. She stretches and lets out a protracted yawn. The empty glass is still balanced in her hand, her fingers tightly clasped around the smooth thin stem.

She stands up, her limbs weak and watery, and places the glass on the coffee table with a dull thunk. The thump in her head accelerates as she leans forward, a large rock rolling and banging against her skull, making her feel sick. It's time for bed. She staggers through the living room, exhaustion weighing her down.

Deciding to not look at the clock for fear of it being so late that she suddenly discovers she has only got a few hours left until it's time to get up again, she turns off all the lights and checks the front door, shuffling her way through to the hallway. To her horror, she realises that it's unlocked. Her chest is tight, her flesh suddenly ice cold. She fumbles around for the keys, dipping into her bag that is slung over the newel post, her fingers cold and clumsy as she drags them across the bottom of it, scraping and fumbling, panic stripping away her dexterity. They're not there. A handful of old tissues and a rogue lipstick is the best she can come up with. Dropping everything onto the floor in a messy heap, Emily spins around, eyes wild as she scans the small shadowy hallway, eventually finding the keys on the console table, hidden behind a stack of mail. She grabs them and locks the door, her palms slick with perspiration.

Forgetting to keep the noise down and to avoid the creaky step, she runs upstairs and races around the landing, peering into bedrooms looking for intruders, stopping outside Joel's room to catch her breath. With a hand placed on her breastbone in an attempt to still her thrashing heart, she pushes the door ajar and lets out a rasping staccato breath when she sees him lying there, curled up safe in his bed, still wrapped in the strong nurturing arms of sleep. Thank God.

Her own carelessness is surpassed only by her stupid habit of worrying endlessly then doing nothing to alleviate it. If anything, she makes difficult situations worse with her weak thoughtless behaviour, being slapdash and forgetting to lock doors when a child in the next village has gone missing, possibly, in fact most probably, taken against his will. And on it goes, the vicious circle of fecklessness and fretting that is her life.

Tomorrow, she tells herself, she will not drink. She will make sure the door is locked and she will routinely check all the windows. She will close every curtain, every blind, do what she can to keep the outside world at bay. Her son is her life. He is everything to her. She cannot risk losing him.

She doesn't miss having a husband and she definitely doesn't miss Samuel. What she misses is the security another person's presence provides when things get tough. Aside from that, what Samuel's absence actually does is keenly remind her of how irritating he was, how final and unyielding he could be as he threw out lists of demands that were impossibly rigid, from making sure she left impossibly straight, perfectly symmetrical lines in the grass every time she mowed the lawn, to never allowing his name to be shortened by anybody, even his own wife.

The memory of trying to tiptoe around the house in the early hours with a newborn baby in her arms so she didn't disturb his precious sleep still jars. It was a traumatic time made all the more difficult by Samuel coming home and telling her that he no longer wanted to be married, saying that fatherhood and being a husband was no longer for him.

She can't remember how she reacted. She does, however, recall feeling sick and the room tilting as she struggled to take in his words, to slot everything in place inside her head whilst holding a screaming baby. She recalls watching his mouth move, muffled echoey sounds coming out as he told her things she thought she would never ever have to hear.

But now with hindsight, she can see that he did her a favour. She is not and never will be the austere, clinically minded woman he wanted her to be. She is the sort of woman who falls asleep with a glass of red wine balanced in her hand. She is the sort of woman who leaves the pots piled up in the kitchen sink because she is too tired and lazy to wash them immediately after eating. She is the sort of woman who leaves the front door unlocked when there's a predatory individual somewhere in the vicinity who has taken it upon themselves to snatch children away from their unsuspecting parents; parents who are trying so damn hard to hold down a job and raise a child in the best way they know how.

Newspaper reports have painted a picture of a less than perfect mother who was late picking up her son on a regular basis. On the day he vanished, she had left work a couple of minutes later than usual and had become caught up in heavy traffic. Reading about it damn near broke Emily's heart. It resonated with her, striking a chord deep within her, giving her crippling déjà vu.

Joel is collected by a childminder three days a week. The two days that Emily picks him up are fraught with difficulty and tension. She cannot count the number of times she has been late, held up in traffic, trapped in meetings that have run over, cornered by customers needing to speak with her about issues that could easily wait until the following day.

There are days when it feels as if the world is determined to stop her getting to Joel, refusing to allow her two days when she is afforded the pleasure of standing at the school gates along with the other parents who are fortunate enough to not have to work and are able to collect their children in a calm and measured manner, whereas she inevitably arrives late and flustered, wishing that for once, life would go her way.

A pebble-sized lump sticks in her throat, borne out of exhaustion and weariness at a cruel and judgemental world that allows such wicked people to exist, the sort of people who take children and do unspeakable things to them, whilst pointing the finger of blame at the parent who was just trying to make ends meet.

Already, the trolls on social media have made their feelings about the mother of little Leo known. *Lazy, thoughtless, feckless.* Just a few of the repeatable adjectives being bandied about to describe her. Like none of them have ever had a bad day and turned up late for an appointment. Calls have been made for social services to intervene and question her actions. Little or nothing has been said about the perpetrator. Their actions haven't been called into question. They are a faceless individual, anonymous and ghostlike. Like a thief in the night, they spirited away a little boy, stole somebody else's child, somebody's baby, and yet the press and public are hellbent on blaming the mother. She's a tangible entity, unlike the offender. She has a name, a face, a home; something they can cling on to, something the baying mob can lodge in their heads and hold fast whereas the person who did this terrible deed has managed to slip away and escape, their reputation unblemished.

Emily swallows and blots out all thoughts of Leo and his mother and the crazy backward world in which they all live. If she is to get a good night's sleep, clearing her head of toxic news and the endless possibilities of what could fracture her little family is essential otherwise she will lie awake through the wee small hours, raking over the past, present and future until she can no longer think straight. She sighs and rubs at her eyes with her knuckles. She needs sleep and she needs it now if she is to face the world tomorrow with a clear head.

Slipping in between the soft cool sheets, she drifts off almost immediately, all thoughts of Samuel and their short-lived marriage forgotten, all the horrid dark images of little lost Leo and an unidentifiable nameless being, soon relegated to the back of her mind. She replaces them instead with thoughts of Mo and his recent text, imagining his kind warm face and soft voice and soon feels her body become weightless, as light as air.

5

LYNDA

'Jesus Christ. I know it's a terrible thing to say but I'm so relieved it didn't happen here.' Isaac dunks a biscuit in his tea and shoves it into his mouth with a savage like intensity that both fascinates and repels Lynda in equal measure. He resembles a man who hasn't eaten in months.

Registering the disgust on his colleague's face, he quickly chews and swallows it down. 'I mean, imagine how fucking terrible it must be for the staff at that school. They must be getting some stick over their methods. I'll bet they're having a safeguarding meeting as we speak. They'll have the bigwigs in from the local authority, maybe even Ofsted, who will crawl all over the place looking for cracks in their policies, searching for somebody to take the rap.'

Lynda rolls her eyes, trying to turn away from him, the top half of her body twisted at an unnatural angle so she can't hear his words or see the line of spittle that has formed at the corner of his mouth. Retirement can't come soon enough. She no longer understands this place or these people. Her young colleagues are on a different wavelength to her. She sees no humour in their jokes, has no clue as to what makes them tick.

She is a stranger in this place, the building in which she has worked for the past forty years. Things have changed, morphed into a system, a regimented organisation that she no longer recognises.

Teaching at Priory Place Secondary School used to be easy, effortless. For sure, there were badly behaved pupils, errant youngsters who didn't want to learn, certain that they knew everything there was to know, and that she could deal with, but it now feels as if the odds are stacked against the staff. They are bound by bureaucracy and endless lists of recently implemented policies, targets and government requirements that are impossible to keep up with and meet.

One more year. That's all she has to aim for. Keep going for twelve more months and she can kick back and relax, potter about in her garden, attend the local choir more regularly, see the few friends that she has more often than she is currently able to, and generally do whatever she wants to do whenever she wants to do it. In the meantime, she has to adhere to school rules and policies designed – purportedly – to keep youngsters safe and further their learning whilst having to sit in the company of people like Isaac who, although barely out of university, seem to know everything about everything. She can't recall the last time he actually sat and engaged in a proper, decent conversation, or even stopped to draw breath.

A rumble of discontent growls deep within her chest. She is being uncommonly hostile and unforgiving towards her younger colleague, but just lately the small things about her everyday life have begun to irritate her. Perhaps it's her age. Perhaps it's the job. Or maybe it's recent events that have set her on edge, making her feel out of sorts and uncomfortable about the life she used to take for granted.

'So, what do you think will happen next then, Lynda?' Isaac is staring at her, eyes wide and unassuming as he waits for her to reply to a question she chose to ignore. Lynda stares at this man, at his pinprick pupils and dull featureless gaze before looking away and placing her hands in her lap.

She clears her throat and makes an attempt at being both polite and bland, hoping her answer will satisfy him, quench his thirst for idle gossip and tittle-tattle about anything and anybody. That's all he wants to hear, sweeping generalisations about recent events, not the facts of the matter in hand. 'I'm not really sure, Isaac. Although I'm sure you're right,' she murmurs. 'About everything.'

His eyes give nothing away. Either she has hit the mark or he is too dim to realise that she is fudging her way through this interaction. He smiles and nods his head, seemingly satisfied with her response. 'Right,' he says a little too fervently as he slaps his hands on his thighs and stands up. 'Got to get on. Things to do. Too much work and not enough time.'

Lynda watches his retreating figure, relieved by the moment's silence his absence leaves. Sometimes she finds it easier, less arduous to just sit here alone and gather her thoughts rather than become embroiled in the chit-chat that swirls aimlessly around the staffroom. It helps her to focus, sitting alone and pondering over things that matter to her rather than joining in with the talk and camaraderie that surrounds her.

It feels disingenuous to engage with the rest of the staff when, if she is being completely honest, she doesn't particularly like any of them. Far better to sit contemplatively and focus her mind for the lessons she is about to teach. She would rather give the pupils the better side of her nature after she has had time to relax and gather her strength, to sharpen her knowledge and teaching skills after a period of peace and quiet and a mug of hot coffee than turn up to class, frazzled and exhausted after being forced to make small talk about inane subjects that hold no appeal for her. Besides, she has always been happy with her own company, never needing to be surrounded by other people.

She has her clubs that she attends a couple of times a week and that is enough for her. Having never married, she has grown used to doing things her way and compromise isn't something she is acquainted with. She is too old, too set in her ways to start conforming to the needs of others just so she can feel as if she belongs and can be neatly slotted into somebody else's idea of what constitutes standard social behaviour.

She thinks of what lies ahead of her this evening. A frisson of excitement runs through her. She has a new class to attend – an art class in town – and the thought of it gives her goosebumps. This is why she rarely mingles with the others here. They wouldn't understand. They would see her as antiquated with her strange ideas of what passes as normal.

While they are all glued to their TV screens, watching the latest reality shows that list celebrities she has never even heard of, the sort of people who cavort about in front of the cameras making fools of themselves for eye-watering sums of money, she is visiting her local church for choir practise. Or she is at her local history society meeting studying the origins of the earliest settlers in the village, tracing the earthworks discovered by examining satellite imagery available online.

It's not everybody's cup of tea, she knows that, but it's how she chooses to spend her time and telling others would simply be like opening up a vein and allowing them to watch her bleed, so she keeps her private life private, banishing any interest from other members of staff.

But now that the local history group has closed down for the next few months, she has this new class to attend and it has given her something to look forward to. She will be surrounded by like-minded people, others who, like her, love drawing and painting and seeing their visions appear on the canvas, viewing it as a way of unleashing their inner creativity, pouring out their heart and emotions and watching it morph into something real, something tangible that they can call their own.

She is planning on attending with her neighbour and close friend, Moira. They rub along nicely together, knowing each other's foibles and eccentricities. No explanations are ever necessary. They come from an era when respect was respected and folk knew when to remain silent rather than harping on about nothing in particular just to fill a silence, or so they could hear the sound of their own voice. Times have changed so much and she's not entirely sure it's for the better.

A movement nearby alerts her to the time. It's 10.45am. Break time is over. People brush past her, barely registering her existence. She is invisible, a dying breed. The sort of teacher that joined this profession because they had an unshakeable faith in the education system. She came to it armed with a need to impart knowledge to young growing minds. These days, it is all she can do to read out of a textbook without wanting to scream to the heavens above that none of the things that they teach kids these days is important. It seems to her everyone has lost their way, becoming caught up in the competitive need to espouse how brilliant their child or school is, publicly shaming those who fail and championing those who fulfil the criteria of a rigid government tick sheet that in no way furthers a child's learning, but rather straitjackets them, sucking them dry, obliterating any interests and aspirations that would serve them well in life.

She stands up, thinking that perhaps she should reconsider her retirement date, bring it forward. She is of no use to anybody with this sort of negative attitude and no amount of protesting will change the system. It is too big a machine; unwieldy and often unmanageable, something that despite its many obvious flaws, keeps on moving and grinding. She is a tiny cog, too insignificant to be of any real use. Still, there are some happy bright children in her classes. They are the ones who keep her going, lighting up her otherwise dull day. They are the ones who, despite their hormone-fuelled urges and behaviour, make her smile and give her hope that people, underneath it all, are actually quite decent.

She collects her bag, straightens her collar and heads off to class, thinking that she shouldn't ponder so much. It causes her unnecessary stress. She should be like the other members of staff here and let problems wash over her.

A year, she murmurs as she turns into the corridor that leads to her class. *Another year and this place will be no more than a part of my history.*

6

It isn't what it used to be, this road, this village. Things have changed. She used to be happy here, secure and settled, but small occurrences and subtle changes in the dynamics have made her uncomfortable, left her feeling as if things that she once held dear are slipping out of her grasp.

People she knew have moved on and their houses are now occupied by nameless faceless individuals who barely acknowledge her presence. She doesn't want or need special treatment or a standing ovation whenever she passes them in the street, but a simple greeting or a smile wouldn't go amiss. Everything around her is awry, out of kilter, the usual courtesies of village life now lacking. The sparkle seems to have left Middleham and been replaced by a dourness, a gritty wash of nothingness that no longer holds any appeal for her.

She still knows a few people close by – Alf and Alice, the elderly couple next door, quiet respectful folk who rarely venture outside, and then Moira from a few doors down. Moira, pillar of the community, active in the local choir, eccentric and unconventional with wild wiry hair and unpredictable behaviour. A harmless enough woman, handsome in her youth with a striking bone structure that used to turn heads, she now slouches about in baggy old clothes and wellies.

And then there's Lynda. Lynda, with her poker face and sharp grating voice. A stickler for routine, Lynda is often to be seen supervising the gardeners from the local council, demanding that they trim the edges of the small village green with greater precision, barking orders at them from her front lawn while they sweat and toil in the scorching heat. Sarah has heard that she is an amazing teacher, one of the best, but imagines she gets results by forcing draconian rules and regulations on the pupils. *Still*, Sarah thinks resignedly, *every school, every village, every town needs a Lynda to get things done.*

And then there's Emily. Sad little Emily who spends her entire life in a spin, running from one place to the next, always behind time, yet still managing to look perfect and flawless as she loads bags in and out of the car, shouting at her son that he will be late if he doesn't get a move on. Sarah can hear them every morning – Joel traipsing along the pavement behind his mother while she scurries ahead, calling his name, shouting that they won't get to school on time if he doesn't move it and pick up his feet and walk properly instead of dilly-dallying. Sarah used to find it amusing. Now it sours her morning, the sound of Emily's boorish squawking voice making her skin prickle with annoyance as she stands at her window and watches them. Recent events should make Emily appreciate her young son a little more, but it would appear not. She is unmoved by it all, untouched by the disappearance of that boy as she continues chivvying and shouting at Joel, forcing him into the car with her palm pressed hard into his back.

Sarah rubs at her face, letting her hand drop to her mouth while she chews at a loose piece of skin next to her nail. She nips it between her teeth and tugs, wincing at the line of pain that shoots up her finger as it comes away. A tiny ruby pearl appears.

She makes her way into the kitchen and holds her finger under the cold tap, noticing that the sink is dirty. How did she miss this? Ignoring her throbbing finger, she takes a bottle of bleach and pours it around the rim, savouring the pungent smell as it hits her nostrils. Life can be so terribly unfair at times. Taking a metal scourer, she attacks the sink, scrubbing ferociously until her muscles begin to twitch and her arm is sore from the effort.

Why does the like of Emily have a child while she is denied the privilege? How is that right or just? And then there is the woman whose child has been taken from outside the school in the next village to theirs. Another useless good-for-nothing individual who put her own needs before that of her young son, turning up late day after day, leaving him alone, vulnerable to the malevolent predators that seem to be ever-present in this day and age.

Sometimes people sicken her. Even folk who appear kind-hearted and genuine have ulterior motives. She should have been on time, that woman. She should have left work earlier, told everybody that her child comes first, made sure he wasn't left alone. A pain shoots up the back of Sarah's neck as she scrubs at the now gleaming sink, the noxious odour of bleach swirling about the air and filling the kitchen. Life isn't fair or just, she knows that; but once, just once, would it be too much to ask for things to go her way?

She stares down at her hands, red and cracked from being immersed in water too often. This cleaning regime is killing her skin. She knows it, but it is the only thing that she can cling on to, the only steady thing that offers her reassurance in an ever-changing and often perilous world. The one thing she has desired for all of her adult life is denied to her and here she is, surrounded by women who don't care about their children, shouting at them, leaving them exposed to all types of dangers. Sarah would never do that; she knows it for certain. Her child would always feel safe and wanted and needed. It's the least any decent adult can do. Perhaps that's why Emily is alone. Perhaps her husband saw her for what she really is and took flight before she ruined his life as well.

Her phone rings. Her hands sting as she attempts to rub them dry before the caller gives up and she misses it. It will be Malcolm. He's due home this evening. It's been a long and worrying week without him. What with the recent abduction and then receiving a stream of non-committal missives regarding her job enquiries, she'll be glad when he gets back and she can relax properly. She snatches up the handset.

'Hi, it's good to hear from you.' She tries to keep her voice light, to keep out of it the bitterness that is raging in her belly.

'Ah, yeah you too.' A pause as he clears his throat. 'Thing is, I need to stay on for a few more days. I told my manager that you wouldn't mind. It's just that we need to finish this project and we're not quite there yet with the final paperwork.'

Time stretches out in front of her, a long stream of seconds, minutes, hours with her sitting here on her own with nobody to talk to, nobody to turn to when her worries and anxieties threaten to overwhelm her. 'It's fine,' she murmurs, fighting back tears. 'You do what you need to do.'

'Yeah, thanks. I knew you'd understand. It's not easy being away but it's not for forever, is it?'

'Hopefully not,' she says, her own voice echoing around her head, strong and thunderous as it pulses through her ears.

'Right, well, I'll call later when I've got a definite date for coming home. You take care, yeah?'

Sarah nods. She wants to hear him say that he loves her but fears that those days are long since gone, so far behind them in fact, that they are all but invisible. Those love-filled hedonistic days when their dreams were enough to keep them going seem like a lifetime ago. Twelve years they have been together. Twelve years four months and three days if she is going to be precise and pedantic about it – which is what Malcolm called her during their last argument.

It had been about the usual – their lack of children. She had claimed that he was being selfish, denying her the right to be a mother with his refusal to get his vasectomy reversed and he had replied that no child would want to live in such a sterile environment with a pedant for a mother.

'One whiff of a shitty nappy would be enough to send you into a meltdown,' he had shouted. 'You're so bloody hung up on cleanliness and making sure nothing is ever out of place that having a baby here, messing the place up, would tip you over the edge.'

He doesn't get it. He never will. She cleans because she has nothing else in her life, nothing and nobody to throw her energy into. She is alone. With Malcolm working away so often, there are days when she feels as if her world is about to implode.

He chose to have a vasectomy without telling her shortly after they met and although it was a shock to her, it wasn't a particularly big problem as she felt no pressing desire at that point in her life to have any children of her own. But with the passing of time, her need to become a mother has grown and intensified to the point that there are days when it is all she can think about. It consumes her every waking moment: the thought of what their baby would look like, what they would call it, how she would dress it and the sort of healthy food she would cook for their precious child.

And then, like a bucket of cold water being tipped over her, it dawns on her that it will never happen. She will never know the warmth of their child's body or smell the aroma of their soft unblemished skin. She will never know what it feels like to carry a child inside of her, to experience that first kick and feel that first twinge of pain that would signify that she was in labour, about to become a mother for the very first time. And all because Malcolm, the man she committed herself to for the rest of her days, refuses to consider going back on a decision he made without even consulting her.

She could foster or adopt, but doubts he would want that, and if she is being frank, neither does she. She wants her own baby, something that has grown inside her, not another person's child. She wants their baby. Something that will tie them together, cement their already crumbling relationship. Because it is crumbling. She's not stupid. She can spot impending disaster, has a nose for it, and if she doesn't do something about it, her marriage to Malcolm may well come undone and unravel completely.

All she needs to do is shift her focus elsewhere, stop her constant clingy behaviour, develop her own interests and become her own person instead of standing at her window day after day, staring out at the world, analysing the lives of other people and putting the word to rights. She wouldn't feel the need to do it if she had another person to pour her love and time into.

As it is, she spends her days rattling around this house with too much time on her hands. Too much time to think is what she has. With no current job, she needs to find an outlet for her energy and anxieties before she says or does something unfortunate that will bring her marriage and her life as she knows it, to an abrupt and premature end. If she can shift her thoughts away from babies to something more productive, perhaps things will change. Malcolm will start to have more patience with her. She has talked about little else and nagged him relentlessly for the past few years. Little wonder he chose a job that takes him away from home so frequently. She isn't an idiot and yet finds it so damn hard to switch her attentions elsewhere, hormones fuelling her need.

Her biological clock is ticking. She loathes that phrase with a passion but knows that it is true. She is thirty-five years old and every month, every year that passes squeezes at her gut, condensing her bitterness and frustration into a tight little knot deep down in her belly. She has so much anger and resentment stacked up inside of her, there are days when she can hardly breathe. Anything and everybody sends her into a rage.

The knock at the door takes her by surprise, fizzing her blood, making her heart thump. She rarely gets visitors. With family who live away and few, if any, friends, she is unaccustomed to the loud banging that is echoing throughout the house.

This, she thinks, *is how insular I have become.* It is indicative of how sad and pathetic her life actually is, that a random caller in the middle of the day is enough to send her into a state of confusion and panic. This is what she has turned into – a ridiculously lonely housewife who is marginally paranoid and neurotic.

She visualises a man standing outside, knife in hand. The same man who took that child a couple of days ago from the village down the road. He could be anywhere right now – still loitering in Atenby or here in Middleham, right outside her door, waiting for her to open it so he can pounce.

Holding her hand to her chest to quell the rising terror that has her in its grip, she slouches through the hallway, grabs the handle and opens the door.

7

ASHTON

I t's three o'clock and he is already prepared and ready to go. Too early. Once again, he is too damn early. The class doesn't start until seven. Another four hours to kill. Four hours of sitting worrying about how it will all turn out. Four hours of that wrenching gut-sinking feeling that everything will fall apart before it's even begun. He wishes that he had no reason to feel so anxious. He has planned this to the nth degree. And yet deep down, he knows that he does actually have every reason to worry. Now he is back home where it took place, he can never truly relax. People have long memories and short tempers. They rarely forgive and almost always remember.

The bottle of beer in the fridge looms large in his mind, beckoning him. Not now. Later perhaps, after it's all over. Once the class is finished, he can come home, unwind and crack open a bottle or two. Maybe even three if things go well.

The ticking of the clock behind him on the bureau booms in his head, chiming in time with his rapid heartbeat. He gulps down air, tells himself to stop it, to get a grip and calm down. Maybe it's being back here, in his hometown after spending so many years away that's doing it. This is a small place, not geographically perhaps but mentally. It's a large populace with small minds. Unforgiving small minds that refuse to comprehend or let go of the past. Even the smallest of misdemeanours are frowned upon, judgements doled out by the bucketload, by people who've been nowhere and seen nothing.

Still, he's back now, part by choice, part forced due to financial reasons. Living away from home while earning just above the minimum wage proved to be too much for him and after contacting his mum, he made the decision to leave Lincolnshire and head back north.

With his stepdad out of the picture, he banked on things being easier. And so far, everything has been fine. Better than fine really. No problems or issues to speak of. A little tension perhaps in the first few weeks but he supposed that was to be expected. Now they've got a routine sorted, he and his mum, a way of going about their daily business without impinging on one another's space, life seems easier.

His presence was bound to bring a small amount of darkness, an awkwardness that only time can erase. He missed her while he was away. He missed her smile, her warmth and positive attitude even when faced with the most trying of circumstances. That's just how she is. He thinks of what he put her through – what they were both forced to endure – and thanks God that she stuck around for him.

It was his mother's idea to start the classes. Her faith in him, in his skills and abilities, gave his flagging confidence a much-needed boost and he jumped at the idea but now, two months down the line, his nerves are kicking in and part of him is wishing he had refused, wishing he had thanked her for the idea but insisted that his day job was enough.

The day job that is so mind-numbingly boring, there are times that he feels like picking up his coat and bag and walking out of the factory doors never to return. Inspecting food at the end of an assembly line, searching and scrutinising for lumps of stray plastic or grit or anything alien that may have become lodged in it, isn't exactly the most scintillating way to spend the day. In fact, after three hours of examining tray after tray of confectionery, he sometimes feels as if he is having an out of body experience, his solid form remaining on the floor while his mind and spirit wander free to escape the drudgery of the task in hand.

It's the thought of the money that keeps him going. With only a tiny amount of board and lodging he uses to pay his mum for his keep, he's now got a tidy little sum tucked away and hopes that soon he will have enough to use as a deposit for his own place. What he really needs to do before that time is find another job, if possible one that doesn't make him feel as if he is losing his mind. There are days when he feels certain that sticking hot pins in his eyes would be infinitely preferable to what he has to do hour after hour, day after day in that fucking awful factory.

He took today off, using one of his precious holidays to prepare for this evening. He didn't expect such an uptake for the classes. After it was advertised by the community centre, he received ten replies within days and knew at that point that there would be no backing out.

He's hoping to keep it as casual and informal as possible. That's his way. He's never been one for formalities and unnecessary procedures, preferring a relaxed environment in which to work. Gaynor, who helps run the community centre, is a friend of his mum's. She has been at the centre of this, printing leaflets, placing them in windows, mentioning it on their Facebook page.

For so long, it didn't feel real that it would happen, that his mum's idea for him would come to fruition, and now here he is, nervous, with a growling roiling stomach and sweaty palms, counting down the hours until he takes an art class for which he is desperately under qualified. He lets out a snort of derision. Desperately under qualified is an understatement if ever there was one. He has a diploma in art & design. No tutorial experience or certificates to back up his knowledge. All he has is his sketchpad, pencils and paints, and a paintbrush.

'Honey, we're the local community centre, not the Royal College of Art,' Gaynor had said with a smile when he told her he wasn't really qualified to teach adults. 'We provide the required insurance. All you need is your skills and that lovely easy manner of yours that your mum is so proud of telling everybody about.'

He had felt his face flush at her words. Compliments have never sat easily with him. He has spent the last twenty years trying to get on with his life, getting his head down and making a living the best way he knows how. With only one relationship that petered out a few years ago, he has focused his energies on getting his life back on track, achieving things that he once thought never possible. Even the tiniest of accomplishments have been like climbing a mountain. Beginning life on the bottom rung of the ladder has been difficult to say the least, but he is starting to get somewhere and somewhere has to be better than nowhere.

Reaching into his bag, he checks that he has the necessary equipment. He'll need a pen and pad for a register. That much he does know, that he has to take names and numbers for fire regulations. It's not as if ten people are going to push their numbers over the limit but he wants to get it right. Sticking to the rules is important to him. He learnt the hard way that breaking them comes at a price.

A spear of discontent and anxiety twists in his gut. A memory flashes into his head. He bats it away. Now isn't the time for such maudlin behaviour. He needs to stay focused, get it right, not drive people away by presenting himself as a mumbling miserable figure who doesn't know his arse from his elbow. He has to appear confident, slightly brazen even. Nobody wants to watch a bumbling idiot who can barely string a sentence together because they're so wracked with nerves. They want to be taught by somebody who oozes charisma and confidence. Somebody who knows exactly what they're doing. He has to be that person.

Now definitely isn't the time for his own memory to start bashing him over the head, trying to remind him that deep down, he's a nobody, a damaged individual who, it seems, can never forget. He wishes he had the type of brain that would allow him a moment's reprieve from it, but he doesn't. It's there every morning when he gets up and is stuck in his head before he goes to sleep every night. Maybe it's a lifelong thing that will never dissipate, an internal barometer of how messed up he really is. Maybe he is beyond redemption and this thing will follow him around for the rest of his days. He likes to think not but then sometimes in his darker days, he wonders if what took place was nothing to do with his upbringing and everything to do with him, with who he really is, the wicked malicious Ashton that lurks deep in his soul.

The minutes turn into hours as he sits, trying to ready himself for this thing. He has tried watching the TV, listening to the radio, listening to his music on Spotify. Nothing has worked. Nothing has managed to soothe him, to ease his state of angst. To others, taking an art class with a handful of local people would be as easy as breathing, but not to him.

He goes over everything in his head, pre-empting their queries, thinking up answers to questions that haven't yet been asked. This is what he does. He has spent his whole adult life planning out his days to preserve his well-being. He has come too far to let everything come crashing down around him, has worked hard to get to where he is, which, compared to many, isn't so far at all, but for him it's been a global trek. He's walked the length and breadth of the earth a thousand times over to reach this point in his life. *This is why,* he tells himself, *I have to get it right, to not allow my nerves to get the better of me and blow it before it's even begun.*

He stands up, stares at the hands of the clock as they move around the silver face. 5.30pm. Soon his mum will be in, exhausted after another day at work, standing at a production line in another shitty factory that pays minimum wage for back-breaking work. Still, it's far better than how life used to be when he was a kid. He bites at the inside of his mouth, tells himself to stop it. He's at it again, harking back to those days, to that time, to that fucking miserable period in their lives when everything went so horribly wrong, tainting his existence, staining it a murky shade of grey.

As soon as he gets in later, he's going to have that beer. He thinks of how it will keep him going; the thought of that cold liquid, the yeasty flavour, the creamy froth, how it will put a haze over everything, a welcome blurring around the edges of his life. Just the thought of it makes his mouth water.

'Hello, love.' His mother's voice rings through their dingy little hallway with its peeling paint and mouldy wallpaper. There was a time he wouldn't have noticed these things. Now they seem to be paramount in his mind. He thinks, perhaps, that he now sees this house for what it is – somewhere that contains a pile of filthy unwanted memories. A place where bad things happened. Terrible revolting things. For now, it is somewhere to live, a place for him to sleep and eat. It has saved him from a life of near poverty in Lincolnshire where his wages barely covered his rent but he knows that it's bad for him, living here. Too much hurt. Too much damage. This house and the things that went on in it all those years ago were almost the undoing of him. He doesn't blame his mum. What could she have done? Besides, he gave her as much misery in the end. His behaviour, what he did, it all added to their downfall. He was just as much a part of it and now he has to repay her for standing by him, for never questioning him or turning her back on him. She was always there for him. Still is.

'In here, Mum,' he shouts, glad of her presence, relieved that her arrival has broken the wicked spell he was under, his mind refusing to shut down and allow him a moment's peace.

'Oh,' she says, giving him a broad smile as she kicks off her shoes and steps into the living room, 'it's good to see you, son. What a day it's been.' She flops down on the sofa and closes her eyes. 'What a bloody day.'

8

SARAH

It was his long beard that caused it. She didn't mean for it to happen, for the gasp to escape. She tried to stop it with her hand but it was too late. He had already spotted it. She could tell by his expression, by the quizzical look he gave her as she stepped away from him farther into the hallway, that he thought her ill-mannered. She didn't mean to be. She isn't a rude person by nature. It's just that she isn't used to receiving visitors, and he was so dark, his gaze so piercing. And the beard. It was all so unexpected.

She can see now that her reaction could have been misconstrued as impolite but that wasn't how she intended it to be. She hopes he doesn't hold it against her. If there's one thing she prides herself on, it's that she always tries to do the right thing, even if the right thing leaves her standing alone. She believes that being principled is an admirable trait and it is one that she is rather proud of. Malcolm doesn't always agree, calling her unbending and severe but at least she can say that she sleeps at night with a clear conscience.

'So, you don't mind taking it and handing it over to her?' The man at Sarah's door is staring at her, his hand outstretched as he thrusts a small attractively wrapped parcel towards her.

'No, of course not,' she replies, all the while wondering who this man is and what is inside the gift-wrapped box. She can't remember the last time she received a present, especially one wrapped as beautifully as this with its gold ribbons and soft cream tissue paper.

'As I said, I wanted to hand it over to her myself but I've been called away to work and won't get to see her. I'll message her to let her know you've got it. She'll probably pop over for it once she gets in from work.'

He is smiling now, his teeth gleaming as he watches her for a reaction. She manages a weak smile in return, nodding as she takes it from him, noticing how slim his fingers are, how long and perfectly manicured his nails are. No callouses or grazes. Not a manual worker then.

'Anyway,' he murmurs, his eyes sweeping over her as he turns to leave. 'Thanks for this. It's nice to know that Emily has such thoughtful neighbours. You can never be too sure, can you? It's a lovely village this one.' He stops and sucks at his teeth. 'Sorry, I'm rambling. Anyhow, it was nice to meet you.'

'I'm Sarah,' she calls after him as he heads down the path towards the gate.

'Mohammed,' he replies. 'But people just call me Mo.'

She flashes him a smile and closes the door, leaning back on it, the box clasped close to her chest. The soft thump thump of her heart seems to fill the whole house as she heads through to the kitchen where she places the present on the kitchen top, eyeing it with more than a small amount of envy. When was the last time Malcolm surprised her with a box of chocolates or a bunch of flowers? Too long ago to remember, if at all. He prides himself on being practical, not the sort of man who would ever make false promises; not the sensitive sort at all, which can be interpreted as cold and selfish depending on your perspective.

She thinks about Mohammed, or Mo as he called himself. She's seen him around recently but hadn't realised his connection to Emily. He must be a recent addition to her life. Her new partner no doubt. Either that or he's a random friend who has taken it upon himself to drop gifts off at her house. Even that sends a stab of jealousy through her. Despite Emily's lackadaisical attitude and tardiness, she still manages to snag a man who is thoughtful enough to bring her gifts in the middle of the day. She will come in from work, tired and frazzled and be greeted with whatever is inside this box. Whatever the contents, Sarah herself would be overjoyed to receive it. Jewellery or chocolates is her guess. It's the right size, the correct weight. She's usually pretty good at guessing these things. Not that she's had much experience when it comes to receiving them of course. Not with Malcolm and him being the way he is.

The way he is. She considers that phrase and then thinks about spending more nights on her own while he works away doing God knows what with God knows who. A hot fetid breath shudders out of her. She stops, silently reprimanding herself. That was a few years ago and as far as she is aware, Malcolm has never been unfaithful since.

As far as she is aware.

Because of course, it's all about trust, isn't it? When your husband has a job that conveniently takes him away for long periods of time, you have to switch off to the possibilities and all the temptations that are out there. She has told herself this many times to reassure herself and also to move on from his previous indiscretion. Either that or every time she has a glass of wine to try and unwind, it will all come spilling out, every hateful thought, every spiteful poisonous idea that she has had about divorcing him or stabbing him while he slept, would slip

43

from her mouth unbidden. And then, with Malcolm being the practical no-nonsense type, he would up and leave her, unable to take her toxic corrosive ways, unable to put up with her horrid malicious words. He would make a clean break and start a new life without her.

So after it happened, she made a conscious decision to forgive him, to move on and try to be the best wife she can be by being biddable and compliant, acquiescing to his demands to stop him straying again. If they go for a meal and he wants to go to a certain restaurant then they will visit it without question. Should he wish to go for a night out with the boys, he will go and she will make no demands on what time he will be returning.

She does her utmost to be pleasant, to be the sort of wife he wants to be around, to keep her distance and not interfere in his affairs while managing to always be there when he needs her in the hope that it's enough to keep him by her side. But there are times when it proves difficult. When he extends his time away for instance, or when she gets bored at home after taking redundancy from her job at the local council. Or if she sees other women getting treated with gifts when she can't remember the last time her husband bought her anything at all.

She fights back tears as she recalls how he forgot their wedding anniversary earlier in the year. And of course, rather than nag him about it, she chose to be silent, to simply hand over the card she bought for him and accept his limp apology as he ripped open the envelope and placed the specially chosen card on the mantelpiece without even reading the message inside. Still, at least they're together. An affair would have been the end of many other marriages, but they have ridden the storm. They have lived to tell the tale as the saying goes.

Sarah trails her hand over the smooth tissue paper, stopping to stroke the gold satin ribbon. Her fingers itch to untie it, to rip open the paper and see what's inside. The contents might reveal the nature of Mo and Emily's relationship, the depth and intensity of it. But she can't. It would be a terrible invasion of privacy. Tipping it upside down she can see that it's neatly wrapped, precisely so with sharp exact corners and not a rip or tear in sight. There's no way she would be able to unwrap it and then rewrap it again without it looking as if it has been tampered with.

She is still sitting there, staring at the box, her third cup of coffee in hand when another knock comes at the door, sending her into a flurry of activity. Slipping down from her stool, she sloshes hot coffee over her lap and onto the floor.

'For Christ's sake!'

The cup rattles as she slams it down on the kitchen top. Wiping herself down with a nearby cloth and cursing under her breath, she hears the knock come again, loud, insistent, sending her into a near meltdown.

By the time she gets to the door, her cheeks are flushed, sweat prickling at her neck and scalp.

Emily is standing there with her boy. He is holding his mother's hand and staring up at Sarah and now she suddenly feels terribly self-conscious, aware of her red face and coffee stained clothes.

'Hi!' The sound of Emily's voice makes Sarah want to scream with frustration. She sounds and looks so perfect, so very different from the howling creature that she morphs into every morning as she leaves the house. Emily is standing there smiling, happy. With her child. Does she have any idea of how lucky she is? How fucking fortunate and privileged she is to have a child? Sarah doubts it. People don't realise these things. They simply plough on with their lives, unaware of how their status and presence affects others around them, unaware of how miserable they are making their friends and neighbours feel because they are so wrapped up in their own blissful existence that they have little or no time to notice or care.

'Mo said he left something here for me? I hope you don't mind,' Emily says, her eyes sparkling, her full mouth glistening with carefully applied lipstick. 'When he said he was calling round, I mentioned that you might be in. Sorry if it's been an inconvenience for you.'

'No,' Sarah replies insipidly, 'it's not an inconvenience. Not a problem at all.' Her heart is battering beneath her sweater as she gazes at her neighbour, knowing she should invite her in. The boy is a sweet thing, all eyes and teeth and a creamy complexion. He gives her a wide smile and leaves go of his mother's hand, turning around to look over the road at his house, at their terraced cottage with its Georgian-style windows, and stylish trellis over the doorway, and of course the obligatory climbing rose curling up it to complete the picture. It's a nice house, cute and picture-perfect but Sarah prefers her larger detached property. It might not be older, a Victorian build like Emily's, but it was constructed in keeping with rest of the houses in the village. It fits in well and she is more than happy with it. They have a large garden and a lovely picture window at the back. It's everything she will ever need and more.

'I'll just go and get it for you.' Sarah turns and leaves them standing there on the doorstep. She can't ask them in. The place is a mess with coffee on the floor. She's not sure she wants Emily in her house at the moment while she is feeling this low. Not while she is feeling this envious of her life and her child, and even though she knows this is a cruel and uncharitable thought, she can't stop it. It's how she feels at this moment in time and if she is going to be frank, she is getting to the point where she is sick and tired of quashing her own feelings to satisfy other people and spare their sensitivities. It's as if she isn't allowed to have any ideas and thoughts of her own anymore after spending so long pleasing Malcolm, hoping her malleable amiable nature will soften him, make him more pliable so she can get her way and make him change his mind about the reversal. It's a two-pronged attack. She has also worked hard on her own behaviour to stop his wandering eye. If he's happy at home, why would he ever want to be with somebody else?

She grabs at the box and heads back to the door, clutching it a little too tightly, loosening her grip as she reaches Emily and that little boy of hers, that delightful little boy who spends his days being harangued by his own mother.

'There you go. Hope it's what you wanted!' Her voice ratchets up a notch. Not how she intended it. It comes out as a screech; an excitable childlike squawk that causes her face and neck to flush with embarrassment. Her armpits prickle and itch, her palms are suddenly damp with sweat.

'Oh, I think I know what it is. Nothing too expensive. Anyway, thanks again for this.' She swings around, takes a few steps, the boy scurrying along beside her, then stops and half turns to face Sarah before speaking. 'We should get together for coffee sometime. You know you're always welcome at mine. Work seems to take over my life but it would be lovely to see you for a chat. We need to stick together, us villagers, don't we? Especially after... well recent events, shall we say?' She nods down at the boy and heaves a small sigh, biting at her lip and shaking her head despondently.

'I know what you're talking about, Mum,' he says, a touch of exasperation in his tone. 'Everybody was on about it in school. A boy went missing in Atenby. We had an assembly about staying safe and now we're not supposed to walk home on our own anymore unless the school gets a letter saying we're allowed to.'

Sarah sees Emily squeeze his hand. That's what she would do if she were his mother. She would keep him by her side at all times. She would shower him with love and kisses, smother him with affection. He would feel wanted and needed at all times. Safe and cosseted. He would want for nothing. She hopes Emily provides her boy with all of those things. He deserves that much and more.

'A get-together for coffee sounds great.' Sarah has no idea why she is saying this but it sounds right and came out spontaneously, no thought behind it. No planning or over analysing. Just a natural reaction to a simple statement.

'Really?'

Sarah feels her face burn at Emily's response. She seems genuinely happy at the thought of it. Not what she was expecting at all. She imagined a cool retort before Emily headed home, closing the door behind her and getting on with her busy life. And now she has this – a positive reply. She feels duty-bound to say something in return. It would be rude not to.

'Absolutely. How about I arrange something for over the weekend? I could even invite a few of the other ladies from the village.'

Emily's smile lights up her face. Another surprise that sends a wave of heat through Sarah's veins. With no idea of whether the dynamics of their get-together will work brilliantly or unravel in spectacular fashion, Sarah feels suddenly empowered. She visualises them all, these women, sitting in her kitchen, sipping coffee, eating cake, chatting happily, and finds herself giddy at the idea of it, a mild euphoria rising up her abdomen, swelling in her chest. It feels good to be needed, to have somebody want something from her. No longer the passive bystander, she is here, taking control, making things happen. And it actually feels rather marvellous.

'Looking forward to it,' Emily says as she grasps her son's hand and heads back home.

Sarah closes the door, a pulse rattling in her neck, her nerves jangling, Emily's smile, her reaction playing over and over in her head. Such a small thing and yet at the same time, a huge leap. She is making friends here, being proactive. No longer the meek mild stay-at-home wife, Sarah finally has something tangible in her life. A possible new friendship. Green shoots of hope spring up out of nowhere.

9

THE ABDUCTOR

I administered more sleeping pills for the first day. It was something I just had to do. Not an easy choice, keeping him sedated, but I had no other option. I need him pliable and drowsy, not upset and fearful. Besides, it gave me more time to be near to him, to watch him closely as he slept and drink in every inch of him. Every time he began to rouse, I carried him to the bathroom, put him on the toilet which he complied with without any resistance, then placed him back on the sofa and gave him another couple of sips of his juice.

He's still sleeping and I'm standing here watching him. I've been admiring his expression – so peaceful, so steady and calm. He's going to be a good boy living here with me; I can just tell. He has a maturity about him that far exceeds his years. I always knew he would return. I've had a feeling for so long now and finally, after all the waiting, after all the heartache and bouts of depression I have silently suffered, here he is, sleeping peacefully as if he doesn't have a care in the world.

I look around and a wave of contentment rushes over me. This room is perfect. Timothy's room. I prepared it specially. I hope he likes it when he wakes up. I'm sure he will. He may feel a little reticent at first but once he realises how good he has it here, how faultless this place is, he will settle perfectly. This is it how it is going to be now. This is his new life.

A rustle of fabric makes my blood bubble with anticipation. Every movement, every crackle, every whisper is accentuated in this room. The noise booms in my ears, rolling around my head as I watch him rouse and see his eyelids flicker. Here it is. This is the moment I've been waiting for. He's waking up.

It takes a little while for him to come around fully. Twice I stood here watching as he awoke briefly, then fell back into a deep sleep, twice his eyes opened only for a heaviness to overtake him and pull him back into a state of unconsciousness, but now here he is, rubbing at his eyes and trying to sit up. A pink flush creeps up his face, colouring his pale skin, giving him a healthy glow. An outsider looking in would think nothing suspicious or untoward about this situation. They would see it for what it is – a parent taking care of their child. Because that's all that is going on here. I am a parent nurturing a child who has been sorely neglected. Abandoned, left alone outside. He was asking to be taken. That woman who calls herself his mother deserves all she gets.

'Have I been asleep? Where am I?'

I'm prepared for this. I knew it was coming. I've thought this out, planned for it for what feels like an age. I'm ready.

'You had a nap. You must have had a busy day at school. And you're at my house. I've spoken to your mum. She's been called back to work but don't worry, you'll be comfortable here.' I feel remarkably calm, the words flowing out of me, fluid and coherent. It feels as easy as breathing doing this, keeping Timothy here in my house, telling him a few white lies, making him realise that he is better off here with me rather than with her, that dreadful woman who gives him no love and leaves him alone.

He is still drowsy, kneading his knuckles into his eye sockets and yawning.

'Now,' I say, clapping my hands together lightly, 'time for some food.' I pull the tray closer and place it next to him where he is lying on the sofa. 'I hope you like burger and chips. There's some ketchup here if you'd like it. Oh,' I say, feigning surprise as if I'd forgotten something, 'and your mum said you're allowed another bottle of Coca Cola. Another apology for being held up.' I drag a small bottle out from under the table and pop it on the tray next to his food.

He nods, eyeing the food hungrily before tucking into it and glugging at the fizzy drink, his lips sucking at the neck of the bottle.

'What's your name?' He chews noisily and wipes his mouth with the back of his hand.

I can't stop looking at his eyes, savouring how blue they are; the colour of the ocean on a warm summer's day, and find it hard to stop myself from thinking how wonderful he is, how clear his complexion is, like pure silk. He is everything I hoped he would be and more. A hand squeezes at my heart, compressing it deep within my chest

'My name?' I say, my voice a whisper. 'My name is Trent.'

I have no idea where that came from or why I said it. It was the first thing that entered my head. Some memories continue to linger long after the experience is dead and gone.

'Trent?' he laughs, his face creased with confusion. 'That's a funny name. Are you foreign?'

Bless this child. So innocent. So trusting and unassuming. So utterly perfect.

'No, I'm not foreign, and it's just my name. My parents gave it to me when I was born and that's just how it is. Now come on,' I say, casually clapping my hands together. 'Eat up. There's plenty more where that came from.'

I can hear every mastication, every morsel of food that is crushed between his teeth, the thunder of the liquid as it hurtles down his throat and hits his belly. It rebounds around the room, hitting the walls, echoing and bouncing back again. We are the only two people in the world – our little world – and it feels divine.

'What's that over there, Trent?'

I stop, unaccustomed to hearing that name being said out loud, realising after a couple of seconds that he is speaking to me, pointing over my shoulder. 'Ah, we'll have a look at that later. It can be a special treat for you after you've finished eating.'

He is nodding enthusiastically, his eyes wide now, his features gradually coming back to life after a long drug-induced slumber. Watching him consume his meal is an extravagance I never thought I would ever be witness to. After Timothy, I expected to spend the remainder of my life without him, but now here he is, sitting before me, his beautiful blue eyes full of fire and life. Things are going to work out perfectly. I can just tell. Call it intuition or a sixth sense. Call it whatever you like, I know that this is going to be faultless. It was always meant to be.

'Come on then,' I say as I watch him place his cutlery down on his empty plate with such exquisite care and precision, it almost brings tears to my eyes. 'Let's have a look, see what it is, eh?'

I remove the black vinyl cover to reveal my Epiphone Les Paul Sunburst electric guitar underneath, complete with Marshall amp. I can hardly breathe as I watch Timmy's eyes bulge with shock. His skin grows pink with excitement, his hands itch to touch the neck of the guitar. 'Can I have a go? I mean, if that's okay with you?'

'Yes,' I say, my words tumbling out in a flurry of excitement at the thought of having him here and this whole thing being so damn easy, so wonderfully effortless, 'you can have a go. Of course you can. Whatever is mine is yours.'

I almost call him sweetheart or darling and pull myself up just in time. I don't want to risk getting too over familiar and scaring him away, ruining this new episode of my life before it's even begun.

'Really?' His voice has risen a couple of octaves. I can all but feel the pound of anticipation and pleasure emanating from him as he approaches the guitar, his fingers twitching at his sides, his legs still wobbly as his body gradually wakes up.

'Here,' I say encouragingly, as I point towards the leather stool next to it. 'Sit yourself up here and have a strum. I'll just turn the amp on.'

He stops and stares at me and for a minute I think perhaps I've pushed things too far too quickly. Been too eager and brazen and scared him off.

'Won't it be too loud for your neighbours?' He is almost whispering and I am stupefied, utterly bewildered at how somebody so young can be so thoughtful and considerate.

'Oh,' I reply, my heart filling my chest, augmenting and swelling at this delightful creature before me, 'don't worry so much about that. I've got it all sorted. They'll never complain. You can make as much noise as you like, be as loud as you like. We're quite safe here. Nobody will hear us in this place.' I look around at the room, my room – our room – and smile. 'Nobody at all.'

10

LYNDA

She looks dreadful, with her hair askew and her dressing gown hastily wrapped around her body and roughly knotted into a big bunch. Lynda stares at Moira's pale waxy skin and thinks that perhaps her friend needs to go back to bed and sleep off whatever bug or virus she has picked up.

'Oh, Moira. Poor you. Have you been to see a doctor?'

Moira lets out a rattling cough and sniffs, running her hand through her thick wiry hair as she shakes her head dolefully. 'No. I'm sure it'll clear up in a few days. I just need a hot toddy and an early night. A couple of days and I'll be fine. Really sorry to let you down, Lynda. I was so looking forward to tonight as well.'

'Can't be helped, my dear. I'll pass on your apologies to our new artist friend.'

'Thank you. Hopefully I'll be fighting fit next week.' Her voice croaks as she stops and coughs again, bringing her fist up in front of her mouth, her body angled away from her concerned friend. 'God knows where I picked it up from. The farthest I've been this week is the bottom of my garden. Must be an age thing,' she says as she grips on to her towelling robe and ties it tighter around her waist. 'Since I hit fifty, I seem to be susceptible to every illness going.'

'Just make sure you rest up and don't be going outside tending to that bloody massive garden of yours.' Lynda raises her hand and points her finger in Moira's direction. 'I've told you before that you need to get somebody in to help look after it. It's far too large for you to manage on your own.'

'I know, I know. When I'm well, it's not a problem though. I enjoy getting out there, even in the middle of winter, I love nothing more than sitting on the bench, staring at it all, willing spring along.'

Lynda looks up to the sky, reaches out her upturned palm to catch a droplet of rain. 'Hmm. Looks like you'll have a long wait for that with this weather.'

Moira shrugs, turns and coughs into her hand then moves back and gives Lynda a weak smile.

'Right, well, you know where I am if you need anything,' Lynda says, her voice shrill and authoritative. 'And I'll let you know how tonight goes. Anyway, best be off. I need to get parked in town and it might be a bit of a bugger. There's some sort of small music festival going on. Damn stupid council with its plans to use the high street as a concert venue.'

She gives Moira a brief wave and heads down the long path and out onto the pavement where her car is parked. She and Moira have been friends for eight years now, ever since Lynda made the move to Middleham after spotting the cottage she now lives in, for sale.

She hadn't planned on moving but it seemed like the right thing to do. Her other Victorian property suddenly felt too big for her to manage and Prosper Cottage was such a quaint thing with its Georgian windows and climbing roses snaked around the front door. It looked and felt perfect, like slipping into a comfortable old shoe.

She had resigned herself to being single after a brief relationship with a woman called Jean who neglected to tell Lynda that she actually had a husband and three children and had no plans to leave them. And so Lynda was ready for a new start, somewhere quieter, off the beaten track where she could enjoy a slower pace of life and not feel like a stranger in her own home. Middleham was still within travelling distance of work and to this day it is a move that Lynda hasn't regretted. It has also given her a little bit extra in the bank for when she retires. The village is much as she expected with its peaceful location, eclectic mix of people and fair share of nosey neighbours. Meeting Moira at the local history society was a bonus. Like Lynda, she is reserved, living a quiet dignified life, dismissing gossip and drama, preferring instead to pour her efforts into matters of the mind; intellectual pastimes that tax the brain.

Lynda sniffs and climbs in her car, wishing there were more Moiras around, more people who respected the needs of others. She thinks of the missing boy in Atenby and feels a stab of fear. It's so close to Middleham. She's surprised they haven't seen any police around the area. After the initial announcement on the news that he had gone missing, probably abducted, she half expected to wake up to a flurry of activity and was more than a little shocked to discover that nothing had changed. Life in the village ticked along at its usual pace, as if nothing had taken place. As if a small boy hadn't just vanished only a couple of miles down the road. Perhaps the police already have their suspicions and have homed in on a suspect.

Lynda starts the engine, hoping that that is indeed the case. She feels sure that they know what they're doing. *Hope so anyway*, she thinks. *Faith and trust in people and the police is all we have when it comes to dealing with such cases, isn't it? The affected family can only sit and wait, hoping and praying for a positive outcome.*

The car growls as she pushes the accelerator a little too far, before swinging her vehicle around and heading out of the village towards the main road into town.

~

The chill in the air catches her by surprise. Lynda pulls up her collar and shuffles through the crowds towards the community centre. Finding a parking space wasn't half as bad as she expected. The cold has probably kept a lot of people away. She puffs out her cheeks, wondering why anybody would choose to stand outside in this weather, listening to music they could listen to at home. She's too old for all that nonsense, too rigid and unbending in her dislike of large crowds, too intolerant of stupid people who would undoubtedly get in her way and spoil her enjoyment of the evening.

She isn't miserable and grouchy, as some have suggested, neither is she unapproachable nor frosty. Experienced is what she is. She knows people, can anticipate their every move, their every thought, work out exactly what is going on inside their heads. She isn't an expert but is usually pretty close to the mark when it comes to fathoming their mindsets. There have been a few who have caught her out in the past, left her floundering, but not many. A couple of troubled challenging pupils have tested her capabilities for sure, made her doubt her own intuition after she missed the signs, but in the main she is usually fairly accurate.

She spots the lights of the community centre in the distance, around a corner and away from the gathering throng of freezing people who have obviously underestimated an early spring evening, some of them with thin jackets and some not wearing any warm clothing at all, garbed out in only T-shirts and low slung jeans. The thought of it makes her skin prickle and shrivel. Youth really is wasted in the young, as the saying goes, and yet she wouldn't want any of it back. She prefers the wealth of knowledge and experience she has stored up in her head as opposed to being driven to achieve the ultimate hedonistic lifestyle sold to her though the television and social media. Her routine, her job and her interests are what keeps her going. Everything else is just piffle and waffle.

A blast of warmth greets her as she opens the door and steps inside, into a flood of ochre light and a small huddle of people of all ages, all shapes and sizes. Her chest expands with relief. Not too many and a goodly eclectic mix. Already the place exudes an air of conviviality, a welcome atmosphere that is tangible as she slips off her coat and steps forward into the middle of the crowd.

'Hello. So glad you could join us.' A woman in her mid-forties is smiling at Lynda, her hand outstretched. 'I'm Gaynor. I help run the community centre and just thought I'd hang around for a while to help Ashton since this is his first session here.'

Lynda offers her hand and recoils slightly at the cold dry skin of this woman. Her palm is like parchment, with deep grooves and a dull coarse feel to it. 'Pleased to meet you, Gaynor. I'm Lynda. I'm sure your presence here will be very much appreciated by everyone concerned. These initial gatherings can be a bit intimidating at first, can't they? Until everyone becomes familiar with one another, that is.'

'Indeed,' Gaynor replies, her voice deep and reassuring, belying her diminutive svelte frame and elf-like features. 'That's why I offered to stay behind, to help Ashton set everything up and get the introductions over with. That's the hard bit. He's a lovely talented guy and I'm sure you're all going to really enjoy your time here with him.'

More people arrive, bustling in behind her, the sweep of the open door bringing in a blast of cold air that blankets the room. More introductions are made, more conviviality takes place until eventually, a young man appears through a door carrying a small black satchel. Under his arm is a large blank canvas. Lynda guesses that he is probably in his late twenties or early thirties. *How strange*, she thinks, *that the roles have been reversed, and that she, in her early sixties, is now being taught by somebody who is possibly half her age.* Still, sometimes it's rather relaxing to switch off and be led by somebody else, rather than having to take the lead and be in charge all of the time. On occasion, it is exactly what a person needs, to be able to watch and learn rather than constantly scrutinising, hoping your words are going in, becoming embedded and having an effect on a young person, giving them a positive trajectory in life. Being a teacher can become an all-encompassing vocation, smothering your own needs, stifling your own creativity in order to breathe life into somebody else's.

She watches him as he sets up his easel, notices that his hands are trembling and feels a pang of pity for this poor chap. Teaching adults is in a different league to teaching children, and she should know. The strategies required for gaining attention are completely different. Standing at the front, clapping and making silly noises to acquire everybody's attention, whilst working for many in a class full of children, would be deemed as silly and inappropriate when teaching adults.

Lynda looks around at the rest of the class, willing them to listen to this young man, willing them to be kind.

'Welcome, everybody,' he says, his voice breaking slightly as he looks at them with a degree of caution. 'I'm Ashton and I'd like to welcome you to my little art session.'

A small round of applause breaks out from the back of the

hall. Lynda turns to see Gaynor standing there, clapping at Ashton's words.

'We're delighted to be here,' Lynda says a little too loudly to drown out the noise. *Silly and unnecessary. Let the man get on with it for goodness' sake.* She is sure it is well intentioned but it is also overly dramatic, drawing attention to his nervous state and flushed complexion.

He clears his throat and begins to speak, telling them about his qualifications and experience, then displays some of his work, pointing them towards an array of pictures lined up on the back wall. Despite his limited credentials, it is apparent that he is a talented man, predominantly self-taught and able to emulate some of the great artists' work with such precision and startling accuracy that a silence quickly descends as they scan his pictures, a palpable air of admiration and respect evident in the room.

'What a clever thing you are!' one woman says as she stands, eyes narrowed while she stares at his copy of Van Gogh's *Sunflowers*.

'I have my own work as well,' he pipes in quickly. 'It's just that I feel more comfortable displaying these as I think they are of a higher standard than my own stuff.'

Lynda nods, comprehending what he is saying. It's easier, more comfortable to hide behind the identity of somebody else, rather than open yourself up to the scrutiny of others by revealing your own thoughts and ideas. Showing everyone your paintings must feel like exposing your own personal diary to a crowd of onlookers and asking them to read it aloud. The thought makes her shiver. Far better to stay in the shadows and keep your own private thoughts to yourself. She can understand why he has brought these particular paintings along. They are a group of strangers to him, not nearly familiar enough to allow them to see his personal work, to allow them to step inside his head and be privy to his innermost thoughts.

Smiling, she steps away, understanding his rationale, connecting with his way of thinking, feeling sure that she and this young man, Ashton, are going to get along just fine.

11

I t's a bracelet. An involuntary shiver runs over her skin. She was expecting chocolates. Or maybe even a box of miniature drinks. But not this. Definitely not this. It feels so sudden. Too soon even. And yet, a small part of her is flattered, a sliver of excitement pulsing through her at the thought of having somebody in her life who cares enough to do this, to go to the effort of choosing, buying and wrapping this exquisite gift. This is a new phenomenon. Something different. Something exciting.

The other part of her is fearful, worried and anxious that this new feeling, this new relationship will come crashing down around her taking her emotions with it, blackening them, leaving her a husk of her former self. She can't go through that again, another break-up. She just can't. Even though she would never want Samuel back, the emotional turmoil at the time was almost unbearable.

Since Samuel, she has had only one other attachment to another person, if you can count two dates and a peck on the cheek an attachment, and it was she who ended it after deciding there was no attraction there, no spark at all. It felt like she was dating her own brother. And now here she is, feeling a deep connection to somebody before she has had a chance to work out whether or not it is the right thing to do.

Her hand hovers over the small velvet box, her fingers quaking as she sweeps the tiny silver bracelet up into her palm in one quick movement. It's beautiful, there's no denying it. A small ruby stone sits in the centre of the silver bangle. Slipping it on, she realises that it's a perfect fit on her slim wrist and wonders if Mo had it altered specially. It would be just like him to go to such lengths. Emily's heart leaps around her chest as she pictures his face, thinks about the smoothness of his voice, then worries that this is all too good to be true, that everything will go terribly wrong at some point leaving her heartbroken and bereft for a future she hoped and prayed would happen, but didn't.

She places the bracelet back in the box and rests her hand against her chest to stem the rising panic that is creeping up her throat, squeezing her windpipe closed and making her head thump. She has to stop this. Plenty of people have good easy relationships where they are kind to one another. Samuel has tainted her view of what constitutes normal, made her think that tragedy lurks around every corner.

She feels as if she has spent the last few years waiting for the hammer to fall, just waiting for that time when a new start full of possibilities and promise will come to an abrupt and untimely end. This is how people operate after they have been mentally bashed about by former partners. She has been in self-preservation mode for so many years now, she doesn't know how to break out of it. It's a shield that surrounds her, a suit of armour she wears to keep herself safe from those who wish to hurt her and her boy. But perhaps now is the time to remove it, to be her real self. To expose her softer side rather than being constantly on red alert, wondering where the next crushing disappointment is going to come from. Isn't that how other people live their lives? With an easiness and acceptance that everything will always turn out for the best? And if so, why shouldn't she also be allowed to live that way? Expecting the worst from every situation has become a habit she is finding difficult to shake, but shake it she must if she is to move on, otherwise she will be stuck in this rut indefinitely and that is not how she wants to be. She wants a good easy life for herself and her boy, not this stilted existence where she lives in a constant state of readiness, waiting and braced for the next major blow.

'Mum, I'm hungry. You said we would eat when we got in and now my belly is rumbling and I feel sick!' Joel's voice drags her out of her musings, bringing her back into the sharp light of reality.

'Okay. I'm on it,' Emily shouts as she tucks the box into her pocket, the small container giving her a warm glow inside as it presses against her skin. Dare she allow herself to feel happy and wanted and desired? Maybe it's time to put the past behind her and to start thinking positively. She feels she has earned it. She feels it is time.

Pizza is hardly a nutritious and healthy meal, she knows that, but it's fast and tasty and to see Joel's little face as he tucks into it, his small hands holding the gooey cheese-laden slice, is worth it. 'How's your tummy?'

Joel nods, his lips coated with grease as he shoves another slice in his mouth and chews it hungrily like a child who hasn't eaten for months. 'Better,' he says, his mouth full.

'Good. Glad to hear it.' Emily sits back in her chair, replete, a thought dangling in the forefront of her mind, words presenting themselves, waiting to be said out loud. She swallows and wipes at her mouth with a serviette then closes her eyes briefly before speaking. 'You don't have to answer me if you don't want to...'

Joel stops chewing, his hand poised halfway to his mouth, a large triangle of pizza bending and dripping as he watches her carefully, listening to what she has to say. 'I was just wondering what you thought of Mo? I mean I know you've only met him a handful of times but I just thought–'

Emily wants to laugh and cry simultaneously as Joel's face breaks into an impromptu smile. 'He's ace! I think he's really cool. Why?' Joel asks innocently. 'Are you going to marry him?'

She shakes her head and wags her finger at her young son, unable to hide her delight at his response. 'Not so fast, young man! Not so fast, eh?' Her stomach clenches at the thought. Perhaps her son has spotted something between them, an invisible link that draws them together.

'Anyway,' Joel continues as he takes another sloppy bite of his pizza, 'Mo said he would take me out one day, maybe fishing or to the football match. Me and him and maybe some of his mates.'

Emily swallows, rubs at her forehead, smoothing out the lines there. She isn't used to this. Her parents live abroad for half of the year and Samuel, apart from the allowance he pays towards Joel's upbringing every month, is an absent father in every sense of the word, having not seen his son since he was a baby. Besides, Mo hasn't mentioned any of this to her. This is all new, alien. It will take some time to digest.

They continue eating, a solid silence between them as she considers the possibility that Mo will also grow closer to Joel if their relationship advances at this pace. Is that such a bad thing? Perhaps she is being overprotective having had her son all to herself for all this time. Maybe it's time to loosen the apron strings, give her son some space and allow Mo the chance to form a bond with her boy. It makes sense and seems like the right thing to do, a natural progression from near stranger to possible stepfather. A sudden bout of dizziness takes hold at the very idea, at thinking those words, allowing them to roam freely in her head. Her eyes fill up and her skin grows hot. Even thinking about it, considering it as a possible future, causes her to sit up that bit straighter. She will ring Mo later, see if he's available and thank him for the bracelet. She might even mention his possible venture with Joel and see what sort of reaction it provokes. Not that she is necessarily against the idea. It's just that she needs some time to get her head around it, to absorb the fact that her boy is growing up and becoming friends with somebody that she herself is very fond of.

'Right,' Emily says as Joel finishes off the last slice of pizza, 'time to clear up. Tell you what, I'll sort out the dishes if you do your homework. What have you got?'

He screws up his face in distaste. 'Maths. Miss Simpson said we have to practise our times tables.'

'Ah. That'll be easy.' Emily leans forward and gently strokes his hot crimson cheek. 'How about we strike a deal? You can have the TV on in the background if you like. But you have to really practise those eights and nines. They're the ones you found hard last time, remember?'

He nods sullenly and is off his seat and heading into the living room before she can say anything more. She listens to the blare of the television in the distance and smiles as she visualises him desperately searching for the remote to lower the volume so she doesn't have to shout through to him to turn it down. This is their routine, their life. This is what keeps her world balanced and in sync.

Clearing the kitchen takes only a matter of minutes and by the time she marches through to the living room, Joel has already emptied his schoolbag on the table and is still searching for the remote. Emily feels her skin crawl as she listens to the news reporter speak about Leo Fairland and the fact that he has now been missing for nearly two days. She spins around looking for a way to mute the TV. She doesn't want Joel hearing this. He is a child and doesn't need to be subjected to such things. The news about this incident has reached a whole new level of toxicity, slating and slandering Leo's mother, asking neighbours and purported friends about the veracity of her story.

'I'd heard he was often left home alone.' A toothless elderly woman is staring at the camera, clearly relishing her fifteen minutes of fame. Her hair is a tangle of grey curls and although she can't see her feet, Emily feels almost certain the woman is being interviewed in the street while still wearing her slippers, possibly even still in her pyjamas.

'I think it's about time these so-called working mothers stayed at home and started looking after their kids properly. If she'd been there at that school gate when the bell went, none of this would've 'appened.' A bald-headed man with pockmarked skin shakes his head at the reporter who thanks him for his time and comments before swinging back to face the camera, his microphone obscuring the lower half of his face as he battles to be heard against the howling wind.

'Well, there you have it. Just a few of the heartfelt comments from people in the nearby town who have been hit hard by this terrible occurrence.'

Emily has heard enough. She finds the remote on a top shelf and frantically scrolls through the channels until she lands upon a cartoon for Joel to watch. Any cartoon. It doesn't matter. Anything is better than the drivel being spouted on the news by people who know nothing about anything yet are convinced they know it all. They stand there pontificating about how bad a mother that poor woman is when they know nothing whatsoever about her or her life.

Emily is willing to bet her bottom dollar that those people

have waited all their lives for something like this to happen so they can snag a couple of seconds in the limelight and talk utter drivel to a watching world. It sickens her. They sicken her. People can be vile and disgusting without a thought for what others are going through.

She is so grateful that her life is back on track after all the shit that Samuel put her through. She is fortunate enough to earn a decent enough wage that allows her to employ a childminder a few days a week and is also lucky that Samuel did the one honourable thing in his life and agreed to help pay for Joel's upbringing. Without his input into her monthly finances, she may well be in the same position as that poor woman who has had to spend her days dashing away from work in a blinding hurry to collect her son from school. All it takes is a line of slow-moving traffic, an awkward customer who refuses to let you leave on time, and the whole deck of cards comes toppling down, that carefully constructed, flimsy edifice that is her life – and the lives of many working people – can collapse into an unrecognisable sorry heap of nothing in an instant.

Driven by a sense of injustice and a need to hear the voice of another person, Emily snatches up her phone and punches in Mo's number, hoping he has finished his shift in his taxi and is at home studying. One year left and he will have his maths degree and will then hopefully be able to start applying for other jobs. He's a good man, a kind and thoughtful man, she knows this and suddenly feels guilty for doubting his intentions when he mentioned spending more time with Joel. Any issues she has with it are hers and hers alone. She is the one making problems where there aren't any, not him.

His answer machine kicks in and Emily leaves a message thanking him for the gift, telling him what a lovely and generous thought it was to buy it for her. She ends the call and flops down onto the sofa, her body heavy with the woes of the world.

'Come on,' she says to Joel, clapping her hands with more positivity than she feels. She suddenly feels worn down by the bitterness and negativity on the news and social media. Why can't people just pull together and be kind? 'I'll give you a hand with your maths homework. Right, what's seven times six?'

12

Sweat blooms under his armpits and gathers around his hairline. It's going well. Everyone is being polite and they all seem impressed with his collection of sketches and paintings. So why does he feel so fucking nervous? His body feels as if it's vibrating, his shirt doing little to disguise the solid beat of his heart. He stands behind his easel, suddenly remembering that he has forgotten to do a register. *Damn it.* He can do it when he's finished this little talk. The place isn't going to burn down in the next few minutes. Except Gaynor is here and now he feels even more compelled to do the right thing, to adhere to the rules and regulations of the place.

'Sorry folks,' he says sharply, his voice carrying over the room, pinballing off the bare walls, bouncing around and causing everyone to stare at him. 'I just need to do a register for fire purposes and go through a few housekeeping rules. If I can just take your names and then let you know where the toilets are and the nearest fire exits, then we can carry on and enjoy the rest of the session.'

'Ha!' a voice shouts from behind him. 'We definitely need to know about the location of the lavatory. We have a collective age of a thousand in here tonight.'

There's a short titter followed by a prolonged silence. His heartbeat increases. Sweat runs down his back, pooling at his waist, darkening his bottle green shirt.

'Right okay, toilets are through that door and to the right. The fire exit is the set of double doors behind you and if I can pass around this sheet of paper, could you possibly write down your name and hand it back to me when you're done?' His voice sounds disembodied, as if it's coming from another room. It ricochets in his head, strange and unnatural.

The rustle of the sheet as it's passed from person to person, rips through the silence. Why did he have to stop? Despite his nerves, it had all been going really well. Everybody seemed at ease, and now an atmosphere has settled on them, a darker more sombre ambience that has shattered the previous tranquillity. He waits until everybody has signed it then quickly scans the sheet and pushes it into his bag. He'll look at it later, get to know their names, but for now he wants to get on, to break this awkward silence and get people back into a more relaxed frame of mind.

'Okay thanks, everyone. Now, what I thought we would do is start the evening by sketching some still life.' He steps away from the table that contains an array of random objects – an apple, a water bottle, a wallet and a pepper pot. 'You can draw all of them if you wish or just focus in on one or two objects. It's completely up to you. That's the beauty of art. It's all down to interpretation.'

A murmur of appreciation ripples around the small gathering, people nodding and smiling. He allows himself to expel a small breath of relief, his chest swelling and expanding as he gradually controls his breathing, stemming the panic that had threatened to overwhelm him for most of the day. *This is going to be fine. It has to be.* He will make it fine. They seem like a friendly bunch. He wishes Gaynor would up and go and leave him to it. For all she thinks she is providing some backup and support for him, her presence makes him feel nervous under the extra pair of eyes, as if she is keeping watch for any mistakes and taking note of them.

The class set up their sketch pads, some standing at easels, others sitting at small tables next to the display. The initial easy feeling returns as everyone sets to, concentrating and becoming ensconced in the process of drawing.

Ashton wanders amongst them, giving advice, making positive comments, wondering how the hell he ever got here and whether or not they will see through his façade to the terrified boy underneath who lives every single day in fear of being recognised and found out.

'That's a fascinating interpretation.' He is standing next to a middle-aged lady who has short greying hair and sharp features. Her cheekbones are angular and slightly equine, but she has soft welcoming eyes. She has drawn all of the objects piled on top of each other. Each of them is stacked smallest to largest with the pepper pot at the bottom and the bottle of water at the top. 'Is it symbolic?'

The woman gives him a quick glance and nods, then turns her attention back to her artwork but not before he sees it – a rapid flushing of her face, the darting of her eyes to evade his gaze, the stiffening of her spine. Once again, he is plunged into a sea of uncertainty; his pulse beginning to race, perspiration prickling him, a slight blurring of his vision. Does he know her? He doesn't think so but then, that period of his life has been shifted to the farthest corners of his mind in a deliberate attempt to forget it ever happened. Like he ever could. The actual incident is crystal clear in his memory. It's just the peripheral things he has tried his best to forget; the people, the minutiae of that time, he has worked hard to shove it all away, to compartmentalise it so it doesn't intrude on his everyday life. Sometimes it works and sometimes it doesn't. There are days when he wakes up refreshed, ready to face the world and then there are other days when he stirs himself from the arms of sleep feeling as if the weight of the world is on his shoulders, dragging him down to the dirt, right where he belongs.

The heat in the room seems to rise. He rolls up his sleeves and moves on, chatting to the other people, giving as much advice as he can, pointing out artistic merit where it is due, and all the while, the grey-haired woman sits squarely in his mind. He tries to sneak glances at her, to work out if she is familiar to him. Something tells him that she could be, then another part of his memory tells him to stop it, to end this perpetual cycle of metaphorical self-flagellation. It's not healthy to live like this, constantly looking over his shoulder, worried that somebody might remember him from way back when. It all happened a long time ago. He was only eleven years old, for crying out loud, too young to know what he was doing, and yet according to those around him, old enough to know better. Old enough to be prosecuted.

Ashton nips at the flesh on the end of his fingertips, his thumbs and forefingers twisting and pulling until he manages to find a loose section, a thin thread of skin that he tugs at until it comes away in one satisfying piece. A streak of agony shoots up his finger, a throbbing painful reminder that he is still here, torturing himself over something that is best forgotten. He cannot, no matter how hard he tries, draw a line under it. He is his own worst enemy.

While the rest of the world has moved on from that dreadful period of his life, he is still there, re-experiencing it, his life stuck on a loop. He has relived it so many times now, he wonders if the day will come when the thoughts and memories will stop and allow him to be free. For a while in Lincoln, the sensation dissipated, but now he has come back up north, back to his hometown, the fear of bumping into somebody and being remembered for what he did, overshadows everything. And now, here he is, with a chance to start afresh doing what he loves and already it has come back to bite him.

Perhaps this lady is simply nervous, or maybe she is concentrating, or maybe – just maybe – it is all in his head? A figment of his imagination. Maybe she didn't change, her eyes didn't flicker, her skin tone didn't change. Telling himself that that is the case, he moves on, trying to forget the look in her eyes, that quick flicker that he is convinced signified recognition, and speaks to the other people in the group, attempting to lose himself in his thoughts, all the while reminding himself that he is here to teach these people, to make a good impression and not end the evening like a gibbering wreck.

This is a way out of his mundane factory job, a way into the world of art. It doesn't pay but it will look good on his CV. What he really wants is to work in a college, teaching others, but knows that it's out of the question with his past. A criminal check would soon rule him out. There are other jobs out there in the art world however, he just lacks the required experience. This place is his leg-up, his helping hand. He just has to make sure he doesn't fuck it up before it's even begun.

The time passes so quickly that the caretaker arrives to lock up the centre before everybody has even finished packing away their equipment. Ashton stands by the door, waving everyone off, nodding and chatting until at last they have all disappeared, even her, the middle-aged lady, who he managed to avoid by discussing brush strokes and shading with another lady, making sure their conversation lasted long enough until she was safely out of the door. Especially her. Cowardly for sure, but by next week, he will have plucked up enough courage to face her. He has a week to sort his head out and tell himself that it was nothing, just a quick nondescript glance that he misread and blew out of proportion.

'Sorry for keeping you waiting.' Ashton approaches the ruddy-faced man and pulls the piece of paper out of his pocket that contains the names of his tutees. 'Do you need this?'

'Eh?' The caretaker glances over his shoulder as he runs a brush around the floor and sweeps it all into a dark corner. 'Not for me, big fella. That's for you to keep. Or you can hand it over to Gaynor. She sorts all that sort of stuff out. I just come in to sweep up and lock the place up, as a favour, you know?'

Ashton nods sagely and stuffs it back into his pocket, relief that it's all finally ended washing over him as he slips on his coat. It wasn't so bad after all. He actually rather enjoyed it. He kind of hoped that there would be some younger people present, but at least almost everyone turned up and they left looking fairly content so he counts it as a win.

'Right, well I suppose I'll see you next week?' The caretaker doesn't reply, responding instead with a curt nod as Ashton heads out into the chill of the night.

Only when he has reached the bus stop does he dare to reach for the list of attendees. He runs his eyes down it and stops at one name. It looks familiar, but he can't be sure. Maybe it's better that certain memories are unobtainable to him. Maybe he should ignore the whole thing, get on the bus and forget about the look that she gave him. Or maybe he should try to remember, to work out whether or not he needs to do anything about it. Not that he can do anything aside from giving up the classes, which he really doesn't want to do. As nervous as he is about taking them, he also knows that this is his chance to better himself, an opportunity he cannot afford to miss.

His head is tight, his shoulders hunched and knotted by the time the bus arrives. Sloping off upstairs to be on his own,

Ashton takes a closer look at the name, squinting, raking through old memories, trying to get them to resurface. By the time he gets off at his stop, he has convinced himself that it's her, his old teacher. The one who had to testify against him in court.

He had so many teachers after Miss Croft; a series of adult faces, one after another after another – police officers, psychologists, family liaison officers – that they all blur into one in his mind. Too many to count. And yet her features have stuck in his head. The way she looked at him, her reactions every time he caught her eye. She recognised him. He knows it now. There's no other explanation. There's a connection there, a link to his past. A past he would sooner forget. A past he is deeply ashamed of. And it seems that apart from not turning up next week, he is stuck with this situation. There's not a damn thing he can do about it.

13

LYNDA

An unforgiving blustery wind catches her unawares as she steps outside, hitting her full in the face, cooling her hot reddened cheeks. The sound of her heels clicking on the pavement booms around the now empty street. The crowds that had gathered to watch the music festival have since parted, leaving the area almost empty. A half-crushed tin can rolls along the road, resting in the gutter with a metallic clatter. In the distance, a dog barks, its gruff timbre reverberating through the darkness of the town.

Lynda hurries along, pulling up her collar against the bracing cold. Spring still feels a long way off even though it should be here by now. The calendar no longer seems to dictate the seasons. The weather is ferocious and unpredictable and everyone is at its mercy. A nearby awning flaps in the breeze and a sad neon sign above an empty pizza shop flashes erratically in the distance.

This is a lonely old town, thinks Lynda as she picks up her pace and hurries to the car park, head dipped against the gusts that slap at her skin. Her head begins to ache and her back stiffens as she tries to half twist away from the freezing squall. She lets out a juddering breath. *It's not him. It can't be.* He was in her mind before she entered the place, her thoughts full of those kids that she missed, those lost disillusioned pupils that she overlooked and let down and now she is putting two and two together and coming up with five. And yet, she can't stop thinking about him. It was the eyes. Those piercing blue eyes that could cut glass. Of course, if it is him, he has changed his name. He was an Andrew, not an Ashton and she is almost certain Andrew Gilkes didn't have any siblings, so him being a brother to the boy she once knew is out of the question.

By the time she reaches her car, she has convinced herself it cannot be him, that lad from that terrible time. The boy was sent away. Surely, he would be living out of the area after what happened, after that dreadful incident? Although of course, it was what – twenty years ago? He will have moved on now, be a grown man, living somewhere far away from here, if he has any sense, that is. Lynda remembers the details of the court case, the abuse he had suffered before the attack. There were no winners in that case, just a string of sad helpless victims.

The heater takes some time to get rid of the chill that has wrapped itself around her ankles and settled deep in her bones. It's at times like this that she feels ready for retirement. An academic year feels too long to wait to get her life back. But she knows that in the morning, once she has slept and rested, a day at work or a weekend pottering around the garden doesn't faze her in the slightest. The world feels like a brighter happier place.

She puts her foot down, pleased the traffic is light. Maybe it's dredging up all those memories that is pulling her down, making her feel a hundred years old. It was a sad time for sure, an awful traumatic time. And even if it is him, there is nothing she can do about it, not a damn thing. The boy paid a heavy penalty for what he did. If only she hadn't been dragged into the whole sorry mess then she wouldn't be thinking about it now. If only he hadn't done it in the first place.

Her breath feels chunky and ragged as exhaustion gets the better of her. She doesn't want this to get in the way of her enjoyment of the classes. Whether it is him or not should be irrelevant. It's over with, all in the past and best forgotten. She shakes her head, switches on the radio and turns her thoughts to the programme playing, focusing only on the road ahead.

The car crunches over the gravelled drive as she approaches her house. Something occurred to her on the drive here. Shuffling out of the seat, she grapples with her keys and locks the driver's door. Once inside, she combs through a pile of documents stacked next to the bread bin, searching for the piece of paper that may just answer the question that is still roaming around her head, refusing to leave her be. It takes two attempts to find it, her fingers fluttering, her head beginning to ache at the base of her skull as she opens the slip of paper that advertised the class. The graphics are basic, possibly done on a home printer, but the link to Ashton is there. His name. Ashton G. Andrews. It's too familiar, too close to his original name of Andrew Gilkes for it not to be him. Had there not been a resemblance, then perhaps she would put it down to coincidence, but not with the striking likeness. *Those eyes. That gaze.* She takes a long breath and swallows. *It's him. It's definitely him.*

Lynda drops onto a nearby chair, a rickety wooden structure that scrapes and groans under her weight. She needs to make a decision. Does she continue with the classes or is she so scared of revisiting that period in her life, so scared of cracking open those difficult memories that she has to stop attending?

Cross with herself for allowing her emotions to dictate to

her, she stands up and brushes a line of imaginary dust from her lap. She must continue with the classes. Of course she must. It is the only decent thing to do. The boy paid a hefty price for what he did.

And so did you.

She pushes the thought away. A year of sleepless nights leading up to the court case is nothing compared to what that boy had to endure in his sad little life. She was an adult, more than able to handle such a difficult situation. He was just a child. She wasn't, and still isn't, entirely sure that he knew what he was doing at the time, that what he did was wrong and illegal. He was a deeply troubled boy, damaged and broken by a brute of a man who knew exactly what *he* was doing.

Dear God. Lynda allows a lone tear to escape. After all this time, the boy she once knew is here, back in her life, and for all of her knowledge and experience, the persona she projects to the outside world of being a capable strong woman, she is sitting here, alone in her kitchen with no clue of how to handle this situation. No idea of what she should do next.

She boils the kettle, makes a cup of strong tea, allowing the tannin to coat her mouth and spur her brain into action. It's too early for bed. That's where she wants to go but knows that she will then wake up at 4am with this issue still whirling around in her brain when what she really craves is a full night's sleep, a leisurely restful slumber that will give her a clear head and allow her to think in a more linear fashion.

The tea is hot, burning her throat as she sips at it and swallows, gulp after gulp until the mug is empty. Lynda stares at the clock. 9pm. It's at times like this she thinks how wonderful it would be to have a partner, to have somebody to talk to, somebody to share her problems with. Being alone has its benefits but with that comes many downsides, and a lack of comfort and sympathy in times of need is one of them.

'Damn it.' She stands up, rinses her cup, places it upside down on the drainer and switches off the light. She no longer cares whether or not it's too early. Her bed is calling. She is bone weary, so tired she feels like she could sleep for a thousand years.

The stairs appear to move from side to side under her feet as she climbs them, her feet heavy and cumbersome, her body like lead. *Perhaps it's the shock*, she thinks as she climbs into bed without even attempting to wash her face or brush her teeth. She thought that that whole nasty business was behind her, all done and dusted, and now here it is, staring her in the face week after week after week when all she wants to do is learn how to draw and improve her painting skills. Life can often be a difficult winding path, the journey difficult to navigate.

And then she thinks of that poor missing boy and how dreadfully guilty his mother must feel and suddenly her problems don't feel so bad after all. *There is always somebody out there far worse off than yourself*, she thinks. *It's just that sometimes, we have to put everything into perspective and look at the broader picture, put our own purported problems into context.* That's what she needs to do right now – forget about the past and focus on the future. Even if it is him, he is obviously happy and settled and trying to make something of his life. That has got to be a good thing, hasn't it?

The last thing Lynda sees before sleep takes her is his childlike face, staring up at her as she catches him with the other boy, doing things no child should ever do, forcing her to see something no sane rational adult should ever have to see. Then hour after hour of darkness as she slumbers silently.

14

I leave him alone in the room, strumming the guitar, experimenting with different sounds. When he's ready I will show him some chords, perhaps even teach him how to play properly. He doesn't notice me leaving, which is a positive thing. He's comfortable, at home, and that makes me happy. More than happy. I'm bordering on delirious but am fighting to suppress it, to keep my real feelings under control. I need to keep a healthy distance for now, maintain this aura of professionalism as if I'm no more than his temporary carer. Soon he will realise that I am so much more than that and then we will form a lasting bond, one that can never be broken. Not by anybody.

Closing and locking the door behind me, I head upstairs into the bathroom where I shower and change into clean clothes. At some point he will have to get used to being left alone. It's just how it is, how we will have to live until things calm down and we strike up a routine. This is a new situation for both of us. It's down to me to reassure the boy, my little Timmy, and convince him that this is now his home, the place where he belongs. I feel certain that he will adapt. He's a clever boy, well-mannered and advanced for his years, not like many youngsters nowadays who are coarse and uncouth. He has a way about him, a subtle ability to suss out new people and situations. I've seen it in him – that look, the trusting expression, his aptitude to see beyond the obvious. Not many children have that capability, but Timmy does. He's a good boy, a special child and I'm blessed to have him back in my life.

I do know that at some point I will have to face the outside world, not salt myself away to keep an eye on him here. I don't want to raise any suspicions. My day-to-day comings and goings will appear stilted and noticeable if I break with them. People are naturally suspicious, always ready to point the finger, to intrude on the lives of others instead of taking a close look at their own.

When I let myself back into the room, he is sitting staring at the door, his eyes wide, his skin slightly flushed. 'Where have you been? Have you been in touch with my mum yet?'

I'm ready for this, knew it was coming. It was inevitable that he would start asking questions, but it doesn't matter because I'm prepared. 'Sorry. I just had to take a phone call. That was your mum. She said that she's really sorry but she has had to stay on late at work. They've had a bit of an emergency and she's been told that they need her at the hospital.'

I watch his face change, see a flicker of recognition. The news reports have their uses, informing me that Timmy's mum is a nurse at the local hospital in town working in the trauma unit. 'There's been a huge car crash involving two HGVs and over a dozen cars on one of the main roads.'

His expression changes from mild anxiety to shock. 'Really? That's terrible. What's going to happen?'

'Well,' I say, trying to feign concern, 'I'm not entirely sure but I suppose they'll have to work around the clock until everyone receives the correct treatment for their injuries.'

'To me, I mean,' he says, his eyes still heavily focused ahead as he looks to me for an answer to his question. 'This happened once before and I had to sleep over at a friend's house. Mum had to ring one of the parents even though she didn't know them that well, and ask if I could go there. Is that what's going to happen again?'

Such a sweet innocent soul. I smile and cock my head to one side. 'No, you won't have to go there again. Your mum asked if I could keep you here for the night, if that's okay with you?'

Without waiting for an answer, I wander over to the corner of the room and pull off another cover to reveal a large drum kit underneath. 'There's plenty to keep you occupied here, isn't there?'

He nods and smiles but I detect an air of reserve about him, a wariness that has crept into his expression, into his gait as he walks around the drum kit eyeing it greedily. He is unsure. That's understandable, but we're a partnership and he has to learn to trust me.

'Trent?'

I turn to face him, hoping my expression is one of compassion combined with neutrality, as if I don't know what's coming next. As if this situation is new to me too. 'Yes?'

'Where will I sleep? And I don't have any pyjamas or clean clothes for in the morning.' He steps forward and trails his hand over the leather stool and up onto one of the cymbals. It vibrates ever so quietly causing him to move away as if burnt. The low metallic shiver of the cymbals gradually peters out, leaving a ghostly silence. I can hear my own heartbeat, every movement from within my body, the surge of blood as it rushes around my veins, a gushing reminder that there will be more questions to follow. The difficult part is yet to come – the settling in period when it dawns on him that he isn't ever going home.

'Firstly, it's Saturday tomorrow so you can wear whatever you like. No uniform needed. You can sleep in it if you like.' I give him a comical wink and am relieved to hear him giggle. 'And secondly, how about this for convenience?' I move to the corner of the room and open what looks like a small built-in wardrobe. I flick on the light and gesture for him to follow me.

'Whoah! This is like one of the coolest rooms I've ever seen.' His voice is an excited squeak. 'A music room with its own bedroom and bathroom.'

'Only the best for my good mate,' I say, giving him a small nudge and holding up my hand for a high five. He responds immediately, slapping his palm against mine and I know that I'm getting there with this boy, earning his respect and admiration. Everything is going to be just right. We're a perfect match, me and him. We always have been.

'I need to pop out for a short while, but I know you'll be fine here,' I say dismissively, not wanting to alarm him at being left alone for too long. He is nodding at me, his eyes shining with exhilaration. 'You can have a go on the drums. Get some practice in if you like?'

'Really?'

'Really,' I say as I ruffle his hair. I expect a slight recoil and am almost moved to tears when I'm rewarded with a small tight hug, his thin arms circling my midriff before he breaks away and slides himself onto the stool, his face a sight to behold.

'I always wanted drumming lessons but Mum said they were too expensive. We don't have much money now that Mum and Dad have split up, and my dad is out of work as well. That doesn't make him a bad person though. He's not lazy.' His eyes are sweeping over the kit as he talks.

'Of course he's not,' I murmur, thinking of a way to change this topic. I don't want him thinking or talking about his parents. I need to break that connection. I'm his family now. But I guess something as powerful as this will take time. A strong relationship that has built up over so many years will take quite a bit longer than just a couple of days to sever. 'I'll be back shortly,' I say, giving him a wide smile. 'Just you make sure you get stuck in and enjoy yourself.' Then I back out of the door, remembering to lock it behind me and get on with my everyday life.

15

'For one day? That seems a bit silly, doesn't it?' Sarah stares at the handset as if it holds the answer to her husband's piece of unexpected and unwelcome news.

'It can't be helped, I'm afraid. Complete change of plan. Or at least a slight alteration. I thought you'd be pleased that I can manage to get away for a day. I can stay on here if you like and not bother coming home at all?' His voice is clipped.

'No, of course not. I'd much rather you were home, here with me. Even if it is only for twenty-four hours.' Sarah stares at her nails, thinking how short and stubby they are. She has let her appearance slide recently. No wonder Malcolm works away so much with her looking like this, a shabby mess of a woman. She needs to start taking more care of herself, put more effort into her appearance. These things count. For all everybody talks about beauty coming from within, it's expected that people should look the part, especially women. Magazines and newspapers, billboards and the internet are full of images designed to shame those who don't bother with the latest shampoo or conditioner. Monster-sized pictures of impossibly glamorous females wearing skimpy clothes whilst also managing to cook a cordon bleu meal and look after small children – they're everywhere.

Sarah stares at herself in the mirror, flicks a stray hair away from her face. Maybe they have a point. A little slick of lipstick and the occasional haircut wouldn't go amiss, would it? God knows, she has enough time on her hands now she isn't working to make the effort and look nice for her husband. Nothing too ostentatious but painted nails and the odd application of make-up could make all the difference to his indifferent attitude towards her and ultimately her own flagging self-esteem.

'Right, well I'll be home tonight, then back at work tomorrow,' Malcolm says huskily.

'That's lovely, Malc. I'll cook you a meal.' She thinks about what she has in the freezer that will be easy to prepare. 'How about some salmon?'

'Sounds fine. Anyway, got to get going. Don't want to be too late.' And with that he is gone. No goodbyes, no whispered messages of love. No words to placate her and ease her troubled mind.

Sarah stands, phone in hand, wondering what is going on, what it is that caused his rapid departure from the conversation and why he is now coming home rather than staying on at work. She shrugs, places the phone on the table, walks through to the kitchen, a dark sinister thought niggling at her. Opening the fridge door, she refuses to allow herself to go down the route of worrying and making wild inaccurate guesses as to what his motives are. Malcolm is a grown man, free to do as he pleases, as is she. Not that she does. This house is her life. Standing staring out of the window, keeping check on what her neighbours are up to, watching their movements and making sure life in Middleham ticks along as it should, is her life. It's not much, but it's all she has.

She tugs at the package wrapped around the fish, the oily

slimy sensation causing her stomach to clench. She gags, suppressing a retch that rises up through her gut. The walls of the kitchen lean in drunkenly, forcing her to sit down at the table while she unwraps the salmon. At some point, she has to accept that Malcolm once had an affair and it is now behind them, and that she is the one clinging on to that fact, treating it as a recent threat, fearing that it may happen again. She can't continue to put herself through this every time he says or does something that feels slightly awry. And yet part of her knows that he has a wandering eye, is a natural flirt and has that alluring twinkle in his eye that attracts females. But so what? That doesn't mean he is out there sleeping with every woman he meets. He's handsome for sure and can charm people with just a smile but shouldn't that be something she is proud of? She is lucky to have somebody like that as a husband.

She continues preparing their meal, taking her time, making sure everything is as perfect as it can be, then leaves it to marinate, thinking about his journey home and how she can use the time to make herself look half decent for a change.

The shower is hot as she steps into it, the citrus scent filling the steamy air of the cubicle. She scrubs at her body and washes her hair, keen to remove any lingering cooking smells from her skin. She has to look good for her husband tonight. Sitting in the house day after day has led to her becoming slovenly. She has thrown her efforts into making sure the house is always perfect and neglected her own appearance. Now is the time to put it right. He deserves that much.

She puts on her favourite cream wrap-over dress and ties up her hair, swirling it into a loose bun, the style Malcolm always loved all those years ago when they first met. Her throat contracts as she thinks back to those times – she an impressionable young thing with limited life experience and Malcolm, older, wiser, a member of a local band that played in all the clubs in town. The age gap didn't put her off. Twelve years meant nothing to her back then when she was young and desperate to impress and be impressed, and still doesn't. All the girls flocked to Malcolm but she was the one he chose. Out of all the women in town, he chose her and married her. How has that warm glow that bound them together grown so cold in the past few years?

The radio is playing in the background as she heads back downstairs, checks the food and puts a few finishing touches to the room. She dims the lights and sets the table, using her best starched tablecloth, laying out the cutlery and even lighting a couple of candles for the full effect.

'Impressive.'

Malcolm's voice takes her by surprise. She spins around, wiping her hands down her old apron, then suddenly aware of how grubby it looks, whisks it off and stuffs it in a drawer out of sight. 'You're home!'

'I'm home,' he says with a sigh, dropping his briefcase onto the floor by his feet and pulling at his tie wearily, dragging it from side to side as he yanks it loose and loops it over his head.

'You look tired.' Sarah steps forward, runs her fingers through his hair and gently kisses his forehead. She wants to ask; every fibre of being screaming at her to get him to tell her why he made a rapid departure from work only to return again in the morning, but doesn't. She won't enquire. He's weary, lines creasing his face as he slips off his coat and dumps it over the back of the chair.

'Here,' she says, picking it up and whisking it away, 'I'll take that. You get comfortable and I'll shout you when it's ready.'

'I'm going to have a shower. Won't be long.'

She detects exasperation in his voice. Or is it exhaustion? She definitely won't ask. All that does is rile him and then the evening will be spoilt. She will let him lead the conversation and she will simply follow, let it go wherever it takes them. She's just pleased to have him home. No point in spoiling their short time together. Her questions can wait.

His jacket is heavy, a recognisable masculine tang of fatigue and old aftershave emanating from it. She hangs it up in the cupboard, leaning down to retrieve a crumpled letter that falls out of the pocket, fluttering to the floor and landing directly at her feet. The temptation to open it is such a powerful sensation. It is marked confidential and has Malcolm's name and home address printed on the front. She wonders when he received this particular missive. She has no recollection of it arriving and is usually pretty well organised when it comes to household matters. Her heart flips about in her chest as she slips the piece of paper out of the envelope and opens it up.

'Everything okay?' Malcolm is standing behind her, his frame silhouetted in the shadows of the confined space of their hallway.

'What? Yes, sorry, just hanging up your jacket.' Without missing a beat, she surreptitiously slips the paper and the envelope back into the pocket in a crumpled ball. Later she can sort it, straighten it out and place the letter back in its envelope. *This*, she thinks, *is what happens when there is a lack of trust and one of the partners is forced to pry. This is how a relationship crumbles.*

They eat, the ambience easy, the food perfect as Malcolm tells her about his journey back from Huddersfield and how he is convinced the roads are full to breaking point, the infrastructure groaning under the strain.

'So, how's the project going? Everything on track for completion?' Sarah has no idea why she is asking. Their projects rarely seem to get finished on time. As a telecommunications engineer, Malcolm's talk of work leaves her cold, his esoteric language sweeping over her head in an indecipherable blur.

His face changes, a subtle shift in his expression as he takes a sip of his wine and pushes his salmon around the plate. 'Oh, you know. Same old, same old.'

She nods as if she understands, when in truth she has no idea how he spends his days, what it is he actually does for a living. It pays the bills, and she supposes that that is all she needs to know.

They eat the rest of their meal in near silence, an uncomfortable feeling settling in the pit of her stomach. There is nothing she can pinpoint, nothing she can grasp at and hold aloft, but it is there, a sickly sensation that is spinning and churning aimlessly in her gut, an indiscernible atmosphere between them that tells her that something is very wrong. They only have this evening together. Tomorrow he is away again. Back on the road to a place she has never seen, working with people she has never met to do a job she doesn't understand. They have become strangers. This is not how she wants it to be, their marriage. She wants love and tenderness and compassion. She wants a sense of well-being on both sides, a lasting contentment. To outsiders, they have it all – a big well-furnished house with all the latest mod cons, a long sweeping garden, a shiny spanking new car. Apart from the lack of children, they have everything anybody could ever need or want. So why does she feel so lonely? There is something terribly skewed here. She is many things, but she is definitely not stupid. Her instinct immediately flits to thoughts of another woman. Always that. Everything always leads back to that one indiscretion. Will it ever leave them?

With no idea of how to even approach the subject of what it is that is going on in his life, what it is that is bothering him, she stands up and clears the table. He doesn't ask for dessert. She doesn't offer any.

Once she has cleaned the kitchen and loaded the

dishwasher, she makes her way back into the living room to see him sitting there, his face screwed up in concentration as he studies his phone.

'What time are you setting off tomorrow?'

He all but throws his mobile into the air before tucking it deep into his pocket and turning to face her, doing his utmost to look composed and calm, but it's too late; she saw that look, that expression that confirmed her initial fears, telling her that her suspicions are correct. Something is happening. Something she knows nothing about. Something that could shatter her world.

She makes her decision there and then. She will wait until he is asleep, then come down here, look at that letter and take a look at his phone. And then she will know and perhaps wish she didn't.

16

TRENT

It doesn't take long. I arrive back from the shop with my purchases and head straight into his room clutching his new clothes and a set of pyjamas under my arm. I am practically giddy with excitement as I unlock the door and all but hurl myself inside. I'm greeted with a deathly silence. A cold finger of dread traces its way down my backbone as I look around the empty room. Then I see that the door to the bedroom is ajar and tiptoe over to peek inside. It's heart-warming to see Timmy's little body safely tucked up in bed. His school uniform is neatly folded up and has been placed over the chair. Such a sweet boy. Such a sweet and polite little boy. I knew that this was going to work out for the best. I had no doubts about it and now here we are, like a new family, him feeling so comfortable and so at ease that he had no qualms about climbing into bed of his own volition. His new bed. In his new room. This is perfect. Better than I ever hoped it could be.

I place the new clothes and pyjamas next to where he is lying and pick up the perfectly folded uniform. I will wash it, not that he needs it anymore. That school was never a good place for him. He will learn more by being here with me. I can teach him how to play musical instruments. We will learn about the world together, studying landscapes and history. I will read the classics to him – *Treasure Island, Robinson Crusoe, The Jungle Book*. We will explore the environment, finding out about the natural earth and how we evolved as a species. The possibilities are endless. He has a curious mind; I can just tell. He's a sharp thinker, an astute little boy. I will teach him everything a young lad needs to know. He will be so happy, so enthralled. He will never want to leave here.

I'll make sure of it.

He's groggy, confused and disorientated. That's all it is. There are bound to be snags. He's just a child after all. I'm late bringing him his breakfast. This is all my fault.

I look at his tear-stained face, at his wiry little body as he stands next to his bed in his vest and underpants, staring up at me, and feel my heart begin to pound. I've left him alone for too long. He has slept here all night on his own and now he is disorientated and frightened. I need to learn from this, be the best that I can be for him.

'Can I go home now?' His mouth is trembling as he speaks, his cheeks red, his hair plastered flat against his head where he slept.

'Ah, you need some breakfast. I got you some Coco Pops and toast. Would you like jam or butter? Or you could have both if you like.' I keep my voice soft, angle my body to one side to appear less dominant, less intimidating. 'You can have as much as you want. No school and no limits.' I cringe at my words. I'm trying too hard to be cool, to be his friend. I need to back off a bit, dampen my ardour and remember that he needs a little time to adjust.

'I'm not very hungry.' His voice is soft, a whisper in the silence of the room. He looks so helpless. I want to scoop him up, to stroke his hair, inhale the scent of his little body, tell him that he is safe here with me and that there is no need for him to feel upset or scared.

'I think perhaps you should have a little something. Oh, look,' I say, trying to inject some enthusiasm into my tone, 'we've also got some strawberries.'

I pop one into my mouth and make appreciative noises as I eat it, then busy myself with laying out his new clothes and making the bed, humming softly, keeping my timbre gentle and non-threatening. Making a point of keeping my back to him, I sneak a glance and see that he is staring at the tray of food. Before I turn around, I catch sight of him as he sits down and picks up a slice of toast then grabs the knife and dips it into the butter, spreading it on his toast liberally.

I heave a silent sigh of relief. Mornings are always going to be the hardest. He is tired and vulnerable, seeing the world through sleepy anxious eyes. As the day progresses, things will improve. He will become accustomed to our new routine and perhaps even enjoy it. That part will take time. I'm no fool. There will be more tears to come, but once we get beyond that point, then our lives will take an upward turn. He will realise that here, he is cared for and safe, not left alone when everybody else has gone home. Here is the best place for him. He just doesn't know it yet.

'Eat as much as you like.' I stay over the other side of the room. It's all about space and timing and making sure I don't overdo it. Scaring him senseless with my eagerness and desperate need to bond with him would be a terrible thing to do. It would undo everything we have achieved so far. I have to remember the advances we've already made. Many children in his position would have screamed and cried, being taken home by a complete stranger and spending the night alone. But not my Timmy. He's one of a kind, a brave boy.

'When is my mum coming to collect me?'

I've been expecting this but it still makes me suck in my breath. It's imperative I get this part right. He has to believe me. 'She's in bed after a hectic nightshift. She called to say that she's really tired and that they might need her back at the hospital later on once she's had a rest.'

My words are met with a contemplative silence. He continues eating and I take that as a sign that he isn't overly distressed by what I have just told him. Perhaps he is used to this? All the more reason to keep him here with me, to make sure he is given the care and nurturing that he needs and deserves.

'Once you've finished your breakfast, you can have a strum on the guitar if you'd like? Or perhaps you'd prefer the drums?'

'Am I allowed to play out?'

He pours himself a bowl of cereal and I listen as he adds milks and slurps and crunches, spooning large helpings into his mouth. 'Not at the minute. Maybe at some point you can have a kick-about of the football in the back garden but not right now. Besides, it's pouring down outside.'

I don't like being untruthful to him, but it's not a proper lie. I'm saying these things to protect him. There are some cruel thoughtless people out there. He needs to be kept apart from them. It's my job to protect him now. I'm his responsible adult, his main carer. This is his new home.

He belongs to me now. He is all mine.

17

She has her reservations. This isn't how she planned on spending her weekend. Not that she had any real plans, but she doesn't want a neighbour dictating how she will utilise her precious time.

'So, as I said, everything will be ready by eleven o'clock if you want to join us?'

Lynda stares hard at the creature before her, this near-stranger who appears to be trying too hard by being overly jocular and too bouncy; just too damn bubbly by far. It is irritating and insincere and is getting under her skin. 'Sorry, can you run it past me again? I'm a bit slow on the uptake this morning. Had a busy week and the old grey matter isn't what it used to be.' She taps the side of her head with her index finger and tries to muster up a smile.

Sarah cocks her head to one side and nods, as if she can comprehend what Lynda is saying and thinking, like a young girl who is allowing the sweet old codger before her more thinking time to process what is going on around her. Lynda hopes Sarah can't really work out what is going through her head. She might not like what she finds there.

'It's just a little get-together,' Sarah says, her voice now beginning to knock at Lynda's head like a hammer against her skull. 'A sort of coffee morning if you like, for some of the ladies in the village. I thought it would do us good to touch base and chat about things that are going on in the local community, you know?'

No, I don't know, Lynda wants to say but instead smiles and nods, wishing she could shut the door and get on with her day without feeling beholden to somebody who, if she is being truthful, irritates the life out of her.

'I'm about to knock and mention it to Emily and was thinking I could ask Moira as well?'

Lynda thinks about Moira and how pale and wan she looked yesterday, as if all the life had been sucked out of her. 'Perhaps I should ask her for you? I know she's not been well lately.'

'Aw, that's a shame,' Sarah says in a voice that reminds Lynda of nails being dragged down a blackboard. 'But you never know, a few hours out of the house might be just what she needs.'

A sigh rises up Lynda's throat, tries to force its way out of her mouth. She clamps her jaw shut until her teeth ache, suppressing it and holding it in. 'Perhaps. I'll knock and ask her later, see if she's up to it. Eleven o'clock, you said?'

A small amount of guilt nips at Lynda as Sarah's eyes brighten, her lip curling up into a smile, a genuine sparkle of gratitude evident in her expression. 'Oh, if you could, that would be amazing! You know her better than I do and if she's not been well, then I don't want to disturb her. But as I said, sometimes getting out and about and keeping in touch with other people can do us the world of good, don't you think?'

Lynda doesn't think that at all and would much rather be sitting in her armchair sipping a cup of strong coffee than mixing with a group of women she barely knows and doesn't care about, but remains silent instead, nodding and smiling at this woman, wishing these encounters were less intrusive, less draining and half as rewarding as Sarah claims them to be.

'Right, well, best be off. Need to go and ask Emily if she can make it. I was going to ask Alice but I think perhaps she's not really up to it? What with her bad legs and everything.'

Lynda thinks of poor old Alice; tiny frail Alice with her failing eyesight, uncontrolled diabetes and leg ulcers and thinks that sitting in Sarah's kitchen is quite possibly the last thing on earth that she would want to do and yet somehow this unfortunate deluded creature is too dim-witted to see it.

'Will your husband be joining us or will it be a golfing day for him to escape the cackling ladies that are all gathered in his house?' Lynda makes a point of staring over at Sarah's empty driveway, at the large dry patch where his car usually stands, then turning to look at the flush that rapidly colours Sarah's cheeks. He is a strange one, Malcolm. Evasive, elusive. Always working away from home. Keen to avoid any contact or neighbourly conversation. Lynda has met his type before – slick and shifty, as if he has something to hide.

She watches the lump in Sarah's throat bob up and down as she swallows repeatedly and grasps at a stray hair, dragging it out of her eyes and pushing it behind her ear with pale clumsy fingers. 'He was home last night but had to set off early this morning.' Her words are like rapid gunfire as she looks to her feet then over at her own house and that large and glaringly empty gravelled driveway. 'He's got a big project on the go at the minute but once it's complete, we're hoping to book a holiday somewhere exotic and hot. Somewhere with a nice long white beach that has a bar that sells cocktails, I hope!'

Lynda nods knowingly, thinking once again that she is being unnecessarily mean and antagonistic. She has no idea why people infuriate her as much as they do. For all she knows he is a perfectly nice man, a good and caring husband and here she is thinking ill of him when in truth she barely knows him. It's as if her tolerance levels have completely eroded leaving her on the cusp of being tetchy and permanently angry, ready to fight the world and everybody in it.

'Well, that sounds perfectly lovely. Here's hoping you find somewhere nice to visit.'

Sarah responds by nodding fervently and fidgeting with the sleeve of her sweater, tugging at it over and over with frantic nervous fingers. 'Okay, so I'll see you and hopefully Moira as well, at eleven o'clock tomorrow?'

'All being well,' Lynda murmurs as she stands and gives Sarah a cursory wave. The door closes with a click and Lynda wanders over to her window, keen to see where Sarah goes to next. To Emily's house. Of course she does. Lynda needs to persuade Moira to go along with her in the morning. Sitting in Sarah's sleek modern house with two young women with whom she has nothing in common fills her with a certain amount of dread. Having Moira there would help ease her tensions, make her feel less out of touch, less ancient and frayed at the edges.

Waiting until Sarah has moved away from Emily's house and disappeared out of sight, she slips outside and heads up Moira's driveway, knocking on her door until her knuckles are sore. Moira lives in too large a house and often doesn't answer, claiming she cannot hear anything from the inside. Lynda suspects it is more down to Moira wanting some time on her own, away from other people. Moira is a good friend with often unfathomable ways that even Lynda struggles to comprehend.

'You need a bloody doorbell,' Lynda says as Moira swings open the door after two rounds of having to bash her fists against it with such force that she now has to rub at her skin to alleviate the ache. 'Something as loud as Big Ben. I'll buy you one for your birthday. Now, I need a favour from you.'

Moira shakes her head and gives her friend a cautious smile. 'Lovely to see you too, Lynda.'

'Oh, hush now.' She glares at her old friend and quickly glances over her shoulder, making sure they are alone, not within earshot of any unwanted bystanders. 'Tomorrow, we have been invited over to Sarah's house for a coffee morning. Now I feel we should go, you know, to show some sort of solidarity with other villagers, but I'm damned if I'm going on my own without you, so I don't care how ill you're feeling, you're coming along with me or I'm never speaking to you again.'

Moira grins, a wave of colour flooding into her sallow cheeks. 'Well, after being asked so nicely, how could I possibly refuse?'

'I knew you'd see it from my point of view. Good woman.' Lynda nods and steps away from the door, then stops. 'You're not carrying anything contagious, are you? Because if you are, I don't bloody well want it. You can wear a mask or a balaclava or any type of face covering that you see fit but whether you like it or not, you are accompanying me into that house.'

'Definitely nothing contagious, you old grump. Just a bad day, I guess. Now shall I meet you there, or are we going to call for each other like a pair of nine-year-olds?'

Lynda narrows her eyes, purses her lips in contemplation. 'I'll call over here for you. Shall we say five minutes to eleven?'

'Right you are,' Moira replies, as she leans against the door frame. 'And then maybe we can come in here afterwards for a coffee to dissect the whole painful event, eh?'

'Oh, you took the words right out of my mouth! A woman after my own heart.' Lynda lets out a barking laugh and begins to walk back home. 'You know what they say, eh? If you don't have anything nice to say about anyone, then come sit next to me.'

~

The morning passes slowly, the house feeling empty and silent. Andrew Gilkes's face pops into Lynda's mind, her stomach tightening at the thought of that time. She has worked hard at putting it behind her, trying to forget what went on. What she saw. The details of the abuse he suffered at the hands of his stepfather before the incident.

She thinks that it is undoubtedly true that many abused people go on to become abusers. That was certainly the case with that boy. It was apparent throughout the trial that he was deeply damaged; disturbed by what he had been through, what he had been subjected to over and over and over until it was so deeply embedded in his growing brain, so strongly internalised, he mistook it for normal behaviour.

She remembers his mother, a meek and mild-mannered scrap of a thing who looked as if a strong breeze would blow her away. She too had been imperilled, put through the vilest forms of cruelty that were listed in court by the defence. Many times, the prosecution tried to shut down their claims and many times they were thankfully, overruled. Nobody in their right mind could have not seen it – that Andrew Gilkes was a catastrophe waiting to happen.

On occasion, social services had been called in to investigate the stepfather, but like all abusers, he was sly and cunning, hiding the damage he wreaked with smiles and an oily charm that exuded out of him in bucketloads, and making outright denials. After the case was over, he moved out of the family home but was never brought to justice for what he did to that boy. And the worst thing is, he is still out there somewhere, possibly ripping apart another family with his fists and smart mouth and his ability to frighten those around him into submission with just a wink and a winning smile.

She needs to block it out of her mind, not sit here going over every tiny detail until her head hurts. Standing up, Lynda grabs at her book but is too twisted up inside, too downright coiled and angry to focus so decides instead to tend to her garden. It's still blustery and chilly out there but immersing herself in something physical might be exactly what she needs to blow away the cobwebs that are tangled up in the farthest reaches of her brain, to rid herself of any haunting memories and painful thoughts that do their best to drag her back to a past she would rather not revisit. She had hoped that that period in her life was behind her, a thing of the past that she would never again have to ever give any thought to, but now here it is, right in front her; his voice, his face, the boy himself, now a grown man close to her, week after week after week. It isn't his fault, she knows that. He's trying to get on with his life, doing his best to rebuild his shattered existence. But now here she is, having to face it all again. That time, those boys. That awful, awful discovery. Andrew Gilkes doing those terrible unspeakable things to another boy.

Lynda strides into the kitchen grabs at the keys and throws open the back door, sucking in a lungful of air, savouring its fresh cleanness as she steps outside vowing to put it all to the back of her mind once and for all.

18

SARAH

S he stands at the door, arms wrapped tightly around her body to stave off the early morning chill that is biting at her face, wondering how he will manage to drive back to Huddersfield having had only two hours of sleep. What a night. A terrible night of tossing and turning, waiting for Malcolm to eventually drop off to sleep so she could skulk back downstairs and read the contents of that letter and scroll through his phone for clues as to what is going on in his life, only for him to be awake hour after hour, lying next to her, sighing and rubbing at his face repeatedly. She tried to feign sleep in the hope he would settle and drop off but it wasn't to be. After a deeply unsettled night, they both eventually fell asleep somewhere around 4am only to be woken by the alarm going off at six.

Her eyes are gritty, her skin flushed and sore. She feels grimy and needs a shower. Breakfast was an ordeal, Malcolm sitting opposite her, eyeing her cautiously as if she might suddenly spontaneously combust, while she sat rigidly, desperate to ask him what is going on, why he had a sudden change of plan at the last minute. What was it that was so important, so pressing, he felt the need to drive all the way home only to spend a restless night, unable to sleep because something was obviously deeply troubling him?

She could have asked, resolved the situation, but the tension in the house was as tight as a drum. The time was never right. She didn't want to ruin their short time together. Not that any of it could have been described as pleasant. It was difficult. She felt permanently on edge, as if he was about to reveal something dreadful, something cataclysmic that could break them apart permanently.

God, she hopes not. For all of his faults, for all of her faults, she still feels there is something worth salvaging from this marriage. Something that they can cling on to in the maelstrom that is trying to drag them under. This isn't the end of them. She won't allow it. She will fight tooth and nail to keep it together. Whether it's another woman or just the usual work-related problems that is pushing him into a corner, making him depressed and unapproachable, she will do her damnedest to stick by him. That's what married couples do. It's what she will do. The alternative is unthinkable.

While he showered, she rifled his jacket pocket only to discover the letter was no longer there. His phone, he placed next to the sink within his line of sight. Either he was being particularly canny, making sure her access was limited, or she is being paranoid, imagining things that aren't actually there. Either way, he is now leaving for another stint away and her worries and suspicions are aroused with no way of dampening them. She will just have to spend the next week, or however long Malcolm is away for, in the dark, doing her best to shift her focus elsewhere rather than spend day after day in a state of near-panic and angst.

And now she is standing here, waving him off like the dutiful wife that she is, as if they don't have a care in the world. Uninformed onlookers would see a loving couple, parting, smiling at one another as the husband leaves for work. What they don't see is the hurt and the anguish and the worry and the constant fear that is lurking in their relationship, the pain of being denied a much-wanted child, the worry and dread of her husband straying away again into the arms of another woman, the absolute terror that he will leave her for good one of these fine days, setting up home with his mistress who is a quiet unassuming glamorous creature that he adores with every fibre of his being whilst hating her, his wife, the woman who once felt like the luckiest girl in the world after snaring the front member of a once successful band. How times have changed. How far they have fallen.

Tears burn at the back of her eyelids as his car crunches its way off the drive, and he swings onto the road and disappears out of sight.

Closing the door, Sarah is tempted to go back to bed, to curl into a foetal position and cry until there are no more tears left, but what good would that do? It wouldn't make her feel any better, leaving her feeling, very possibly, a hundred times worse. No, she must keep on keeping on. She has to rise above the apprehension and the fear and get on with her day. That's important to her. Her routine is her life. It's all she has. Without that she is an empty shell, a nobody.

She sees him pull up outside Emily's house, stands watching from her window as Mo slides out of his sleek black car and makes his way up the path, pausing initially before trying the handle of Emily's front door and then marching inside. A shiver runs through her. Everybody's door should be locked. Especially Emily's with a child living there. What is she thinking? Where is her concern for her son, knowing there is an abductor about?

Leaving her house unsecured like that is tantamount to neglect. Sarah knows that she herself would never do such a thing. Any child in her care would feel safe and loved. Emily should know better. Disappointment ripples through her at her neighbour's lackadaisical attitude. No man would be allowed to march into her home without first being asked. They haven't been in a relationship for too long, that much she does know, certainly not long enough to really know him. And what with–

Sarah stops herself, refusing to think such a thing. It's wrong on every level to even consider it. She quashes the thought, pushes it away, wishing she didn't have the type of brain that went around in circles, second guessing every bloody little thing, making wild assumptions when in actual fact, none of it even concerns her.

And yet, if anything were to happen to that boy, little Joel, and she could have put a stop to it by being just that little bit more caring, more street savvy and aware than his own mother, she would never forgive herself. In this day and age, even people you think may be friends, need to be vetted. They have to prove themselves before they can just muscle their way into your family, before they can take advantage and just walk straight in without knocking. Still, she won't allow her views to be known. Not yet anyway. People wouldn't necessarily see it as she does. She runs the risk of being cold shouldered, told that her views are unfashionable and extreme when all she is trying to do is protect a neighbour's child from possible harm.

So for now she will keep it to herself as best she can, be the happy smiling lady that people expect her to be, but she will also keep watch because that's the only way she can really feel safe. In this increasingly turbulent and often dangerous world, somebody has to remain alert, to filter out the undesirables, the perverts and the downright deluded, and if that person happens to be her, then so be it. She has plenty of time on her hands and isn't afraid to show her true colours if it means that she is keeping people safe, especially somebody as young and as vulnerable as little Joel. It's the least she can do.

Deciding to seize the moment, she leaves the house and heads over to see Lynda. With Malcolm gone again, sitting in the house on her own all weekend looms over her like a big dark cloud. She promised Emily that she would arrange a get-together and that is exactly what she intends to do.

Lynda opens the door and Sarah is greeted with Lynda's usual frosty and marginally sarcastic manner. Why does this woman always make her feel inferior and silly? Sarah may not have a rack of qualifications to speak of, but surely she deserves a modicum of respect instead of being treated like one of Lynda's errant pupils. Lynda agrees to attend Sarah's get-together, assuring her that she will ask Moira to accompany her. Feeling relieved that the conversation is over, Sarah makes her way over to Emily's house, a knot of tension pulling at her stomach. Mo's car is still outside. She could leave this conversation until later, let them have some time together, but why should she? It will only take a few minutes. That's all she's asking for – just a couple of minutes of Emily's time.

The door is opened before she even has time to knock. Mo is standing there, keys in hand, a bag casually slung over his shoulder. 'Hey!' he says with a broad smile. 'Hello again. Thanks again for the other day and taking in that parcel for me.'

Sarah feels her hand being touched and tries to pull away but it's too late. Mo is shaking it vigorously, his other hand placed on top of hers making it impossible for her to move away. His skin is warm next to her cool fingers as he pulls her into the tiny hallway, turning around to shout over his shoulder. 'Hey, Em. You've got a visitor!'

She does her best to remove her hand to no avail. Only when Emily appears as a silhouette in the doorway to the kitchen does he loosen his grip, allowing Sarah to extricate herself from his vicelike grasp. Pulling her hand tightly to her side before quickly shoving it deep into her pocket, she nods at Mo and gives Emily what she hopes is a genuine smile that conveys her true intentions. She would actually like to be friends with this lady, even though they are very different people. The least she can do is try.

'Hi, Sarah. Good to see you. Everything okay?'

'Yes, yes. Absolutely.' She swallows to stem the panicky feeling that is rising up her throat and pulling at the sinews in her neck. 'I was just wondering if you'd like to pop over mine for a coffee in the morning? Moira and Lynda are going to be there. I just thought it would be a good opportunity for us all to have a chat. Time always seems to be against us, doesn't it?'

Emily shuffles towards her, wiping her hands on a cloth before turning and throwing it onto the kitchen counter behind her. 'That sounds lovely. Thank you for asking. Can I bring Joel with me?'

A flutter takes hold in Sarah's gut at the mention of his name. Her reply that she would be delighted to have him in her home is thwarted by Mo's voice as he breaks into the conversation, his voice booming around the confined space in which they are standing. 'Hang on. Joel can come with me, can't he, Em? I've been promising to take him out for a while now. We can go for a kick-about at the new football area in the park. A few of my mates'll be there. He'll love it.'

Sarah's spine stiffens, a rod of ice spiking through it. 'It's no problem,' she says, trying to keep her voice even, to not display the growing dread and fear that is ballooning in her chest making it difficult for her to breathe properly. Mo barely knows the boy. Surely Emily will refuse? It's her duty as a parent to have her son's best interests at heart. This feels wrong. Her nerve ends are shrieking at her to stop this situation, to halt this offer Mo has made, before it spirals out of control. 'He is more than welcome at mine, Emily. I've got juice and biscuits and he can have the run of the house while we sit and chat in the kitchen. Not a problem at all.' She struggles to keep her voice even. Blood is pounding through her ears, throbbing in her veins.

'The new football area?' Joel's voice takes everyone by surprise. 'Can I go with Mo, Mum? Please, please let me go!' He is standing at the top of the stairs watching them all, his eyes glistening with undisguised excitement.

'Honestly, it's not a problem for him to come to mine,' Sarah says quietly, knowing that she has already lost this particular battle. The boy's mind is made up. To force the issue would make her appear too controlling, a dominant busybody when all she is doing is trying to protect him, keep the lad safe from an unknown faceless predator who is roaming the area. This is so difficult, so damn exhausting having to be the voice of reason all of the time, the person who can see the big picture while all around her people sleepwalk into avoidable disasters. She feels alone on a choppy sea of uncertainty; her marriage, her life in this sleepy village all under threat and it appears that despite her constant levels of vigilance, watching out for possible threats and changes in the daily pattern of life, there is not a damn thing she can do about it.

Joel begins to jump up and down, the floor vibrating under his feet. 'Please, Mum! Please let me go to the park. All the other kids at school go there. I'm the only one who's never been. Please!'

Emily shrugs her shoulders at Mo who gives her a wink. A rosy hue colours Emily's cheeks. She looks away at the floor before glancing up at Sarah and smiling.

'Okay,' she says meekly. 'You win. The park it is.'

Joel races downstairs and hugs Mo's legs before running over to his mum and giving her a kiss on the cheek. She feels a tension of opposites stir deep within her, a deep well of envy and apprehension that mixes and merges, leaving her feeling faint and queasy. This family life, this apparent fusion of tenderness and trepidation could unravel at any time. Mo is practically a stranger to the boy. And as for introducing Joel to Mo's adult friends? It is madness. How, in the current climate of fear, can Emily even begin to think that this sort of parenting is acceptable? It is dangerous and reprehensible is what it is and as fearful and angry as she is, Sarah knows she will have to keep her thoughts to herself. Being labelled as the village meddler, the toxic spreader of gossip is not what she wants. All she can do is use a more subtle approach, perhaps speak with Emily about similar cases, talk to her about how grooming actually works.

'What time?' Emily is staring at her, waiting for a reply. Sarah observes her mouth, watches how it moves, sees her neighbour's quizzical expression as she waits for her response, but is too lost in her own thoughts to do anything. 'The coffee morning tomorrow? What time do you want me there?'

Snapping out of her stupor, Sarah musters up a smile, a grimace of a response, her head pounding as she tries to shake away images of dead mutilated children, little boys used and abused and discarded like bits of old rag. 'About 11 o'clock?'

'That okay with you, Mo?' Emily steps forward and touches his hand lightly, the look between them causing Sarah to look away, her skin hot with shame as if she is intruding on a private moment.

'Certainly is. And then we might go to McDonalds afterwards. You can work up quite an appetite kicking that ball around, you know!' Mo is smiling, his face tilted towards Emily's serene gaze.

'Right, well I'll be off then.' Sarah pushes past Mo and grabs at the door handle, her fingers suddenly slippery with perspiration. 'Bye, Mo.' She peers over at a startled Joel. 'Bye,

Joel. Enjoy your kick-around tomorrow.' She catches Emily's eye and manages a tight thin smile. 'And I'll see you tomorrow at eleven o'clock.'

Slipping past them she wrenches at the handle, swings open the door and steps outside into the welcoming westerly breeze.

19

TRENT

Evening is creeping in and he is becoming fractious again. We have spent most of the day playing on the instruments but his interest will only stretch so far. He's a young boy, a child. He needs more.

'Mum will be up out of bed by now. You should try calling her again.' He is standing in front of me, a demanding expression settling on his features. I'm prepared. I knew this would happen. I didn't for one minute think this would all slip into place with the greatest of ease. We're in a period of transition, an evolutionary point in our lives when our previous identities are slowly being erased only to be replaced with our new ones. Soon he will forget all about his feckless mother and her negligent slipshod ways. She is already a thing of the past. When I made the decision to get Timmy back, I knew it wouldn't be easy. Nothing in life worth having ever is. But the rewards will be heavenly. And one day he will thank me for it, but not just yet. There is still a lot of work to be done to reshape and restructure our lives, to phase out little Leo, the abandoned lonely boy and replace him with Timothy, my boy.

'Trent?'

I keep my expression impassive. 'Yes? What's up?'

He suddenly bursts into tears, his eyes bulging with sorrow and panic. 'I want to go home! I want to see my mum.'

A fist squeezes at my heart, clutching it so tightly, I think I may never be able to breathe again. 'Hey!' I say softly, reaching out for him and pulling him closer to me. 'What's all this about then? We're friends, you and I. You're perfectly safe here with me, you know that, don't you? There's no need to get upset.'

'It must have been a really bad accident,' he says, sniffing and dragging his soft little knuckles over his eyes. 'Why can't they call one of the other nurses in to help?'

Fire flares under my skin. Seeing him sad and scared like this is killing me. I knew it would happen, knew what his reactions would be to this situation as time passed. What I didn't prepare for was how I would feel. How his sadness and torment would affect me, making me feel ridiculously low and helpless. I guess this is just something we will have to work through together as a partnership. I need Timmy just as much as he needs me. Our relationship is symbiotic. We are an inseparable pair. I would die without him. I know that now. He is here and now that I've had a taste of what it's like to have him here, with me in my life, I steadfastly refuse to let him go. I will fight as hard as I can to keep him, do whatever it takes to keep this wonderful little boy by my side. I lost him once and I'm not prepared to let that happen again. He is here to stay. My boy, my life. This was always meant to be.

'Tell you what,' I say, daring to reach out and stroke his hair. 'What say we have some crisps and lemonade?' I am loath to move away from him, from the soft feathery feel of his silky hair that is making me giddy with love and excitement, to his creamy porcelain like skin. Every little thing about him is perfect. 'It's just over here,' I say quietly. 'I brought it in earlier.'

I can feel his eyes boring into my back as I walk towards the small tray of food I put aside earlier in anticipation of this happening. Reticence and fear were bound to dawn at some point. I needed a contingency plan and this is it. 'Here we are,' I murmur softly as I place the tray in front of him. 'Tuck in.'

I take a crisp and pick up my tumbler, taking a long drink of it and smacking my lips together dramatically, then wait, my heart leaping around my chest, my head buzzing with expectation and a small amount of fear that he will refuse, that he will shake his head and demand to be taken home.

The seconds tick by, an interminably long and agonising stretch of time as I wait for him to make a decision. Taking another crisp and putting my tumbler up to my lips, I am able to exhale secretively as I watch him snatch up a crisp and then drink the lemonade in a series of long thirsty gulps.

It doesn't take long for the effects to kick in. I feel a small amount of guilt at resorting to these measures, but until such time as all memories of his mother are erased from his mind, then I am left with no choice. As I said, I will do whatever is required to keep him here with me. He is, after all, mine now. I am free to do as I please with him.

I pick up his sleeping body which is as light as air and twice as precious and change him into his pyjamas before placing him carefully in his bed. I blow him a kiss, bid my beautiful boy goodnight and back out of the room.

20

EMILY

She has no idea why she is here, why she agreed to attend, apart that is, from being press-ganged into it by Joel and Mo, and apart from the fact she felt powerless to refuse after Mo stepped in and stole her reason for not attending away from her. Having Joel here with her would have given her an excuse to leave. She could have claimed he was bored or had homework that needed finishing, but as it is, she is stuck here, in this huge sleek kitchen that is probably bigger than her entire house and she is feeling out of sorts, rather timid and inexperienced, and acutely aware that she is neither moneyed nor particularly well educated. Not like Sarah with this huge house that looks like something out of a magazine or Lynda who is a teacher and lives in a cottage that isn't huge, but is chocolate box pretty; the sort of house people travel to see, standing outside in admiration at how quintessentially English it is with its climbing roses and thatched roof. Then there's Moira. Quiet green-fingered Moira with her huge house and garden that she tends to at every available opportunity, wearing full length gloves and a large floppy hat and looking like a character out of a 1970s sitcom. Emily feels distinctly out of sorts, clumsy and tongue-tied.

She glances over at Sarah who is flitting about, doing her best to be the genial host. She is always torn between liking and disliking this woman with no real reason to feel that way. Her feelings oscillate wildly depending on whether or not she has had a particularly busy week and is feeling tired and cranky or whether things are ticking along nicely and she has had a chance to spend some real quality time with Joel and Mo. This is unfair, she knows that, but surmises that most people are of a similar mindset. Nobody is friendly and jovial and thinks perfect thoughts every minute of every day. *We are all*, thinks Emily, *susceptible to bouts of anger and jealousy and intolerance.* Still, she is here now and needs to relax and not spend the morning in a tense frame of mind. Her edgy manner will be noticed, which in truth, would horrify her. For all she is wishing to be anywhere but here, she is also keen to appear friendly and approachable.

Sarah has gone to all this effort with lovely rich expensive tasting coffee and an extensive spread of home-baked cakes. The least she can do is be kind and gracious even if she would rather be curled up on the sofa with a good book in front of a roaring fire. Thing is, she didn't really expect Sarah to take her up on the offer of a coffee. She was feeling pretty buoyant that day after receiving a gift from Mo, and grateful to Sarah for taking it in. It was just something she said on the spur of the moment to repay her kindness, and now here she is, wondering how to throw herself into the midst of it and be the type of person that other people want to be around.

Feeling that she is being truculent and churlish, Emily pulls her chair close to the table and leans in closer to listen to what they are talking about. Her skin prickles and stings as it dawns on her what topic is being discussed. She takes a deep breath, wishing she had remained in the relative safety of her own thoughts. She came here to escape this line of discussion, not be a part of it.

'Well,' Sarah is saying, her chest puffed out proudly as she takes a bite of the Victoria sponge, a smear of raspberry jam sticking to her teeth, 'this is the thing. If his mother had turned up on time, then let's be honest here, none of it would have happened.'

A compacted chunk of yellow sponge is lodged in an arc above Sarah's teeth. Emily stares at it, feeling slightly repulsed. She refuses to engage in this conversation. It is unnecessary and only adds to the fear that is already present in everybody's minds. She came here to relax and mingle, not tear apart somebody's life by making uncorroborated claims against a person who isn't present to defend themselves.

A silence takes hold, the air thick with growing disquiet. Emily swallows her mouthful of coffee, the sound of the swallowing mechanism in her throat ringing in her ears.

'I think,' Lynda says at long last, after the protracted silence became too much to bear, 'that there is probably a lot more to it than that, my dear.'

'Well, I'm afraid it might seem like a simple assumption to many, but as far as I can see, had that mother been there on time for little Leo, then he would still be here. The kidnapper wouldn't have had a chance to take him, would they?' Sarah smiles and runs her finger around the plate, sweeping up the remainder of the crumbs before scooping them up into her mouth in one swift movement.

'Have the police said they are sure he's been taken by somebody?' Emily finds herself saying. 'Last I heard, they said they weren't ruling out the idea that he took it upon himself to walk home and then something untoward happened along the way.'

She sees Sarah shake her head and sit up straight,

confidence evident in her stance. 'No, apparently, they've checked CCTV footage on the route he would have taken and he isn't on it.'

'Could he not have taken a different route?' Moira asks, her voice like the chirrup of a small bird.

'Perhaps,' Sarah replies, a look of mild defeat in her eyes. 'But the other route is much longer and it means he would have had to use the small iron bridge that crosses over the river. The river is high at the minute and–' She stops, brings her hand up to cover her mouth realising what she has just said, her face abruptly draining of all colour.

Emily wants to scream at her to shut up, that she needs to stop these unfounded allegations and suppositions. 'I don't want to think about it,' she suddenly pipes up, keen to change the subject. All this talk of missing children is causing her innards to swell and contract. She thinks of Joel out there with Mo and his friends and although she knows he is perfectly safe, probably having the time of his life, a small ribbon of anxiety slowly begins to wrap itself around her skull. What if Mo turns around for just a second to chat to one of his friends and something happens? Something dreadful and unutterably horrid that involves her little boy, irrevocably shattering her life, ripping it into tiny little shreds? She feels their eyes on her, their probing gazes roaming over her, trying to delve inside her head. Her skin flushes hot and cold.

They sit for the next minute or so, sipping their coffee, idly picking at the leftover cakes until Sarah stands up, hands on hips and heads over to a nearby shelf. 'Well, I don't know about you lot, but I'm having one. Sod not drinking during the day.'

She pulls down two bottles of wine, one red, one white and brandishes them in the air with a slight smile. Emily is torn between wanting to get up and leave, to go out searching for her boy, and grabbing the bottle from Sarah and necking it in one long gulp. Why is being a parent and building new relationships so fucking hard?

It's at times like this she wishes her own parents lived closer and didn't spend six months of the year in Spain. Not that they are particularly loving and caring towards her and Joel when they are home. Distant and aloof, her mother and father are more interested in their friends and life abroad than they are in Emily and their grandchild, but at least they would be here, giving her a degree of support. Just knowing they were close by would afford her a crumb of comfort.

She can hear the soft popping of the cork and the light tinkling of wine as Sarah pours out a glass and holds it up on offer. 'Anyone?' she says with a purr.

'Right, well why not, is what I say,' Lynda barks as she takes the glass from Sarah and raises it to her lips.

'Count me in as well,' Moira chips in, her shyness diminishing as she takes a glass of red and swallows two mouthfuls in rapid succession.

Emily bites at her lip, tugging at a loose flap of skin, gnawing and grinding it with her teeth until a burst of pain forces her to stop. 'Oh, go on then,' she murmurs resignedly, thinking that this is a very wicked way to spend a Sunday, but then, what is so wrong with relaxing with neighbours and friends? It's what other people do every week, sometimes every night. It's just that she has spent so long on her own that she has forgotten how to socialise, how to kick back and enjoy herself as if tomorrow is never going to arrive.

Even meeting Mo was by chance. She had a flat tyre and was attempting to pump it up when he swung by in his cab and stopped to help her. Not exactly the most romantic of encounters but just over a month later and here they are, in a relationship, him showering her with gifts, and her too worried and anxious to commit in case it doesn't work out and she is left alone once more, bereft at her loss and having to learn how to live without him. And then of course, there's Joel to consider. Today he and Mo are out there, forming a bond, building a friendship, possibly something more than that, something more permanent. It terrifies her that Joel could be let down by Mo's sudden departure from his life. Emily is permanently wracked with guilt for thinking these dark unwelcome thoughts in the first place, for doubting Mo's intentions and thinking less of him when in truth, it is highly unlikely that he would ever let either of them down. Mo is a good man and she has to learn to trust him.

Sarah fills her glass to the brim. Emily sips at it, savouring the crisp flavour, the slightly buttery taste as it rests easily on her palate. This is expensive wine. Not like the cheap stuff she purchases from the corner shop at £3.99 a bottle. This is the proper stuff that she could only ever dream of buying.

Two more sips and her worries begin to look less threatening. Draining her glass and getting it refilled, she takes another long slug and is surprised to find that she has pushed Joel's absence to the back of her mind. It's the comfortable blurring around the edges that she enjoys, the ability to forget the unforgettable and see things through calm contented eyes.

She is filled with a sense of equanimity, her composure more settled as she listens to the chatter around her – Lynda's sharp authoritative tone, Sarah's nervous fluctuating voice every time she is put in her place by Lynda, and Moira's tiny yet commanding timbre – they all mesh together nicely in her brain. Perhaps she was being uncharitable earlier, wishing she hadn't come. This is actually a really thoughtful thing to do. *Sarah has worked hard at getting all of us together*, thinks Emily as she leans back in her chair and looks around the large kitchen-diner. Getting out of the house more often will very possibly be the making of her, lessening her anxieties, allowing Joel time away from her. He has a life as well. She knows that. It's just that sometimes she feels overwhelmed by the idea that one day she will lose him. He will grow up, go looking for his father, become bewitched by a man who deserted him without a second thought and then she will be left on her own.

She sits opposite Sarah, listening to her talk about her previous job, the redundancy and how being at home on her own day after day is both lonely and draining. Emily tries to muster up sympathy for her but one glance around the house is enough to quash those feelings. She lets her mind wander, the wine having a dulling effect on her reflexes and only snaps back into the present when Sarah stops speaking and sits watching her, as if waiting for a response.

'That can't be right, Lynda,' Moira is saying. 'Surely, you've got it wrong? A case of mistaken identity, perhaps?'

Emily pricks up her ears, something in Moira's tone telling her that this is something they shouldn't be hearing. Sarah too, leans closer, angling her face so she can fully hear what is being said. A slight flush rises up Lynda's face, her usual pale complexion now lightly spotted with pink.

'I mean, I probably shouldn't be saying this,' Moira whispers, a look on her face that tells Emily she has spoken out of turn, said something she regrets and is now unable to backtrack on, 'but is it okay for him to be allowed to hold such a position?' Moira shakes her head and looks away. 'Sorry. Ignore me. I'm just being thoughtless and mean-spirited. Let's change the subject, shall we?'

Emily watches Lynda's sour expression, sees how it takes on a whole new level of exasperation and possibly even fury; emotions that she has never seen Lynda display before now. For all that Lynda is an authoritative figure, one who refuses to suffer fools gladly, she is also reserved and distant, not the type of person to ever wear her heart on her sleeve. Moira too, looks suddenly sheepish having obviously spoken out of turn. She is fiddling with the hem of her skirt, sneaking furtive glances at her friend as she waits for a possible outburst.

Sarah slides closer to the two women, her eyes twinkling with unconcealed curiosity. 'Oh, come on! You've said it now. You can't leave something like this hanging and not tell us what's going on.' She turns and prods Emily in her arm with a small fat finger. 'Can they, Emily? Come on, help me out here. I'm sure you want to know what's happening, don't you?'

Emily swallows, feeling the slight burn of the wine as it hits her stomach. She doesn't want to know what's happening at all. Having seen Lynda's anxious expression, she wishes the conversation would divert elsewhere but knows better than to say such a thing. Instead, she smiles and tips her head to one side hoping this will appease Sarah who is now positively taut with excitement at being privy to the latest goings on in somebody else's life.

If there is one thing Lynda excels at, it is holding a silence for a certain amount of time until the atmosphere in the room becomes so weighted with discomfiture that everyone begins to shuffle in their seats wishing they were elsewhere rather than here, waiting for her reply.

Only when Emily coughs and catches Lynda's eye does she relent, her voice gravelly, lacking in its usual confident flair. 'It's nothing really. I was just telling Moira that it came as a bit of a shock to find out that my new art tutor at the community centre in town is an old pupil that I once had to testify against in court.' She briefly closes her eyes then turns to look out of the window at the neatly cut lawn and rows of perfectly spaced flowers outside. 'It was a long time ago and it just gave me a bit of a shock, that's all.'

'Testify for what?' Sarah's words ring around the room, sharp and probing. 'What did he do, Lynda? What was his crime?'

Emily can hardly breathe. Her pulse is thudding in her ears, the room taking on different proportions as Sarah continues with her tirade. 'I realise you think it happened a long time ago, Lynda, whatever it was he did, but in the current climate, these things can be important. A boy is missing – vanished off the face of the earth – and I believe that every little detail is important. If it was robbery or breaking and entering, then obviously it isn't relevant, but I can tell by your face that it's something more than that, isn't it?' Sarah's voice rises, crashing around them. 'Isn't it?'

Emily can't be sure, but she thinks that she hears a small moan escape from Moira, a high-pitched squeak followed by the rustle of fabric as Lynda shifts awkwardly in her seat, her eyes flicking everywhere but at Sarah, who has practically pinioned her to the seat with her probing gaze and forthright manner.

'Oh, if you must know, it was over twenty years ago and there is no way it has any bearing on what has happened to that little boy from Atenby. No bearing at all.' Lynda stands up, straightens her trousers and stares down at Moira who is sitting, waif-like in her chair, her fingers interlaced in her lap, her small beady eyes darting all around the room.

'How do you know? None of us knows that, do we?'

Emily stands up. She is ready to leave now. She wants no part of this. This is why she shies away from gatherings, why she prefers sitting at home and keeping her own company. One stray word, one sly comment and suddenly everything comes crashing down. Relationships are then fractured, friendships broken, lives ruined. Life is difficult enough, with plenty to fret about without bringing other unnecessary and unwanted problems into the mix. Sarah has no right probing and digging like this. It is none of her business. *This*, thinks Emily, *is why she invited us here – to stir up dirt and cause upheaval. To make everybody feel distressed and uneasy.* She has used that little boy's disappearance to her own advantage, to glean as much information as she can out of people to satisfy her own desire for gossip and scandal. The conversation was always going to be steered around to this and now it has, Emily feels an overwhelming need to escape, to go home where she doesn't have to be subjected to this sort of nonsense. She is not prepared to sit here listening to Sarah in her self-appointed position of judge and jury, deliberating over the case of a man she has never met and knows nothing about.

She hears it as she throws the remainder of her wine down the sink, staining Sarah's beautiful enamel a deep cerise pink; Moira's tiny voice saying those words that still the air around her, tipping her delicately balanced world into free-fall.

'Sexual assault. He sexually assaulted another boy and now he's back in town.'

21

LYNDA

'I'm sorry,' Moira says timidly, her fingers flapping about nervously, her chest rising and falling in a rapid motion that is bordering on hyperventilation. 'It just came out. The atmosphere had turned sour and it was that awkward silence. I didn't know what else to say.'

Lynda sighs and presses her lips together, a series of deep grooves setting into the outer rim of her mouth. 'It's fine, you silly old fool.' She smiles and slaps Moira's arm playfully as they make their way back to Moira's house. 'I should never have mentioned it in the first place. I should have waited until we got back here and then spoken about it. I'm as much to blame.'

'She's a real old gossip-monger, that Sarah, isn't she?' Moira angles her head, stares up at her friend, waiting for a response.

The tension begins to drain from their bodies as they stride past the village green, beyond the postbox before they turn left towards Moira's rambling old house with its long driveway and perfectly manicured garden.

'Oh, you are so right there. She's the worst kind.' Lynda's voice is full of disdain as she wonders why she ever decided to let down her guard and speak so openly about a subject she has kept private for all these years. What on earth has she become?

'I think it was the wine.' Moira rummages in her pocket for her keys, a handful of spare change jangling about in a soft metallic clang. 'It loosened me up a bit too much.'

'Same here,' Lynda says dolefully, thinking this is why she rarely drinks. A worried mind and alcohol definitely don't mix. Throw in a couple of young nosey neighbours and you have yourself a catastrophe. 'At least we did the decent thing and can say we made the effort to socialise with other villagers, eh?'

'We can indeed,' Moira murmurs as she slips her key into the lock and pushes at the door with her shoulder. 'Coffee?' Moira gives her friend's arm an amiable squeeze. Lynda places her fingers over Moira's, thinking how lucky she is to have such a person in her life. While other areas of her life seesaw out of control, Moira is here, always available, unerringly reliable.

'Maybe another time, eh? I'm feeling a bit out of sorts at the minute. Think I might just go home and have a lie on the bed, sleep off the alcohol.'

Moira agrees, doesn't badger her into going inside insisting they need to talk about it.

Lynda is thankful for this. Images from that time in her life fill her mind; memories of that poor boy and what he did blooming and multiplying in her head. Memories she longs to forget. Her body suddenly feels heavy, twice its usual weight.

'Right, well you know where I am if you need me.'

'I still think about him, you know.' Lynda swallows down her tears. Crying is for ninnies, for lightweights and the silly people of the world, not for her. She doesn't cry. Never has. Apart from that time, that period in her life when she lost the one thing that ever mattered to her. Then she cried, allowing a river of tears to flow until she was sure she would dry up completely, dehydrate and shrivel into a useless desiccated being, no life left in her.

'The boy from school?' Moira reaches out to touch Lynda's arm again, her fingers barely brushing against the fabric of her shirt before Lynda jerks her body away.

'No. I mean him. My boy.' She didn't mean to say those words. Any of them. They just came out unintentionally, spilling out of her mouth before she could stop them. *Damn the alcohol and damn that Sarah woman for starting all of this.* She has somehow dragged old memories out from the darkest dustiest corners of Lynda's mind and back into the light; old emotions that she has stacked away to preserve her well-being are now making an unwanted appearance. She can do without this. All of it. Dredging up the past is never a good idea.

'Ah,' Moira says quietly, her eyes downcast. 'Are you sure you don't want that coffee?'

The deep rattling sigh seems to come from her boots as Lynda looks at Moira, her eyes heavy with a sudden realisation that things have moved; her life has taken a different trajectory and not one she particularly cares for. 'No. Honestly, I think I'm better off going home at the minute. Once I've had a nap, things will look better. But thanks all the same.'

They part, Moira giving Lynda a meek little wave before closing the door, and Lynda shuffling off home filled with a pressing desire to be back in her little cottage away from the woes of the world. She should never have loosened her tongue and spoken so openly. Maybe it's her age. Maybe this is what happens when you live alone with nobody to talk to: the madness starts to creep in, darkening shadows pushing at your thoughts, nudging you into a place of unending terror.

Lynda thinks that perhaps she should reconsider and not attend any more art classes. It seems that since going there, everything has taken a downward turn, her thoughts caught up in a gravitational pull that she is powerless to resist.

And yet, why should I not attend? she thinks sullenly. She enjoyed the latest session. He seems to be trying to make a go of things, this Ashton lad – although she still doesn't know for certain that it's him, even though every fibre of her being is screaming at her that it is. Too many coincidences and similarities for her liking. She's no fool and despite shoving it all away, pretending it never happened, her memory of that time is sharp. With every passing day, she feels more and more certain that it's him.

Letting herself into her cottage, she pulls off her jacket and slumps into a chair, a dull ache developing at the base of her skull. She massages her neck with the palm of her hand, thoughts of her own boy still lingering in her mind. It was such a long time ago, so long that she feels as if it happened to somebody else. It was a hundred lifetimes ago when her boy was taken from her, whisked away before she had chance to get to know him properly.

He will be forty-nine now, a grown man with a life she knows nothing about. He may possibly have children of his own. She could be a grandmother, have grandchildren out there that she will never get to meet. A surge of anger rises up her abdomen at the injustice of it all, flexing itself within her diaphragm and exiting her throat in an echoing howl. Her scream ricochets off every wall until she slumps, spent, no energy left in her.

She thinks of her mother, her long-dead mother, insisting that the baby be adopted, telling Lynda she was far too young to care for a child when she was still one herself, neither realising nor caring about whether or not Lynda wanted to keep the baby, not giving a thought to her daughter's wants or needs. Her emotions were shoved aside by a woman who thought she knew better.

Lynda recalls that overwhelming love for her child, an all-encompassing emotion that has stayed with her. The bond with him was immediate, an invisible thread that nobody – especially her own mother – should ever have broken. Having her child removed from her arms was like having a limb amputated. She remembers trying to nuzzle him in, to hold him as tightly as she could only for him to be rudely snatched away from her breast by an inconsiderate domineering matriarch who was convinced that she was doing the right thing, refusing to give her daughter's feelings a second thought.

It was only a matter of seconds, their time together, but she remembers his smell, the feel of him, the chill of his absence as he was whisked from her arms leaving a cavernous void within her that would never be filled. Even to this day, she can picture him, recall his scent, still be startled by how frail he was, how utterly breathtakingly beautiful he was. He was hers. Her baby boy. And her own mother stole him from her, passed him on to another family who, she was sternly informed, would take better care of him and love him more than Lynda ever could. Like her own cold calculating mother knew the first thing about tenderness or love.

She stands up, clutching at her chest, thinking how shitty and unfair life can be. The floor tilts under her feet as she shuffles to the door, needing to do something, needing to get out of this room. The walls are closing in on her, the ceiling squashing her down. She hasn't had an episode like this for so long now that she thought it was all behind her, that that part of her life was neatly locked up after she threw away the key, vowing to never ever allow it the light of day, but now here it is, presenting itself in all its sickening and ugly glory.

The stairs creak and groan as she marches up, ready for a lie down on the bed. Shutting out the world is her aim now. Wrapping herself in her own cocoon is what she will do.

A sudden idea jumps into her head, dragging her out of her thoughts. She realises that the wine has dulled her thinking, made her forget about something important. An addition to her life that has helped her cope. How could she possibly forget? What sort of a person is she that she would completely overlook such a significant thing – something that has recently brightened her life, helped her to cope with the darkest of days.

Another creak and groan as she turns and heads back downstairs, the heavy veil of gloom gradually dissipating at the thought of seeing him again. He has a way of lifting her spirits. Simply having him around the place, just knowing he will be there when she gets home, helps her to put things into perspective. She pushes open the door down to the basement, treading carefully through the shadows, her hand trailing over the wall as she searches for the light switch before flicking it on and staring over to the corner of the room.

'There you are,' she says softly, her mood lifting at the sight of him. 'I'm so glad to see you. Have you missed me?'

22

TRENT

I'm having to administer the sleeping tablets more often than I would like, to help stop the tantrums and tears. Soon they will cease. This level of animosity and rebellion cannot continue indefinitely. The drugs help to calm him down, to make him more malleable. He's a sweet boy deep down, but at the moment he is going through the painful process of separation, something that can't be hurried and will take some time but something that also has an endpoint. Sometime soon, he will come out of the other side of this and everything will seem brighter. He will see sense and be glad that he is here.

I am trying to keep things on a level, to keep everything as peaceful and reasonable as it can be. It's difficult, however, to get a routine set up while he is in this frame of mind so I am just having to bide my time and be patient, be the strong reliable adult he needs me to be.

'When can I go home, Trent?'

The tremble in his voice almost breaks me. I want him to be happy, I really do, but the thing is, I want him to be happy here, with me, not to be constantly pining after her, the woman who calls herself his mother, the same woman who abandoned her own son. Soon he will see through her false promises and poor parenting. Once he sees how loved he is here, his need to be with her will be a thing of the past. And that's when he will turn to me.

'We spoke about this earlier, didn't we?' I want to call him by his real name, to tell Timmy how much I've missed him and that I am delighted he is back here, back home where he belongs, but I know that it would alarm him, rouse his suspicions even further and lower his mood so I remain silent, saying his name only in my head where it can't cause any problems or upset. At night, I lie there, repeating it over and over and over, whispering it into the darkness, enjoying the feel of each syllable as it rolls around my mouth, slipping off my tongue with such ease, it's as if he has never been away.

'You said Mum was at work and then she was asleep and then was back at work again. She must be home by now.' His skin is flushed as he speaks, a sign that he's about to tip over that edge once more, that deep endless precipice where his fears expel themselves in the shape of big fat sobs that wrack his small body.

Oh, how I want to sweep him up into my arms, to nuzzle my face into his neck and murmur into his ear that everything is going to be just fine, that we are a team, he and I, and that we will get through this together. But of course, I don't. He wouldn't understand my actions, would question my motives, think me odd and slightly off balance and it would ultimately drive a wedge between us. I have to remain patient and take my time. He still thinks of me as almost a stranger even though I know him so well, have known him for all of his life.

'Well, as I said earlier, she did say she would call me when she's ready to collect you. There's no need to get upset. Don't you like it here? That makes me really sad, that you don't want to be here when I've tried so hard to help you.' I whisper the words, hoping my martyred expression will have the desired effect and pull at his heartstrings, make him think that I am hurt by his words.

He sniffs and wipes at his eyes. 'I do like you, Trent, and it's really cool here but I miss my mum and I would like to go home now.'

This is the most difficult part, seeing him so distraught and troubled. I feel everything that he feels, can almost climb inside his skin, sense his fear and read his every thought. What I can't do is control any of it. If there were a big switch that I could flick to turn off his memories and make him love me more than his mother, then I would do it without question, but I can't so I am going to have to wait it out, count down the hours, days and weeks until he realises that crying for his mother is futile because he is never going home.

'Look what I've got for you,' I say as I step to one side and present my trump card. An iPad. No internet connection but lots of games for him to play on. I can't risk him stumbling across any news items or getting in touch with his friends but the boy does need to play. I know how much young people love their technology, so am hoping this will appease him, help distract him from his woes and focus his mind on something more positive, more challenging. Something that will help him realise here isn't such a bad place after all.

He steps towards me, slowly, tentatively, and takes the iPad from my grasp, turning it over in his hands before glancing back at me, a quizzical expression on his face. 'Can I message my mum on this?'

My stomach knots. *Damn this need for him to be reunited with that woman.* 'No, I'm afraid not,' I say, feigning sorrow and regret for his plight. 'I'm afraid I don't have any wifi in the house, but there are plenty of apps on there that you can play on to help pass the time.'

His eyes are full of confusion as he steps away from me, clutching the iPad. He is weighing up his options, trying to work out what to say or do next, torn between wanting to keep it and a need to speak up about being reunited with his mother. He is, after all, only eight years of age. A little boy. A confused, worried little boy who is trying to work it all out. I need to remember that, to put myself in his shoes.

'I tell you what,' I say, wondering if this is the right thing to do but feeling that I have no other option if I am to keep him happy and settled, 'later on, you can play in the garden. I'll have a rummage and see if I can find a football or some sports equipment. Won't that be nice?'

'Where are the windows in this room?' he says, turning and looking as if he has just realised that he cannot see outside even though he has been here for days.

'Well, we don't need windows in here, do we? I mean, look around you.' I spin around, my arms outstretched towards all the instruments – the drum kit, the Les Paul guitar, even the not so grand looking piano. 'Look at everything we have here. It's amazing, isn't it?'

He bites at his lip, his eyes flickering with indecision. He interlaces his fingers, locking and unlocking them repeatedly. 'Yes, it's lovely, Trent, but when can I go home?'

This is more exhausting than I thought it would be, keeping him placated and entertained, trying to find new ways of answering his questions with yet more lies, leading two lives; my upstairs day-to-day life and then this life down here with Timmy. I long for a time in the not too distant future when it all comes together, when our lives merge seamlessly and we can move on from this juncture.

'Soon,' I murmur, desperately trying to think of ways to change the subject. 'But first, I'm going to go and find that football and make sure the garden isn't too muddy, and then I'll be back. Tell you what,' I say, giving him a sly wink, 'I'll also see if I've got any Irn-Bru. And how about some sweets? What are your favourites?'

His eyes dart about, confusion addling his poor little brain.

'You like Haribo, don't you?' I'm taking a chance here, casting my net wide and hoping I get a catch.

He nods and I exhale and briefly close my eyes, fighting the fatigue that this charade is making me feel. 'Well,' I say, simulating a level of cheer I don't actually feel, 'it just so happens I have a pack handy. Just you wait here and I'll be back in a jiffy. Tell you what, why don't you get a quick shower and change into those clothes I got for you and I'll go and get everything ready.' I point to the pile of clothing stacked on the chair, still folded after being lifted out of its packaging.

'Can I come with you? To see the rest of the house, I mean.'

I should have expected this at some point. He has an inquisitive mind. A clever boy like Timmy will soon want to explore his surroundings. I can't let him. It's out of the question. For now, anyway. 'Take your shower and get your clean clothes on and I'll be back before you know it. Now let me see if I can find that football.'

I am out of the room before he can protest, locking it behind me and praying he is in a more biddable and positive frame of mind when I return.

23

SARAH

I t's ridiculous really, that there haven't been any police in the village as yet, knocking on doors, searching through hedgerows and shrubbery, looking for that poor boy. They should be here, making their presence known, at least giving the impression that they are doing something, that they are doing their utmost to try and find him.

She moves away from the window, sits down in her favourite leather armchair and turns on the TV. Since Leo's disappearance, she has tried to keep up with all the latest reports, feeling that it is the least she can do, to take an interest and show that she cares. Somebody somewhere has vital information. A member of the public knows where that young boy is, and shame on them for not disclosing it.

The first face she sees sends a ripple of revulsion through her. It's that woman, the boy's mother. There she is, putting on a show for the cameras, her blotchy tear-stained face filling the screen, hiccupping her way through an impassioned plea for her boy to return home. Sarah is sickened. *Are people really falling for this tripe*, she wonders. *Are they really so naïve as to think that she is a caring individual who misses her boy? If she cared that much she would have turned up to the school on time, not left him standing there, unaccompanied and vulnerable.* Sarah thinks about what she said to the other women in the village recently, about his possible route home over the small footbridge that spans the river, wondering if the police have considered the possibility that he may have lost his footing and slipped into the water. They must have. It would amount to gross incompetence to not look into such an obvious possibility. But what if they haven't? What if they are solely focused on searching for a kidnapper rather than considering an alternative theory that he took it upon himself to walk home? A helpline number flashes up at the bottom of the screen, a rolling message, a strapline across her TV screen, highlighted in red.

Sarah picks up her phone, staring at the handset before putting it down again. What on earth would she say anyhow? That they need to check the river for Leo Fairland? As if they haven't done that already. But then, what if they haven't? What if they are focusing on an abduction and Leo is still alive somewhere, clinging on to dear life, his body soaked and filthy, covered in mud dredged up from the bottom of the river. He could still be alive down there by the riverbank, hidden amongst the reeds and shrubbery, hypothermia slowly tugging away at what is left of his life. She imagines how cold he will be, how alone and frightened, and before she can stop herself, she is punching in the helpline number, steeling herself for their questions, rehearsing what she is going to say, the words rolling around in her head over and over and over, tumbling into each other until they lose all meaning.

Heart thumping, she waits, deaf to the recorded voice at the other end of the line that is thanking her for the call and pleading with her to be patient, stating in a muffled robotic voice that an operator will be with her shortly. She shuts it out, concentrating instead on the phrases that are replaying in her head, a long stream of words that may, or may not give the police a morsel of information that could help in their search for the missing boy. That's how it works. She has read about it, seen it on TV, how a passing comment, an insignificant flimsy thread that is attached to a larger tapestry, can help solve the crime. It's like a jigsaw, all the smaller pieces helping to form the larger picture. Every little bit counts. Every tiny piece of information, no matter how small or trivial it may seem, could be the one fragment that helps solve the case. Buoyed up by this, she clings to the phone, hoping she can assist them in some small way. Anything for that boy. She will do absolutely anything to help him get back home alive.

She stands by the window, feeling hopeless, dejected. Her call meant nothing to them, that much was obvious. She offered them her home address, telephone number, email address but was told they had received everything they needed from her and was given a stiff and formal thank you before the line went dead. So much for working together to find him. All the appeals are obviously just soundbites put out to the public to appease their anxiety and growing fury at his disappearance. Whatever happened to community spirit for goodness' sake? At least she can say that she has done her bit, tried to help in some small way, which is very possibly more than many have done; more than the many voyeurs who undoubtedly prefer sitting in front of their televisions, digesting every morbid detail whilst doing absolutely nothing to help bring him home. She is better than that. She has played an active part in the search for him. When all this is over, she can at least hold her head up high, stand tall and proud and say that she tried.

A noise outside alerts her. She moves to the side of the

window, keeping watch. Mo pulls up to Emily's house, sits for a short while in his car before climbing out and heading up her path. Stepping away from the glass, she doesn't want to see whether he knocks or lets himself in, as if he is a close member of their family. Unease crawls about in the base of her stomach. She can't help it, wishes she could, but is unable to stem the restlessness that squirms about in her belly. She wanted to speak to Emily about it last Sunday but was unable to articulate her feelings without coming across as interfering and callous. She wishes there was a way she could get closer to Emily, to form a strong friendship and be in a position to speak to her without any of it appearing confrontational or suffering the possibility of a backlash.

Something about Emily's relationship with this man feels wrong. If she were to talk about it openly, Sarah feels sure she would be verbally savaged and told to keep her unwanted opinions to herself. The thing is, she has read about how these people work, how they manipulate those around them, worming their way into people's lives, showering them with compliments and gifts, and then the next thing they know, the innocent party is left heartbroken after they have been mistreated, their good nature abused and taken advantage of. All she can do is keep watch, make sure nothing untoward occurs in her village.

As if on cue, a police car speeds past, closely followed by a police van. *And not before time*, thinks Sarah, relief expanding in her chest. She had expected a larger presence about the place. A country lane a couple of miles long is all that separates them from Atenby. The police should be swarming all over this place, searching every inch of Middleham, trawling through hedgerows, sending divers into the river, yet she has seen scant evidence of any activity at all.

It's at times like this she feels marginally grateful that she doesn't actually have any children. If this were her boy, she would want a heavy police presence in every village within a ten-mile radius of his disappearance. She would be out there herself, crawling through shrubbery, searching wooded areas, calling out his name until her throat was raw. There would be no lengths she would not go to, to find her child. Perhaps that's why she feels so suspicious of Mo. It's her instinct kicking in, drawing her attention to anything or anybody who has recently appeared around the place. She doesn't believe in coincidences, just cold hard facts. And that's another thing that has kept her awake nights since meeting with Moira, Emily and Lynda – the guy she spoke about at her art classes and his sudden arrival. A man with an unsavoury past appears in town at the same time that a child goes missing. Her hackles rise once more. Definitely no such thing as coincidences. Life doesn't work that way.

Her skin turns cold, her scalp prickles as she considers her options. Why is doing the right thing so damn hard? How easy it must be to follow others, to turn a blind eye to all the ails of the world and carry on with your everyday existence in blissful ignorance. She could do that. She could choose to ignore her gut instinct, disregard the pull of her conscience and act as if nothing is happening around her. And then how difficult it would be to sleep at night knowing she could have made a difference and helped, yet chose to go down the route of denial and apathy simply because it was easier, requiring no backbone or morals.

Without giving herself time to think it through or back out altogether, Sarah snatches up the phone once more and presses redial, then waits for that robotic voice that will tell her she is in a queue and to please be patient, that her call is valuable to them and that they will be with her shortly.

'Hello?' she says, the person speaking on the other end catching her by surprise, 'I have some more information that may be of interest to you regarding Leo Fairland's disappearance.' Her voice sounds hollow, disembodied in the near silence of her own living room. It reverberates in her head, a fuzzy distorted version of herself.

She tells the operator about the new teacher who is running the art classes in town. 'At the community centre; the one next to the car park that is attached to the library. He has a past record for sexual abuse of children. Too much of a coincidence if you ask me,' she says, confidence now beginning to balloon in her chest. The more she talks, the greater and stronger her belief is that there is some sort of connection. 'I think perhaps somebody should look into him, find out why he's here after leaving town for so long. I don't know his name, but I'm sure the police can find that out.' Like a repeat of the previous conversation, the operator thanks her for the information, assuring her they will follow up on all leads before abruptly ending the call.

Sarah replaces the handset, self-worth and usefulness glowing under her skin, buzzing in her head, making her feel alive. An unfamiliar wave of energy pulses through her, throbbing deep in her veins. She has passed on what she knows, said what needed to be said. It was an anonymous call. What happens next is down to the police. As a decent citizen she has alerted them to his presence in town, perhaps even helped to make Middleham and Atenby and every other village in North Yorkshire that little bit safer. That's all she can do, isn't it? With no real power except her ears and eyes and strong intuition, she has put her two penn'orth in and can at least sleep easy at night.

Her mind goes back to Malcolm and his behaviour. And that letter. She realises she hasn't yet checked yesterday's post. Not that it ever contains anything of interest – just the usual junk mail and a handful of bills. She heads through to the hallway to collect it, her head still full of thoughts of her husband and Leo, and Mo's sudden appearance over the road and the new art teacher and his sordid past. She doesn't feel bad about making that call. It was the right thing to do. If he has nothing to hide then no harm has been done, and if he does have a terrible secret lurking in his recent past, then her call was worth it; something the police can use to piece together their investigation and bring it all to a close.

Picking up the stack of mail, Sarah wonders when she will hear from Malcolm about coming home again. His rapid departure still rankles, making her feel out of sorts, as if something dreadful is about to occur. She tries to shove it out of her mind. Badgering him about it while he's working will only exacerbate the problem, lowering his mood, making him less likely to want to return. Instead she will wait for his call, be demure and reserved, hoping he will arrive soon. She shouldn't complain. He holds a senior position and he has a generous salary which affords them this lovely house and a new car. Still, having him home regularly would be good. It might help stem her loneliness, the creeping despair that shrouds her more often than she cares for. Having somebody else around can stop that feeling, put a halt to the dark shadows that regularly filter into her brain. Even if that person is denying her the one thing she craves more than anything else in the world. But she cannot think like that. He has made his feelings clear to her and she now has to accept his point of view. Malcolm is her husband; she is his wife. They are a team. For better for worse, for richer for poorer.

Biting hard at her lip and swallowing down a river of unshed tears, Sarah opens the mail, a way to keep her mind off the sham that is her marriage.

As expected, most of it is junk – leaflets from local companies selling their wares, money-off vouchers for items she will never buy. Only a handful of them are worthy of keeping. One letter in particular feels extraordinarily heavy in her hands;

a large brown envelope with the word 'Confidential' emblazoned across the top. Malcolm's name is printed underneath in thick black ink. An arrhythmic beat starts up in her chest, her heart flipping about under her sternum as she tries to suppress the sudden nervousness that is snaking beneath her skin. She has no idea what this letter is or why it is making her so edgy and uncomfortable. The name of Malcolm's employer is stamped on the reverse with the address of their head office.

Sarah stares at it, concentrating on her breathing, closing her eyes against the tide of nausea that rises up her throat, forcing her to hang on to the wall for balance. Rarely does he receive correspondence from work. This is a new occurrence, something different. Something unexpected. She should open it, call Malcolm and read it to him. It could be important, something he needs to know about right now. But then, head office would contact him to let him know, wouldn't they? Perhaps it's nothing at all. Perhaps this is her imagination, conjuring up possible nasty scenarios into her head. This is what solitude does – it gives her too much time to think, to jump to the wrong conclusions and paint a bleaker picture than necessary, making herself sick with worry to the point where she cannot sleep or eat. After his recent rapid departure, she is making silly assumptions, expecting the worst. She has to stop it. She has just done a good thing, calling the police helpline, telling them of her fears and suspicions. But then, this is also what frightens her. Her instinct is usually fairly accurate, and right now her instinct is telling her that something is wrong with Malcolm. He came home to escape something bad and now that something is right here in their house, causing her to wither with worry.

She props the letter up on the small console table, the sight of his name and their home address jumping out at her.

Malcolm Trent,
26 Greenwoods,
Middleham,
North Yorks

The urge to open it, to read what is written inside is so strong it is a physical sensation; a burning in her chest, a large fist that compresses her lungs and heart and stomach into a tight little knot. She ignores it, shoves her hands deep into her pockets and heads into the kitchen, thinking that despite having done something supportive and constructive, despite feeling buoyant after speaking to the helpline to tell them about the art tutor in town, the familiar curtain of depression is already falling around her. Her head begins to throb, her vision blurring as the beginnings of a migraine sets in. She perches on the chair, staring outside at the birds that peck hungrily at the feeder, thinking that the sooner this day draws to a close, the better.

24

TRENT

The garden is dry and secluded enough for him to have a kick-about. I'm not altogether comfortable with him being out there but the boy needs some fresh air. He's been stuck inside for days and days now and it cannot be good for him. At some point, I am going to have to allow him out of the house. Nobody can be expected to live in just a couple of rooms with no natural light. He needs more than that. He deserves more. And after all, isn't that why I've got him? To give him a better life than the one he had? And now here he is, shut away like some sort of prisoner when all he wants to do is run and play.

I stroll around the garden, making sure there are no escape points. The most difficult part will be keeping the noise down. How can a boy be expected to play in complete silence? At least the neighbours either side are a fair distance away and the tall conifers ensure privacy. And it's not as if there will be an entire team out here, just one little boy. My boy.

I allow myself a small secret smile as the words bounce around my head. All these years without him have turned to dust because now here he is, by my side. We're together again. Back to how it should have always been.

In the garage, I drag out crates and boxes that have stood idle for many years now, hoping to find something that Timmy can play with but am disappointed to find nothing. Why would I have anything suitable here? I have lived a different life since losing him. There has been a big gap, a void in my life when he was absent. I have nothing to offer him and now I have to make up for it.

I will go shopping. It won't take me long to purchase some new items for the boy. It's the least I can do. I must also buy more new clothes for him while I'm there. I am going to need to build up a stack of items for him to wear, a whole new wardrobe of clothes for the future. I am filled with excitement at the thought of it as I get myself ready to leave the house.

The supermarket is thankfully almost empty. I fill my trolley with what I need and am back behind the wheel of my car in record time, my chest tight with anxiety at the thought of being spotted. I'm not doing anything wrong – I sincerely believe that – but other people don't think the same way as I do. Their views of what constitutes right and wrong are very different to mine, but then they haven't experienced what I have experienced and that is what forms us as individuals, isn't it? Our history – the hand that we are dealt in life and what we are forced to cope with – determines our life trajectory, so I cannot be held accountable for this current aberration. Timmy is a welcome addition to my otherwise empty world and I won't allow anybody to do anything to destroy what I now have. Not again. I will fight to the death to keep him by my side. Nobody, and I mean nobody, is going to take him from me.

Timmy is sitting at the drum kit when I let myself back into his room. His face is a fusion of turbulent emotions as I place the sports equipment and new clothes at his feet.

'There you go,' I say breathlessly. 'Take your pick. We've got badminton racquets, footballs, a cricket set and some frisbees. And some new clothes as well, but I suppose you'll be more interested in the toys, won't you?' I'm gabbling now, a streak of excitement running through me. Having him here permanently is starting to feel very real, a tangible force that is gathering momentum. I can feel the crackle of possibility in the air.

He slips off the stool, places the drumsticks on the floor and begins to sift through the pile of toys, a small smile twitching at the corners of his mouth.

'Wow, this is ace, Trent. Thank you!'

'There's just one catch though,' I say, injecting an element of mild distress into my timbre. 'One of my neighbours is very ill so you can't make a lot of noise.'

'Oh,' he says, concern creasing his features. 'What's wrong with them? Is it like when my granddad was really ill and I wasn't allowed to visit him?'

'Well, yes and no,' I murmur, my heart fluttering about my chest, hoping he doesn't become too distressed by what I'm about to tell him. 'It's a young lady. She's only a teenager and she is very ill and needs absolute silence.'

'Is she dying?' he asks, his eyes wide, his mouth puckered into a small O-shape.

'Yes, I'm afraid so.' I dip my head and bite at my lip feverishly. 'She is dying, so when you play out in the garden, you have to be as quiet as you can. Any shouting and you will have to come back inside. I'm really sorry about that, Timmy, but I made a promise to her parents that I would be silent when I was out there and I can't break that promise.'

He stares at me, his brow furrowed. 'Who?'

I try to recall what I have just said to him, repeating the sentence in my head. 'Her parents. I promised them I would keep the noise down and let them have some peace and quiet so they can look after their daughter.'

'Not that,' he says, picking up a cricket bat and inspecting it, running his fingers up and down the length of the handle. 'You called me Timmy. My name isn't Timmy. It's Leo.'

A fist punches its way into my chest and squeezes at my heart. My jaw trembles as I try to steady my breathing. 'Ah, sorry,' I say softly. 'You remind me of another boy I knew called Timmy. You look very much like him. You don't mind, do you?'

He shakes his head and turns his attention back to the array of apparatus sprawled at his feet. 'Can I take these outside now?' He is holding up the cricket bat and a ball. 'We play it at school and I can practise and get better at it. If I'm really good, I might even get chosen for the team. Mr Warwick, our sports teacher, said I'm getting better all the time and just need to perfect my technique. I have to learn how to hold the bat properly and keep it on the ground. If I can do that, I'm in with a chance.'

His eyes are twinkling with anticipation and it's all I can do to not scoop him up and cuddle him into my chest. We have so much to do together, so much to catch up on. My fingers itch to reach out to him, let him know of my feelings for him, affections I have had to hide for an age. 'Right,' I murmur, a tension building within me as I think about the risk I'm taking here. 'We'll go through the back way. And don't forget, not a peep. We don't want to upset the dying girl or her parents, do we?'

He shakes his head and widens his eyes. 'No. I promise I'll be really really quiet. I won't make a sound.' He holds out the ball for me to see. 'It's sponge see, so it won't make a noise when I hit it.'

This boy. So thoughtful. So polite and utterly perfect in every way.

I lead him out of the room, through the long hallway that runs down the side of the house and out into the garden. His attention is focused solely on the cricket set, his fingers tracing the grain of the wood on the bat as if it is made of precious metal.

'Here we are,' I say with a flourish as I push at the door that opens onto the back lawn. I lower my voice to little more than a whisper, placing my forefinger over my lips and making a soft shushing sound. 'Remember. Not a peep.'

Timmy nods, skipping onto the grass like the little boy that he is. I need to keep reminding myself of that fact. He is a frightened confused child. I cannot expect too much from him in such a short space of time. All I want is for him to settle, for the tears to stop and the pleas to be reunited with his mother to cease once and for all.

I stand at the doorway watching as he adjusts his posture and practises his stance, bringing the cricket bat back and forth again and again, his spine rigid, his legs slightly splayed. I walk towards him and bend to whisper in his ear. 'Shall I bowl?'

His eyes sparkle with delight as he looks up at me and I all but melt at his feet. 'Yes please!' His reply is so delicate, so quiet, so heartbreakingly genuine that I almost drop to my knees and take him in my arms. It was some sort of fate that brought us together that day last week. I rarely take that route past the school. There had been an accident on the main road through town so I diverted through Atenby village, and there he was, standing waiting for me. It was kismet that brought us together. Some things are just meant to be.

I throw the ball, making sure it's easy enough for him to reach. It's such a delight to see him happy, his face the picture of childish contentment as the ball flies through the air time and time again. I am more than a little surprised at how quietly he is able to play. This fills me with a great deal of glee, knowing we can come out here more often, knowing my little boy doesn't have to stay cooped up in that room indefinitely. This is progress. A positive step towards a normal existence for both of us.

We spend another half hour outside before I suggest going back inside for juice and a snack. A noise above us draws my attention as I collect the sports equipment and put it back in its package. The choppy whirring sound of a helicopter directly over our heads causes my skin to pucker with fear and dread. Without warning, I place my hand in the small of Timmy's back and chivvy him back inside the house, watching from the doorway as the helicopter continues on its journey to somewhere that isn't here. My stomach shrivels, pain shooting through it as I lock the door to the garden and we make our way back into the room.

25

EMILY

'They want to do what?' Emily feels her heart leap up her throat as she stares at Mo. She feels stricken on his behalf.

He lets out a long sigh, leans back in his chair and runs his fingers through his hair, exhaustion oozing out of every pore. 'It wasn't just me, Em. They want the whole fleet to check their dashcams. It just so happens I was the one who was closest to the school at the time he went missing. It's nothing to worry about. It's my footage they're after, not me.'

Emily feels a strangulated cry emerge from her throat and swallows hard to stop it escaping. All of a sudden Leo's disappearance feels too close to home. The road that separates the two villages feels like a world away compared to this – this calamity that has crept into her living room and tipped her neat little world sideways.

'Did you drive past the school when the kids came out on the day he went missing?' Her voice is almost a screech. She can't help it. This thing is skulking closer and closer to home and she doesn't care for it. If she could, she would close her curtains, lock every door and hunker down in the house until it is all over. Selfish as that may seem, it is how she feels and she cannot help it. She has her life, her family, her sanity to think about.

'No, of course not! Like I just said, I was in the vicinity, which is a certain radius of where the police are searching. I have no idea what that radius is. I'm guessing that sort of information isn't for public disclosure for obvious reasons, but if you stick a pin in a map at the school and have a look around that area, you'll get an idea of how big it really is. Don't forget,' Mo says wearily, 'that Atenby Primary School is in a small village but if you head out of the village itself, there is a main road that leads to the dual carriageway. The world and his wife will have passed that way. If you ask me, they're looking for a needle in a haystack but if it helps, then why not give it a go?'

Emily feels her face flush hot. A sheen of perspiration sits on her upper lip as shame floods through her. It's wrong that she wants to ignore this terrible occurrence but doesn't know how else to handle it. She isn't equipped to deal with such situations. What's next? An army of detectives banging on her door, searching through her garden, asking to look in her loft and shed? Mo being asked to do this feels like they are tainted by association, guilty of a crime they know nothing about.

'Mum, can I play out?' Joel is standing in front of her, his eyes gleaming with excitement as he clutches his football, his small fingers curled around it in a tight greedy grasp. Her instinct is to say no, that he must never ever play out again, that there are dangerous people around, psychopaths who wish him harm and are capable of doing all kinds of terrible things to him without breaking a sweat, but knows that is not the answer he wants or needs to hear.

He is a child. He should be allowed to run and play and shout to the sky above that life is good. He should be free from all of the adult responsibilities and worries that burden those around him. He should not have to shoulder the woes of his mother who is finding it difficult to cope with the fact that a child has gone missing close by. A mother whose partner is now being asked to provide evidence of his whereabouts at the time of Leo's disappearance.

'Come on, bud. Let's go and have a kick-about on the grass outside.' Mo looks at Emily for permission. She nods and sighs resignedly, feeling she has little or no say in the matter. She is coming across as neurotic and overbearing, she knows it, but feels as if her world is shrinking; squashing and condensing her concerns into a tight heavy box that sits deep inside her chest, restricting her ability to breathe.

The click of the door synchronises with the sob that seeps out of her gullet in a rattling gurgling hiccup. She watches out of the window as Joel runs about, kicking the ball, throwing himself to the ground in a dramatic dive at Mo's feet. She should be happy. She has a healthy son, a caring partner and a roof over her head. So why does she feel as if a giant hammer is about to fall and smash her entire world to pieces?

Sitting back down, she wonders what she managed to worry about before Leo went missing. Since that time, it feels like her every fear, every lurking dread that has ever entered her head, has multiplied a hundredfold and is imploding deep within her brain.

She could do with a drink. There's a bottle of Sauvignon in the kitchen. Her fingers itch to open it, to tip the bottle into a glass and drain it in one long gulp. Mo wouldn't approve. He's not a big drinker and definitely doesn't agree with drinking when Joel is around. Emily manages a laugh. He's right of course. Mo is always right. He's a better parent than Samuel could ever have hoped to be and she is blessed to have him in her life. She must never forget that. He is here and is a solid and positive force in her life and Joel's life. Solid, reliable and far more principled than she will ever be. Even on the nights he stays over, Mo is up and dressed and busying himself in the kitchen before Joel has even opened his eyes. The first time it happened, she had to stifle her laughter as Joel made a comment about Mo getting to their house early on a morning and helping to make breakfast, saying how kind it was for him to get up extra early and drive all this way. Tears prick at her eyes, her skin tingling at the memory. She is lucky. Luckier than most. She needs to keep reminding herself that things could be a whole lot worse. Mo has been a wonderful addition to their lives. The best.

The noise from the hallway pulls her into the present. It's not Joel or Mo. The knock comes again, a rhythmic tapping. She gets up, heads to the door and pulls it open to find Sarah standing there, bright eyed and attentive.

'Hi, sorry to disturb you. I was just wondering if you've heard from Moira or Lynda?' Sarah looks behind her furtively, as if she expects to find them near, listening in to what she is saying. 'I was just a bit worried after we were all at mine when it all went a bit – well you know, after what was said.'

Emily steps aside to let her in, part of her sagging inside at the thought of having to sit and listen to more gossip being dredged up by this strange little woman who, it appears, wants to be her friend.

'Coffee?' Emily says, already regretting offering. Mo and Joel will be back in shortly. She isn't quite ready to share her personal life with Sarah and would prefer she weren't here when they arrive back.

'Please! That would be lovely. I've just seen Joel and Mohammed out there playing football. It must be reassuring for you,' Sarah says rapidly, 'knowing that they get on, that there isn't any – well, you know – any friction.'

Emily feels her flesh ruck at Sarah's words, at the inference in her tone and the use of Mo's full name as if to highlight some hidden meaning about his ethnicity. It has got under her skin and although she knows that she should let it go, something about it has put her on edge. It's the use of certain words and phrases that have to be hinted at because Sarah is too cowardly to say out loud what it is she actually means. Emily hopes she is wrong, hopes that her instincts are way off beam on this one and she is being too sensitive but thinks also that she needs to tread carefully around this woman, this annoying unfathomable creature who has her oscillating between feeling a need to form a friendship with her, to being incensed at her presence and every word that comes out of her mouth.

'Why would there be? Mo's a nice guy and Joel loves him. They're both obsessed with football as well so they have a fair bit in common. Anyway,' Emily says, forcing herself to smile, 'I'll just go and get the coffee. Milk and sugar?'

'Milk, no sugar, thank you. Do you need a hand?' Sarah is standing watching them outside, her eyes following Mo as he dives for the ball and rolls on the floor.

A tic takes hold in Emily's jaw. She clamps her teeth together to stop it. 'I'll not be a minute. The machine's already bubbling so I won't be long.'

'No rush,' Sarah calls after her. 'I'll come through anyway,' she says, her footsteps trailing behind Emily who inadvertently picks up her pace to put some distance between them.

'So,' Sarah says with a slight drawl. 'What did you think of what Lynda told us on Sunday?'

Emily wants to shake her head and show Sarah the door. This is why she is here, to spread more rumours. Nothing to do with being concerned about Lynda or Moira and how they are doing. This has everything to do with being a gossip-monger. This has everything to do with smears and lies and ruining people's reputations and she will have no part of it. 'I think,' Emily murmurs as she picks up the percolator and pours coffee into two cups, 'that it all happened a long time ago and that everyone should just forget about it and let that lad get on with his life.'

'But do you not think it's a strange coincidence?' Sarah pipes up, oblivious to Emily's deteriorating mood and lack of patience. 'I mean he arrives back in town and a child goes missing. After what he did, we can't just turn a blind eye, can we?'

Emily wants to scream at her that yes, they can do just that, that they can all carry on with their lives and let people around them carry on with theirs and not go around apportioning blame when they have no evidence to do such a thing, but stands rigid instead, listening to Sarah's crude and artless accusations.

She shifts her position, blood surging and thumping through her veins, roaring through her ears. She pictures herself throwing hot coffee over Sarah, telling her to get out, shouting at her that she needs to get out more and get a bloody life instead of trying to ruin everyone else's.

'Well, I can,' she says breezily. 'I have enough to do in my own life without prying into somebody else's. Anyway, here's your coffee. Chocolate biscuit?' She holds out a plate of cookies and Sarah takes one and shovels it in her mouth, crumbs gathering at the corner of her lips.

The clunk of the front door and the muffled shuffle of feet feels like both a blessing and a curse. Before she can say anything, Joel comes running into the kitchen, grabs at a beaker and fills it with juice, gulping it down to slake his raging thirst. Emily twists around, her eyes scanning for Mo. His voice comes through from the living room, loud, full of clarity.

'I'm off, Emily. Just had a call from work. The police are there so I'm going to go and give them that footage. Shouldn't be too long.'

Sarah practically chokes on her biscuit. Emily wants to laugh as she stands observing while Sarah attempts to swallow it and speak whilst keeping her dignity intact. 'The police? What's happened? Is this related to little Leo's disappearance?'

Emily narrows her eyes, indicating that Joel is still in the room and that she doesn't wish for this conversation to continue, but can see that Sarah is oblivious to such indirect gestures, blind to the levels of social etiquette required around young children.

'Joel, why don't you go and play in your room? You can have an extra half hour on your Xbox.' Emily forces a smile, her face aching as she glances at Sarah.

'Really? Class!' The tumbler is dropped into the sink with a clatter before the boy races upstairs, his small feet a thunderous pounding above them.

'Emily, what on earth is going on?' Sarah's eyes bulge; a crooked vein on her temple pulsates in rhythm with her breathing. 'I mean,' she says, leaning back on the kitchen counter, 'I did want to chat to you at some point about Mo, you know?'

'Really?' *This is it*, thinks Emily. *This is the part when it all comes spilling out, when Sarah's true thoughts and intentions become completely transparent.* 'About what?' *Come on*, Emily thinks, her heart battering wildly under her ribcage. *Just come right out and say it. I'm ready for you.*

'Well, the thing is,' Sarah says, sucking in her breath and puffing out her chest in preparation for her moment of triumph, 'you don't really know him that well. I mean – well, what I'm trying to say is, you have to be careful these days, who you associate with. Some people need to be vetted.'

'Vetted?' Emily hopes her outrage doesn't show in her features, hopes that her skin has not mottled in fury and that her eyes are not wide and glassy with the anger that she is struggling to contain.

'Well, I mean I'm not saying Mo is like this. Not at all, but of course, you don't know who his friends are, and well, you hear about these people, don't you? These grooming gangs.' She lowers her voice, blinks repeatedly, whispers the final phrase, a toxic sentence that causes Emily to shudder with disgust.

She knew this was coming, or at least suspected it, but clung on to the hope that somewhere deep within herself, Sarah would realise it was a step too far and that she would at least have the decency to stay silent. She cannot rescind what she has just said. It is done now, the damage and hurtful insinuation digging deep into Emily's bones.

'So, you're saying that either Mo is a paedophile or his friends are paedophiles? Is that what you're getting at, Sarah? Because of his ethnicity, you've put two and two together and come up with five, making the wild unsubstantiated assumption that he is part of a grooming gang?' Emily tries to stay calm, to be reasonable and measured but it is so damn hard to remain cool and reasonable. She wants to rage at her, at this woman, this fucking deranged neighbour who is nothing more than an interfering poisonous busybody.

'No! Of course not!' A deep mauve flush has swept up Sarah's neck, covering her face and throat. 'All I meant was...' Her words trail away leaving a silence laden with resentment and a deep bitterness that eats at Emily's gut.

When she does speak, Emily's tone is soft; gentle and yet full of such menace that it sounds alien to her, a stranger's voice ringing in her head. Samuel leaving, being plunged into the darkest of times that almost broke her is an era she would sooner forget, but even then, not once did she feel as furious as she does at this moment in time. Lonely – yes, desperate – for sure, frantic – definitely. But never in her life has she ever experienced such unmitigated rage at another human being as the anger she is feeling right now.

'You know exactly what you mean, don't you, Sarah? You're just too much of a coward to come out and say it, that's all. You think that Mo is grooming Joel, don't you? Because of course, that's how it works. If a person has brown skin then that automatically makes them part of something evil, something despicable. Somebody not to be trusted. Is that what you were hinting at eh, Sarah? Is it?'

A huge weight disappears from her shoulders. She has said it now, put those words out there and standing here watching the horror on her neighbour's face, she knows she has done the right thing. It was worth it. 'And for your information, if you're wondering about the mention of the police, because you are wondering, aren't you? The police are collecting dashcam footage off all taxi drivers in the area, not just the brown-skinned ones and certainly not just Mo. Now, if you don't mind, I have a lot to be getting on with...'

She walks over to Sarah, snatches the cup out of her grasp and slams it down onto the table, then using her palm to push at the small of Sarah's back, she propels her towards the front door.

Only when they are on the doorstep does her neighbour's expression and attitude change, her features suddenly cast with iron as she spits out her retort. 'Well, be it on your head. Don't say I didn't warn you! You may not care if your boy is at risk of being kidnapped, raped and maybe even tortured, but I certainly do.'

The slap takes Sarah by surprise, the sting of it causing her to recoil, her hand clutched to the red welt that blooms on her pale skin.

Emily moves towards her, the hiss of her wrath ringing out into the air between them. 'Get out of my house and don't ever darken my doorstep again, you filthy-mouthed bitch, or I will call the police and report you for trespassing. Now fuck off back to your precious little house and make your weird little accusations there, but don't ever come here again.'

Sarah narrows her eyes in what Emily assumes is an attempt to lash out, to counteract the hurt and humiliation that has just been thrown her way. 'I could report you for assault. And while I'm there, I can pass on the details of that boyfriend of yours, tell them about how interested he is in your son. How he takes him for days out alone, doing God knows what to him while you're not there.'

The feel of the soft flesh on Sarah's upper arm is a satisfying sensation as Emily clasps her fingers around it, squeezing tight whilst pushing her backwards off the doorstep, pressing her hand into Sarah's bony shoulder. 'Go home, you sad deluded creature. Go back to your lonely little life and make up lies about somebody else, but stay away from me and my family. And if I hear that you have said anything – and I mean anything – about Mo, I will sue you for defamation of character. You have no right slandering people like this. Now do as I say, you mean-spirited little woman, and fuck right off.'

The slam of the door sends a gratifying dart of relief through Emily. She stands for a second or two, every muscle and sinew, every nerve ending, every receptor in her body twitching and misfiring before the adrenaline swiftly dissipates and she drops to the floor in a sobbing heap.

26

ASHTON

He is just stepping through the door as the call comes through. Gaynor's name flashes up on the screen. Kicking off his boots, he sits down on the bottom step, weariness threaded through each and every vein, running deep into the very core of him. Today has been a long one.

'Hello?' His throat is sore, his tone gravelly after spending the best part of the day having to project his voice to colleagues, fighting to be heard above a floor full of thunderous machinery.

'Ashton, it's Gaynor. I need to see you.'

'I've just got in. I'm getting showered and then I'll be ready for the class later on. What's up?'

The second of silence is enough to tell him that something is wrong. This is what he dreads, that lull in the conversation. It's those sideways glances, the enduring hushed moments – he's had enough of them to last him a lifetime from those who remember him, those people who can easily recall his past. He can sense disaster from fifty paces.

'Can you come down a bit earlier? I've just got here and, well, if I'm being perfectly honest, I think you need to come and see this. Not that you'd want to, but what I mean is, oh shit, this is so bloody hard.' Her voice is vibrating down the line. She is close to tears.

Ashton can imagine what has happened yet doesn't want to. His skin grows hot and cold, his fluctuating temperature meeting and merging under his skin. A buzzing takes hold in his head, a sickness wells up in his stomach. 'Ash, listen, just get here as soon as you can. I'm going to send you a photo of what's happened, okay? You're not going to like it so just prepare yourself is all I'm saying.'

The line goes dead. He stands stock still, his spine stiff, his lungs immobile. He is too afraid to do anything, to look at the photo when it comes through or to even breathe properly. His reflexes have frozen, his mind slowing down as he waits for Gaynor's message. He knew this would happen at some point. It was all going too well. His shitty life had finally taken an upward turn and now it's over. It was a brief period of hope that has been snatched away from him. He should have expected something like this. Good things don't happen to people like him. He thought he had served his sentence, put it all behind him, but of course that will never be the case. His actions on that day, what he did, will last a lifetime. Being taken away from his family at a young age was just the beginning of his punishment. The sentence for what he did to that child will follow him around for the rest of his days, hanging over him like the shadow of death, never allowing him a minute's reprieve. It was wrong, he knows that, terribly wrong, and if he could change the past he would do it in a heartbeat, but he can't.

All he can do is be a good person to make up for his sins but even that feels like an uphill struggle. At what point is he supposed to be able to put it behind him and get on with his life? He is trying – God knows he is trying – but it feels as if the odds are stacked against him, obstacle after obstacle thrown his way to trip him up and keep him down on the ground where he belongs, scraping around in the dirt with all the other lowly creatures.

His phone buzzes, causing him to jump. A picture fills the screen. He needs to look at it but can't, too terrified of what he will see there. Whatever image he has in his mind, he knows this will be worse. Oxygen jangles around his chest, beating its way up his throat as he attempts to control his breathing while holding the phone up in front of him.

He squints and shakes his head, despondency weighing him down. He suddenly feels as heavy as the earth itself. The image confirms his suspicions. A lone tear runs down his face. He wipes it away with the back of his hand and sniffs.

'Paedophile paedophile paedophile' is spray-painted over the doors and exterior walls of the community centre for everyone to see. He thinks of how many people have passed it – all those individuals, driving, walking, cycling, seeing those words there that are directed at him. He may as well have a huge sign over his head telling the world what he did. It won't be long before it is all over social media and he is named online. It was foolish of him to ever think that he could come back to this place and start again, to this small town with its even smaller-minded people. Foolish and naïve, that's what he is. And now, he will have to go down there and help Gaynor clean it up and then everyone will know for sure that it's aimed at him. The class starts in a couple of hours. People will be turning up expecting to take part in an art session and instead, will be faced with this filth and bile and there's not a damn thing he can do about it.

He sends a message to Gaynor, hoping against hope that she has already taken it upon herself to get in touch with the students and let them know that tonight's session is cancelled.

On my way. Can you get in touch with everyone to let them know that tonight's session is cancelled please? Thanks

Checking to make sure he has enough money for the bus, Ashton slips his aching feet back into his boots and heads outside.

~

'No, it is not your fault, Ashton. I'm not having that sort of talk here.' Gaynor is standing, hands on hips looking more furious than worried or exasperated. 'I was shocked when I first saw it and sent you the picture, but now I'm over that and I'm just bloody angry.'

His body feels as if it is about to combust. Despite the chill of the early evening that is setting in now the sun has gone down and the darkness encroaches, sweat gathers around his hairline and neck, trickling down his back in small rivulets.

'It is my fault, Gaynor, and I'm really sorry. You shouldn't have to put up with this.' Ashton thinks about the look of recognition in the woman's eyes last week when she saw him, Lynda Croft, his old teacher, but cannot for the life of him link her with something as base and undignified as this. It just doesn't fit. She was, and very probably still is, an honourable old soul, a mite stately and stiff featured, but she was kind to him all those years ago. That much he does remember. He was told afterwards that she didn't want to testify against him and be a witness for the CPS and had asked if she could act in his defence after she found out about the abuse he had been subjected to at the hands of his stepfather.

He shudders, wishing his thoughts hadn't wandered to that man. Ashton has no idea where he is and doesn't particularly care either. Probably pissing his life away in some seedy pub or sizing up somebody else's child. By the time social services had clicked onto the level of abuse that Ashton had been subjected to, his stepfather had moved out of the family home onto somewhere else and the court case was well underway, too late to change its trajectory. The blame sat squarely on Ashton's shoulders.

'I'll get Roy on the phone, see if he can bring some solvent along to clean it up. As I said, not your fault at all.'

'Will you be able to get in touch with everyone to cancel tonight's session?' Ashton finds himself praying that she's already done it and has to swallow the bitter taste of disappointment as she shakes her head.

'Afraid not. I don't have everybody's number and besides, it's too late to cancel now. People need more notice than this.' She reaches over and places her hand on his arm reassuringly. 'Nobody is going to think anything of this, Ash. They'll think it's daft kids, which is what it probably is.'

'But I–'

She cuts him off mid-sentence, wagging her finger in a matronly manner that reminds him of his own mum when she is on one of her rare rants. 'No. I'll not hear any more of this nonsense, young man. We'll simply explain to people when they arrive that we've had a spate of vandalism, telling them that it's local kids and that's that.'

Ashton is both relieved and horrified. Once Lynda Croft sees this, any suspicions she had about his identity will be confirmed. He is torn between avoiding her altogether, and having a quiet word with her after everybody else has left, letting her know that he remembers her. Neither option is palatable to him, but he feels limited as to what he can do. Pretending his past doesn't exist is ridiculous. It's a fucking huge elephant in the room and now with this act of vandalism, there is no way around it. Better to brave it out and face it head on. The thought of having such a conversation makes his heart thump and his head pound but it's something he's going to have to do. He will see how tonight's session pans out and then take it from there.

Roy is up a ladder, scrubbing at the wall with a wire brush by the time everybody arrives. Gaynor has cordoned off the main door and put up a sign redirecting everybody around the back entrance. Ashton prays that with the area being blocked off, they won't see those words. He cannot bring himself to think about who put them there. Gaynor was being kind, blaming kids for this mess. It's more than that. He knows it; she knows it. More unspoken secrets. More lies.

Gaynor is a close friend of his mum's and knows his background, sticking with their family through both the good times and the bad, although truth be told, the good times were pretty thin on the ground. It was Gaynor who helped to reduce his sentence, testifying in court and describing the horrific abuse he and his mother suffered at the hands of that man. He owes her everything. She insists that he owes her nothing, and here she is, still sticking by him, doing what she can to help him get some sort of life going, helping to alleviate his current misery. If he lives to be a hundred years old, he will never be able to repay her for her kindness.

He spots Lynda in his peripheral vision. There is another lady with her this week. A diminutive woman who looks as if she is here to attend the class. She is busying herself with taking off her coat and opening her folder. There must have been one missing last week. He was too nervous to notice or care. Gaynor gave him numbers of attendees but they elude him. Too much has happened for him to recall the details.

He continues staring at Lynda. Every part of him wants to approach her, to let her know that he is aware of their connection, a shared history he would rather didn't exist. He wonders if she has seen the graffiti, his stomach lurching at the thought of it.

She catches his eye and his blood stills in his veins. She has seen it. She knows. Any fool can see the look of recognition in her expression. It's impossible to avoid. Her shoulders hunch, her eyes darken. Even from this distance, he can see the slight tremble in her hands. And then she does something that loosens the knots in his stomach; she turns to face him and smiles. A warm genuine grin that tells him everything he needs to know. It is a smile that says, *I understand and I'm on your side.*

He is momentarily giddy. All those worries that he wouldn't be able to face her, promptly dissolve. His fears scatter into the ether, carried off into the four winds. There is no need for anything else to be said. Over the years he has become expert at reading other people. It's been his coping strategy, a way to survive the constant terror and strife. Being able to pre-empt others' words and actions has helped him dodge further attacks. He has moved through his adult life, a ghost of a man, watching, assessing, moving on, removing himself from possible conflict, dodging every single bullet that has been fired his way. As a child he had no option but to endure it; but as an adult he at least has the ability to recognise a threat to his well-being and avoid it, to move on and leave it behind.

A possible future presents itself to him. A future where he is forgiven for what he did. A future where he is allowed to just be and not live in fear of being held to account time and time again for actions he can barely remember, actions that were thrust upon him and he unknowingly replicated, thus ruining the life of another child as well as his own.

It doesn't explain the graffiti or who did it. That niggles him, forcing a dart of disquiet through his veins. This isn't a bizarre coincidence. This is aimed at him. Somebody has recognised him and decided to try and destroy the meagre life he has built for himself. It could be anybody and nobody; someone who spotted him on the bus, somebody he passed in the street who saw him come in here. There are any number of possibilities and he has neither the time, the energy nor the inclination to work out who they are.

Despite his initial reaction of wanting to crawl away and hide from it all, he is also armed with a steely reserve, a rod of iron that runs through him, pushing him on. Lynda's smile, her obvious warmth has made him realise that he is tired of hiding away, tired of living half a life, terrified of being recognised and held to account by the small-minded people of this town who will wreak revenge for a crime that they cannot remember and know nothing about. The time has come for him to start again, to live his life as best he can and ignore the haters who wish him harm. If anybody accuses him of being that boy, that damaged, broken lad, he will simply deny it. This – the here and now – is what counts and he refuses to let anybody convince him otherwise.

'Evening, Lynda,' he says, calling over to her as she finishes unpacking her drawing utensils. 'Glad to see you again. Tonight, I thought we would finish off our pictures from last week then take a look at portrait sketches.'

She gives him a look of gratitude and another smile followed by a gentle wink and Ashton's heart soars.

27

TRENT

Things are tricky today. Timmy has cried for his mother again, stating once more that he wants to go home. I think it's slowly beginning to dawn on him that he isn't going to see her anymore and that he is being held captive here. There are flashes of realisation in his eyes that I am not who he thinks I am, that I am an imposter, not somebody sent by his mother to look after him and care for him. I need to tread carefully, not give him any more reasons to be suspicious or frightened of me.

Soon he will forget about his previous life and embrace what he has here, but that day hasn't arrived as yet and until it does, I need to cope with his needs and fears, to alleviate his worries and restlessness. Sometimes I think that we're making headway, like yesterday when we played together in the garden, but then today things have taken a different turn. He awoke in a low mood and it has been difficult to drag him out of it. No amount of cajoling and bribery will console or silence him.

'I'm not hungry. I want to go home,' he says as he sits staring at the plate of toast.

'If you eat your breakfast, we can have another play outside in the garden. It was fun, wasn't it?'

He gives me a sullen nod, his eyes glassy with tears, then says the one thing that I have dreaded hearing. 'You're not who you say you are. My mum didn't send you to look after me while she was at work. I don't believe you.' Tears slide down his face, fat shiny orbs that drip over his chin and land on the table, darkening the rough wooden surface with tiny ragged-edged circles. 'I want my mum and I want to go home.' He lets out a loud howl of protest that tugs at my heart and tears into my soul.

'Please,' I say softly, my own growing desperation obvious in my tone. 'Please don't cry, Timmy. We're happy here, aren't we?'

'I'm not Timmy! Stop calling me that. I'm not Timmy. I'm Leo and I want to go home!' His crying and wailing are more than I can bear. My fingers strain to do something, anything to make him stop. Without thinking, I step forward and hit him across his shoulders – not too hard – just enough to shock him into submission. And it works too, for a short while. He rocks in his chair, wide-eyed and stupefied at what I have just done to him. His mouth drops open, then closes again, his small white teeth chattering together with shock. Then he lets out a blood-curdling scream as if I am attempting to murder him. I can't stand it and bring my hands up to my ears to block it out.

'Stop it! Just stop it!' My words have the desired effect. His screaming stops and there is a sudden silence that is heavy with surprise and despair. This plan of mine is spiralling out of control. I need to be back in charge, to be my usual reserved self and take control. I'm the adult here. He is looking to me for help and guidance as well as love and comfort. He is a frightened little boy and I need to remember that, but today is starting to scare me too. I had hoped that he would be starting to contemplate a life here with me and think beyond the life he had with his mother. I hoped he would begin to view me with a degree of fondness, but it's going to take a little more time.

I stare down at my hand, unable to comprehend what I've

just done. I have just struck him. I hit little Timmy. How could I? I brought him here to love and care for him and I've ended up acting towards him in a violent manner. Shame floods through me.

'I'm sorry. I am so so sorry,' I say, my voice trembling with the horror of what I have just done. This boy is my life. I've waited for what feels like an eternity for him, a lifetime of wondering what happened to my child, and now here he is, perfect in every way, and here I am, being a complete let-down and *hitting him*. I am beyond contempt. I vow to be a better parent to him as I hold my fist to my mouth to stem my cries of disappointment at my own behaviour. 'So how about we play out in the garden for a while, eh?' I don't know what else to say, how to appease him and get him on my side.

He nods, his face wan. 'Yes please,' he replies, his voice a light tremble in the stillness of the room. 'That would be nice.' Oh dear God. He's frightened of me. That's not the sort of relationship I want us to have – an imbalance in our interactions, but he also has to learn to forget about his past and look forward to the future. That's the only way this is going to work. Our characters have to mesh together, be a dynamic force if this new existence of ours is to be successful.

'Right then.' I clap my hands together authoritatively and shoo him along with the gentlest of touches, my hand resting gently on his back. 'Go and get dressed and have some breakfast while I get the football. Come on now. No dilly-dallying. We need some fresh air and to get some colour back into your cheeks.'

I leave the room, my entire body quivering with rising trepidation. *I have to make this work.* We've come too far in our journey to lose focus now. Timmy is mine. I know that other people won't see it that way. They will think ill of me, label me as some sort of unhinged captor, but that simply isn't true. I've earned this boy, having spent so long on my own with nobody to love and now I've got him, I'm not going to let him go.

28

LYNDA

'He seems like a nice guy.' Moira runs alongside her, struggling to keep up with Lynda's brisk pace.

'He is nice. You spoke to him tonight. You saw how hard he is trying to get things right for everyone. He's a good teacher and a bloody good artist, so why, Moira? Why?' Lynda cannot keep her irritation under wraps.

Moira shakes her head and sighs, her voice a whisper, lost in the roar of the wind and passing traffic. 'I wish I knew. I honestly don't know why somebody would do such a thing, Lynda. I really don't get it.'

'Me neither,' Lynda says through gritted teeth. 'Me neither.'

They reach the car and slide in, the drive back to Middleham an awkward one as they sit side by side in near silence, Lynda lost in her thoughts, Moira shrunken and silent as she stares out of the window at the spatters of rain that stream down the glass, crisscrossing and merging into a long wet streak.

The journey seems to go on for forever until finally, Lynda swings the car around the bend and they pass the old oak tree that straddles the field next to the road that leads into

Middleham, its lower branches leaning down like old arthritic fingers, darkening the entire area.

'I'm glad you could make it this week.' Lynda coughs, clears her throat and heaves a long sigh. The engine growls and judders as they come to a stop. She yanks on the handbrake, her fingers clasped around it as she turns and faces Moira.

'I really enjoyed it,' Moira replies, stepping out of the car and leaning down to peer in at her friend. 'Tell you what, why don't you come in for a coffee?' She raises her eyebrows, watches the other woman closely, waiting for her reply.

'Maybe next time. I'm still too chewed up over that graffiti and there's something I need to do before I go home.' Lynda doesn't elaborate and Moira doesn't ask: accustomed as she is to her friend's moods and nuances, she knows it is better to let it go.

There is a silence for a few seconds before she speaks again. 'Do you miss teaching?' Lynda is stretched across the seat. She peers up, her face shadowed, a sliver of light tracing its way over her pale skin giving her a haunted look.

'Oh, you know,' Moira replies, stopping abruptly, her eyes misty as she stares up to the sky, 'I used to think I did. I miss some of the kids I suppose but I don't miss the routine or the rigmarole. Sticking to a strict timetable was never really my thing anyway. After Jack died, I realised I had enough money to be able to stop. I was in too much of a state after he passed away anyway to contemplate going back and by the time I was ready, it all felt too late. I felt distanced and marginalised from everything and everybody. I did some private tutoring for a while but even that felt too difficult, too demanding.' A weak smile twitches at the corners of her mouth. 'I was extraordinarily fragile after his death and it took me a long time to recover. Forty is no age to die.'

Lynda wants to reach across, take her friend's hand, tell her that she cares, that she is here for her and will always be close by should she need her, but knows that words are not needed. They are adept at reading one another, can sense each other's distress and offer compassion without having to speak.

They part with promises of coffee and a chat after next week's class. Lynda rounds the bend with a fire in her belly. She did consider going straight home, not acting out her anger, keeping it under wraps until daybreak, but then decided that this is something she simply has to do. This is a confrontation that cannot wait. Sleep will evade her if she goes home in this frame of mind. Better to act on her instinct, to march right over there and tell that woman exactly what she thinks of her, to inform her of how stupid and damaging her talk is, and that she should keep her loose tongue still, and to stop spreading filthy rumours and gossip without knowing the full story.

With hands balled into fists and her tongue glued to the roof of her mouth with unspent fury, Lynda raps at Sarah's door. The sound echoes around the village, bouncing across the grass, drowning out the gentle cooing of the wood pigeons and soft distant calls of the tawny owls hidden amongst the huge spread of foliage from the squat sprawling sycamore tree that shadows the village green.

The door is opened before she has a chance to knock again. This fuels her anger. It was cathartic, hammering on that solid wood, causing a ruckus, making enough noise to rouse the entire neighbourhood. Standing before her is a meek and distressed Sarah who, it would appear, has been crying. Lynda resolves to not let this weaken her attack. Sometimes, certain things need to be said, and regardless of Sarah's current feeble demeanour, what Lynda has to say won't go away or leave her be. If anything, it will eat at her, a toxic acid that spins through her system, corroding her bones. That is what anger does. It builds and burns within, a fire that cannot be dampened or extinguished. Releasing it is the only way to diminish its ferocity.

'Can I come in?' Without waiting for a reply, Lynda nudges her way past Sarah and stalks through to the living room. The pale cream walls and huge white leather sofa make her feel sick and unsteady. This woman has everything; a house most people could only ever dream of, with luxurious expensive furniture and French windows that allow her an undisturbed view of the North Yorkshire hills. Everything about it is picture perfect, and yet she has to get her kicks by spreading hateful talk and lies, knowing how egregious it is, knowing that it can ruin people's lives. What sort of a person is she?

'I know what you did,' Lynda says icily. 'I've just got back from the community centre in town and I saw it. I saw those words written there. What a despicable thing to do, to go around spreading malicious gossip. I should have known no good would come of telling somebody like you.' She practically spits the words out, her blood coursing through her, hot and viscous, making her unsteady and dizzy. Her finger is outstretched, pointing at Sarah. Lynda is so close she can practically feel the heat emanating from her plump little body.

Sarah takes a step back, slumps down onto the sofa and brings a hand to her mouth. She is shaking her head over and over, her eyes bulging as she attempts to protest her innocence. 'I don't know what you're talking about, Lynda. I have absolutely no idea what is going on here but whatever it is, I can assure you it has nothing to do with me!'

Lynda approaches her. Sarah's distressed state will not stop her tirade. She needs to say this. It's probably long overdue. 'This,' she whispers, the sibilance of her words carrying across the room with just enough menace to make Sarah shrink away from her, 'has everything to do with you. It was here in this house that I made the disclosure about Ashton. Nobody else knows about him. Nobody! How do you explain what has happened if it wasn't you that did it?' She stops speaking. A pulse throbs in her neck. Her breath shudders as she takes stock of what she has just said. Even as she was saying it, doubts had begun to creep in. This woman's soft appearance, her immaculate house, her tormented expression, it doesn't fit with somebody who would take it upon themselves to spray-paint the outside of a public building, daubing it with those terrible accusatory words. She could have got somebody else to do it for her, paid them a princely sum. God knows she has enough cash to do it. This house reeks of money. But that doesn't feel right either. Sarah is the type of person to go to the police with her suspicions, the sort who would plaster it all over social media. She isn't a vandal or a criminal. Something about this isn't right.

'Who did you tell about Ashton? Who?' Lynda's voice has risen an octave. She is almost shrieking.

'Nobody! I haven't told anybody; I swear to you. I have no idea what you're talking about. You have to believe me!' Sarah is crying now, great fat sobs heaving out of her throat, tears running down her crimson cheeks. Her chin wobbles as she sits crumpled, protesting her innocence.

Dear God, thinks Lynda, *she looks like a spoilt petulant child. She isn't capable of such an act. This bovine creature hasn't the intelligence to do such a thing. What was I thinking of, coming here accusing her?* Sarah is many things – dull, pampered, obtuse – but she isn't the one who did this awful thing. She isn't bright enough to carry out such a cruel and vindictive act.

Her skin stings, her mouth dries up. Lynda perches on the edge of the sofa, trying to gather her thoughts, trying to find a way out of this situation. She should feel awkward, embarrassed and more than anything full of regret for this woman's plight and her own shameful accusations yet she doesn't. What she feels is empty, hollowed out by what she saw tonight; those words, those terrible spiteful words written on that wall. Seeing Ashton was bad enough, unearthing memories from a time she would sooner forget, but then to be faced with that atrocious piece of vandalism tonight was about as much as she could bear. Unfortunately for Sarah, she was the only one that came to mind and has borne the brunt of Lynda's anger. And yet if not Sarah, then who? Perhaps somebody else has recognised Ashton from that time. The court case made the papers. He wasn't named, his identity kept secret, but plenty of people knew who he was. Other pupils were aware of what he had done, as were their parents. An army of them upon finding out marched into the school, vigilante style, calling for cameras be put up in every classroom, every corridor, demanding apologies from the headteacher and the governors for having such a boy in their child's school, as if the staff all knew and could pre-empt what Ashton was going to do. It was ludicrous.

Sarah, thinks Lynda, *is like one of those parents, one of the perpetually outraged who feel it is their place to judge and condemn others without knowing the full story.* This is why she has made the assumption that Sarah carried out this act. It was her face, her reaction last week when Ashton's appearance in town was mentioned. She became captivated by the dirtiness of the story, switched on at the thought of dragging somebody's name through the mud. It titillated her, kept her entertained. Lynda could tell by the way her skin flushed pink, by the way her eyes twinkled and shone, as if the whole thing was an episode from a soap opera or a low-budget movie that requires no critical thinking skills to follow the plot.

'I'm sorry,' Sarah says shakily.

'For what?' Lynda snaps, unable and unwilling to disguise her contempt for the forlorn female opposite.

'I don't know. I just think that maybe if I apologise, then you won't think badly of me for whatever it is you think I've done.' Sarah wipes at her eyes, sniffs, runs her fingers through her knotted hair.

Lynda should feel a pang of pity for her. After all, she is the one who has done this, made this unsupported allegation and reduced this childlike woman to a gibbering wreck. But pity is not what she feels. What she does actually feel is nothing. Nothing at all. She is empty. She stands up, unable to verbalise any sort of apology even though every fibre of her being knows she should offer one.

'It's just that I've had a few shitty days and this has put the tin hat on it.' The desperate croakiness in Sarah's voice almost stops Lynda, forcing her to turn and face this miserable wreck of a woman, to tell her how sorry she is, that she should have thought it through before coming around here and mouthing off, venting her spleen on somebody who is obviously already under a great deal of strain for reasons she neither knows nor cares about, but she doesn't. The words won't come. She and Sarah aren't friends, not really. They are neighbours, distant acquaintances who tolerate one another due to their proximity. In fact, if she was being completely honest with herself, she doesn't even like Sarah. Not one little bit. Lynda feels no compulsion to take back her words and express any regret because she feels sure that this woman, although not guilty on this occasion, would have no qualms about dragging somebody's name and reputation through the muck to fulfil her need for tittle-tattle and to make herself feel superior and complete. That's the sort of person she is and Lynda will make no apologies for thinking such a thing. Perhaps she should enquire after Sarah's well-being, ask why the past few days have been so shitty, but no matter how far she digs within herself, she cannot find an ounce of pity for this woman. The look of glee on Sarah's face last week when Ashton's presence was mentioned told Lynda everything she needed to know.

'Okay, well I will leave you to it.' Lynda clears her throat, knows she should say something else, but remains silent instead, counting the beats of her heart as it pulses away under her coat.

'I got a letter,' Sarah continues, oblivious to Lynda's lack of concern, impervious to her frosty demeanour. 'It was about my husband. There's been a terrible misunderstanding where he works. And then I had a bit of a run-in with Emily. I made an awful mistake, said some things about her new partner and we had a huge fallout. So, not the best of days all things considered...'

Lynda begins to wonder if she herself is some sort of calculating narcissist. She should feel something, anything, for this woman, but can summon up absolutely nothing. Not a shred of sympathy. Anybody else would comfort her, sit with her, make tea and tell her that everything is going to be okay, and that she is a decent person who is just having a bad time at the moment, but Lynda can manage none of those things. Instead she begins to walk away, caught up in her own thoughts, her mind focused on getting home, back to the place where she feels secure. Back to the safety of her own four walls where her own idea of comfort and love awaits her, something she gained recently that fills her with joy.

She leaves behind a quietly weeping Sarah, who makes no attempt to follow, just sits instead, crying into a sodden tissue. Lynda cares not a jot about Sarah's husband's predicament or the purported argument with Emily. None of it concerns her. Her mind is still filled with thoughts of Ashton and the mystery person who took it upon themselves to carry out a smear campaign against him. She will defend that lad with every fibre of her being because she knows for certain that he isn't the one behind Leo Fairland's disappearance.

Slamming Sarah's door behind her, making sure it's loud enough to shake her neighbour into a state of restlessness and anxiety, Lynda heads home, thoughts of what is there waiting for her, warming every inch of her cold heavy bones.

29

SARAH

This isn't her life. It isn't her. This is not how she chooses to be. How has everything come to this? It feels as if her well-ordered existence is collapsing around her. She knows now that she should have kept her fears and opinions about Mo to herself. That was a stupid move, speaking to Emily about him. She didn't expect such a vitriolic reaction. She certainly didn't expect such a violent one. It just goes to show how people cannot be judged by their outward character alone, the face they wear in the presence of others. She had no idea that Emily had it in her, that she was capable of hitting another person. Sarah brings her hand up to her cheek, slides it gently over that area, trailing her fingers over her skin, remembering Emily's face, the look of hatred in her eyes. Her own reaction didn't help of course. She should have said nothing, kept her thoughts to herself. But that didn't happen and now there is no going back.

And then she opened that letter. That fucking awful explosive letter that has ripped her world apart. Emily's slap had sent her reeling. She wasn't thinking straight. She opened it when she should have left it well alone. Her emotions were all over the place and she made a bad decision. The worst.

And now Lynda thinks she has spread rumours about that man. It wasn't her. The phone call to the police helpline looms large in her mind. That is a different matter entirely to spreading gossip around. What she did was legal and that matters to her; doing the right thing, staying on the right side of the law. It's important. Somebody has to do it, to be the voice of reason when others are dipping their heads in the sand, pretending nothing is wrong. She has no idea what Lynda was referring to, but knows it had nothing to do with her. God knows, she has enough to contend with at the minute without being falsely accused of something she knows nothing about.

The room takes on gargantuan proportions, a bout of dizziness forcing her to hold on to the arm of the chair for support. She feels tiny, a shrunken version of herself locked in this huge house like some sort of nightmarish *Alice in Wonderland* character. Her vision blurs, the edges of the room misting over as she attempts to stand up before assuming her original position and slouching back down onto the soft leather sofa. She needs to call Malcolm, speak with him about this whole dreadful situation. She deserves to be kept abreast of what is going on. She is his wife, for God's sake. She has every right to know the finer details. It's a mistake, a terrible misunderstanding. It has to be. Malcolm would never do such a thing.

She bites at her nails, chewing and spitting, her usual poise and need for cleanliness no longer of paramount importance. Her fingers tremble as she stops gnawing and reaches for her phone. This is a call she never thought she would ever have to make. This situation, this point in her life feels alien and surreal. She isn't prepared for it, has no well-rehearsed script in her head, no way of navigating her way through what she is about to do and say. The ends of her fingers are numb with confusion and panic, deftness and precision failing her as she punches at the keys, watching the illuminated screen as Malcolm's name flashes at her causing her to swallow any misgivings. At some point she will have to speak to him about this sickening turn of events, so why not now? Easier to do it this way than face to face.

It rings. She counts, realising once she reaches five, that he isn't going to answer. She heaves a sigh, resigns herself to leaving a message, wishing she could hear his voice, be reassured by his words. This is a lonely experience, sitting here unsure of what is going on or where he really is. She is both furious and terrified and needs to find out what has happened.

'Hello, Malcolm. I really need to speak with you. Give me a call back as soon as you can. We have to talk.'

She presses her thumb against the screen and ends the call. Her stomach spins and somersaults. What the hell is she supposed to do now? Sit here and twiddle her thumbs while her life falls apart around her? This is madness. She stands up, determined to do something productive, something that will help her understand what is going on, but is stopped by a sudden pain that flashes up through her abdomen, a tight unforgiving ache that causes her to stumble and lose her balance. The pain increases, a tugging of her innards that propels her forwards, her feet becoming tangled as she rushes to the bathroom, reaching it with only seconds to spare.

Her stomach aches, her throat is raw, her hair sodden with bile and vomit as she heaves time and time again, the contents of her guts splashing against the porcelain, clinging to strands of her hair. Warm pungent air swirls in front of her face. Seconds tick by turning into minutes until she feels well enough to move. She flushes the toilet, stands up, avoids the mirror and slumps down onto the floor, too weak to stay upright.

Pulling off her clothes, she turns on the shower and steps in, letting the hot water run down her face, over her body. She is tired. Exhausted. A cavernous twinge sits in her gut. She washes her body, her hair, trying to rid herself of the stench that clings to her skin. Every inch of her feels dirty, every pore packed with grime and filth. She is unable to wash away the inner dirt that is penetrating her thoughts. She visualises Malcolm's face, his bloodied broken features after she has hit him time and time again for putting her through this; for having a job that takes him away from home for long periods of time leaving her to cope with all these problems on her own, for his refusal to allow her a child, for his mendacious cheating ways and now for this latest piece of devastating news that has blown a hole in her world – a hole so wide she fears it will be never repaired. This could be the undoing of them. Everything they have worked for could unravel, their lives separating and unspooling, their marriage coming apart as all of Malcolm's sordid little secrets come spilling out.

No.

Sarah steps out of the shower, wraps a large towel around her shivering body. She has to stop thinking like this. Negativity is bad for the soul. Negative thoughts are draining, sucking the very life out of her, stripping her of oxygen, poisoning her veins. There has to be a rational explanation for the letter. It's been a terrible misunderstanding, that's all. In time it will all become clear, the situation resolved and she will look back on this time of worry and angst and laugh, thinking how needless it was to have burdened herself with so many damaging thoughts and concerns. Malcolm is a strong-minded individual. A sharp thinker. The company needs him. They need his skills and work ethic. They're wrong. They have to be.

They won't take this woman's claims seriously. Her husband is many things, but the one thing he isn't is a sex pest. Claims that he sexually harassed a female colleague are utterly absurd.

This woman, whoever she is, is probably a spurned individual, somebody who tried to make advances and was turned down, like the time her friend Polly flirted with him relentlessly then threw a hissy fit when he refused to take things further, telling her he was a happily married man. They lived through that particular episode; they can live through this.

The only way she will know this for sure is if Malcolm decides to return her call instead of maintaining an agonising radio silence. All that does is fuel her fears, allowing her imagination to run riot. A million different thoughts will fill her brain, most of them deeply unpleasant. All it takes is a few words from him to reassure her, to tell her that it's all been one huge mistake and to carry on as normal and she will settle. Two days ago the worst thing that was happening in her world was the disappearance of a small boy in the next village and now both she and her husband have been falsely accused, attacked by neighbours and made to feel as if she is wholly responsible for highlighting the fact that a known paedophile is back in town at the exact same time that Leo vanished. Things have spiralled downwards, her good name dragged into the gutter just for trying to do the right thing.

She dresses, tears biting at her eyes, a jagged lump wedged in her throat. She has to pull herself out of this deep dark hole. Sitting fretting is pointless. Until such time as Malcolm decides to get in touch, she has to carry on as if nothing has occurred, be her usual buoyant self, despite feeling as if her life is being slowly torn to shreds.

The village is empty as she stares out across the green, watching the wildlife, wishing she had the power to take flight, to soar across the skies like the swallows and blue tits, her body weightless, her mind free and as light as air. A squirrel darts up a tree. Wood pigeons sit idly on branches, filling the air with their soft cooing calls. On the fence a blackbird sits, its gentle musical chirrup soothing her fretful mind, restoring her faith in all things natural. While the rest of her world slowly falls apart, at least she can rely on the flora and fauna to do their thing. She perches her backside on the edge of the chair, closes her eyes and lets the noises of nature surround her.

30

TRENT

'Don't worry. I'll remember to be silent.' His eyes are dull and expressionless, their usual twinkle concealed behind a cloak of fear and dread. He can barely look at me and I can't blame him for that. What is the point of having him here if all I am doing is making him miserable? He deserves better.

He shuffles along, his small body angled to one side away from me. I have to mend our relationship, to get him to think of me as somebody who cares for him and keeps him safe. One day I hope he will think of me as more than that but for now, I'm content to be his main caregiver.

We make our way along the side of the house and out into the brightness. He eyes me cautiously, his arms clasped around the football. 'I don't mind playing out here on my own. I'll be really quiet. I promise.'

This boy breaks my heart with his liquid doe eyes and heartfelt pleas. I look around at the garden, my ears attuned to every single noise, from the rustle of the leaves as the breeze passes through them, to the distant cries of the gulls, driven inland by inclement weather. He should be fine out here on his own. Just for a few minutes. What harm can it do? He knows me now, knows what could happen if he chooses to break the rules.

I nod at him, relieved when he smiles and straightens up, his shoulders no longer hunched into a ridge of unhappiness and despair. It's only when I see him like this, bright, approachable, that I realise we can do this. We can make it through this rough patch and emerge stronger, facing the world as a team, the two of us together at long last.

'I'm just here inside the house. I've got a few things to do. I'll be back shortly. Remember,' I say, my voice suddenly stern and slightly overbearing, 'about the ill girl. She's dying. You have to be silent.' I lean down to him and whisper in his ear, my own warm breath bouncing back to me as it hits the soft skin of his face. 'You don't want her to die because you're being too loud, do you? Think how terrible you would feel if she passed away and it was all your fault.'

I don't wait around to see his reaction. Timmy is a sensitive boy. I can already guess at what his expression will be, how his mouth will be quivering, how he will be frightened to even breathe too loudly. Soon he will become indoctrinated to my way of thinking. We will be the silent people, floating through this house, each of us in our own little space, isolated and yet very much together.

My heart flutters as I step inside, hoping he does as I ask and doesn't betray my trust. I'm getting to know him, my Timmy, this wonderful, yet still slightly unfathomable creature. If he can do this, we will further our relationship, establish a new level of confidence. He will be complicit in our little game, the plan that I have for settling him here permanently.

Time slows down while I stand in the kitchen at the window watching him kick the ball about. Water gushes into the bottom of the kettle as I fill it, the noise a metallic rattling clatter that reverberates around the room. I turn to plug it in, then swing back around to the view of the garden. My heart stops, contracting in my chest. I am staring outside to an empty expanse of lawn. He's not there. My breath stills, my scalp shrinks against my skull. Timmy is nowhere to be seen. I try to mobilise myself but my feet feel as if they have been glued to the floor. Everything is skewed, my vision distorted. Then I see him. He appears in my peripheral vision, giving me a small wave before he kicks the football across the grass. My smile is askew, my movements trying to catch up with the rest of my brain. He is here. Of course he is. There is no need to worry. No need for panic. I'm being over cautious.

And then I hear it. The scream. The cries for help coming from his mouth. He is jumping up and down, trying to peer over the trees to next door, his wails and shrieks, ear splitting even through the double-glazed window. I watch, stupefied, as he scrambles to climb a tree, his small hands and legs pumping furiously, his face red, his eyes wild and manic.

I spring into action out of my stupor, my hands wrestling with the door handle, and am out and running down the corridor at the side of the house. I all but throw myself at the door that leads out into the garden and am horrified when it doesn't budge. I try again, shoving all of my weight against it, pushing at it with my shoulder until a searing pain shrieks its way up my arm forcing me to stop. A line of perspiration bubbles up on my top lip and sits around my hairline. The screams outside continue, his cries bouncing around the garden. I scrabble around for the key and am aghast to see it isn't dangling from the keyhole where it usually resides. I must have taken it outside with me, slipped it into my pocket or dropped it onto the lawn. Such a stupid move. Careless and stupid and downright dangerous. The noise he is making is loud enough to bring people flocking, powerful enough and emotive enough to bring my plan to a grinding juddering halt. The police would be called, they would take Timmy away, arrest me and my life would be over.

Catapulted into action by such thoughts, I run back into the house, pull out kitchen drawers and empty cupboards to try to find the spare key. I know it's here. I saw it only a few days ago. Everything blurs. I can't seem to think straight. Outside, the noise continues, his screams and cries for help piercing the air, ripping through my every thought, tearing at my brain.

Scraping around the junk drawer, my palm lands upon something solid, something key shaped. My teeth chatter as I scoop it up and run back down the corridor, slip it into the lock and turn the handle. The door springs open, slamming into the wall with a thud. He sees me, braces himself for a fight, his body bent, his arms and legs spread wide, ready for flight. I move towards him, refusing to be beaten by this boy. He continues shouting and screaming that he is being held prisoner here, that he has been kidnapped and that he needs help.

I run at him, throwing my body over his, my hand clamped across his mouth, muffling his cries. We fall backwards into the shrubbery with a crash, small gnarled branches cracking beneath our bodies, leaves rustling as we struggle and squirm. He writhes about, his frail body remarkably strong and resilient beneath my weight.

'Stop it!' I hiss in his ear, flecks of spittle flying out as I speak. 'Stop this right now or I will have to do something that I don't want to do. Something that might hurt you. Don't make me do it, Timmy. Don't make me.'

He carries on thrashing about, his body bucking and bending as he yells beneath my hand, his head twisting and turning in a bid to escape. I press down on him, our bodies tangled together, our limbs knotted and slippery with sweat. Only when he eventually slumps, exhausted, do I take my chance and try to pick him up with one hand, my other hand still clamped over his mouth. He starts to twist about again, his muffled moans and cries still loud enough to draw attention. I have to do something. We need to get back inside and I have to make this noise stop.

Removing my hand, I bring it back and slap Timmy across his face, the sound of flesh meeting flesh ringing in my ears, making my knees buckle. Every part of me wants to crumple to the ground, to tell him how sorry I am and that he gave me no choice, but then he does something that sends me reeling, making me doubt the sort of boy that he actually is.

He spits at me and then sinks his teeth into the side of my hand, pressing down on the fleshy pad on the outer edge of my palm. I push at his head with my free hand, my fingers curling around his forehead as I attempt to drag him off. Only when I grasp at a clump of his hair and pull with such force that I fear it will come out by its roots, does he release his grip. I snatch my hand away, my jaw slack with shock, a groan of pain clawing its way out of my throat.

'You're not who you say you are! You're a bad person, a kidnapper!' His voice is loud. Too loud. I have to get him inside before anybody hears him, that is, if they haven't already. My garden is secluded but it isn't completely segregated and cut off from the rest of civilisation. I have neighbours. People will be alerted to this. He needs to be stopped.

I pull at his arm, my grip firm, and haul us both upright, then drag him across the grass, our bodies damp and dewy after rolling around on the ground. He starts to shout again but I'm too fast for him. Before he can do anything too damaging that will put us in danger, I pull him inside, slam the door and lock it.

'Give me the key!' I am yelling in his face now, losing my cool and forgetting my decorum. I know that he has it. I must have left it in the door when I allowed him out to play in the garden on his own. That was where he went when I couldn't see him out of the window. He snuck around the side and locked me out, stashing the key somewhere.

Timmy shakes his head, tears leaking out of his eyes and spilling down his cheeks.

'The key!' I roar. 'Give me that fucking key!'

Still he refuses, wiping at his face, a look of rebellion in his eyes as he watches me. No longer wide with fear or anxiety, he is now determined, his expression dark with malice and suspicion, hard and unmoving. I am losing this particular battle. I need another angle, a way to break into his mind, to get him to warm to me once again and trust me. Everything is rapidly turning to dust, slipping out of my grasp. I can feel it – my efforts, our relationship – collapsing, crumbling into piles of ash.

'Look, Timmy,' I say softly, my voice quivering with shock at the situation I find myself in, 'you need to co-operate with me. You're here now and whatever you might think, we have to work as a team. I can't have you out there screaming and shouting, can I?'

'I'm not Timmy and there is no ill girl who is dying! You're a liar! You haven't been sent by my mum and I hate you!' He takes a step back then brings his foot up and kicks at my shins repeatedly, his small feet pummelling me with such force it makes my eyes water.

'Stop it! Just stop this behaviour. It's not going to help you, is it? All you're going to do is tire yourself out! Now calm down!' My voice breaks. Panic begins to creep in. I'm losing this. Everything I ever wanted is disintegrating. I grab at his arm and march him down the corridor and back into the room.

He shouts, kicks, tries to bite at me, a wild savage look in his eyes. 'You're mad!' he screams. 'I want to go home and I hate you!' His cheeks are wet, his chin wobbles as he stares at me, saliva dripping from his mouth. 'My mum is going to find me and when she does, you're going to go to jail for the rest of your life. I hope you die in there!'

I step back, shock rippling through me, and slam the door, unable to listen to any more from him. My hands are trembling as I lock it and press my palms against the wall for balance. A pulse throbs in my neck. The floor inclines beneath my feet, the walls rock and shake. I look up to stem the tsunami of tears that threaten to spill out. Above me, the ceiling turns a murky shade of grey as it spins and rotates violently. I hear a low moan and realise it's coming from me. The floor is cold and hard as I slump down and rest my head on the tiles, cool air flooding through me, filling my veins and seeping into my bones. I close my eyes and embrace the darkness.

31

EMILY

Never in her life has she ever been involved in a violent encounter. Before now, that is. Emily is still sitting at the kitchen table, staring at her palm when Mo arrives back, his shadow towering over her. Joel, thankfully, stayed upstairs when it took place, blissfully unaware of what was going on.

'Well, that's that done. I guess we won't hear anything else. They said they would get in touch if they need any more information.' He stares down at her, a line settling between his eyebrows. 'What's up? You look a bit pale.'

She can't speak, has no words, no way of formulating what it is she wants to say. How can she ever begin to explain what happened between her and Sarah to this unerringly kind and compassionate man? How would she be able to say those words to him without causing untold hurt and damage? The simple answer is that she can't. It sickens her to think that there is somebody nearby who thinks so little of Mo, seeing him as some sort of manipulative deviant, some sort of threat when nothing could be further from the truth. She feels his hand rest on her shoulder and has to fight back tears.

'How about a cup of tea? I'm parched and could do with one

myself.' His voice is a whisper; measured and calm as he collects cups and teabags, busying himself while Emily tries to gather her thoughts and steady her nerves.

'That would be lovely,' she replies quietly, her voice a hoarse whisper.

The rattling and clanking of pottery, the gushing of water, the sound of Mo humming softly, all have a calming effect on her, slowing her racing pulse and cooling her hot flesh.

'There you go,' he says as a cup of steaming tea is placed in front of her. 'And a biscuit too, for good measure. Just because we can.' He winks and sits down opposite her, his presence helping to alleviate her fears and anxieties. She is safe here, with him. Everyone else can go to hell.

'Sarah, she–' Emily stops, unsure how to say it, part of her physically unable to verbalise the conversation, to couch it in such a way that Mo is spared from the real intent behind Sarah's words. 'She said a few things that upset me, but I'm fine now. It was nothing. Let's just forget it.'

Mo reaches his hand across the table, covers her fingers with his own, interweaving them, squeezing her hand softly. Heat rises up her neck again, settling on her cheeks. She feels energy begin to flood back into her body. Everything is going to be fine. With Mo here, everything suddenly feels less fraught, less troublesome. Sarah is a nuisance, no more no less. She is a lonely irritating know-it-all with too much time on her hands.

'You don't have to tell me if you don't want to. I just want you to be okay. I'm guessing it was about the missing boy?'

She nods. Tears bob behind her eyelids. She blinks, trying to wash them away. *Fucking Sarah and her toxic mind.* She should forget all about her. As if her words or thoughts mean anything to anybody anyway. She is an irritant, a fly that refuses to be swatted away, constantly swarming around people, looking for shit to feast on. It hurt though, what she said, her inferences and hints about Mo, her suggestions that she was putting Joel in harm's way. Those hints and accusations fucking well stung and Emily isn't sure that she can ever forgive her. What she can do is ignore her, cut off all future contact and pretend that that toxic woman with her malicious thoughts and spiteful words doesn't exist.

'It's all a bit stressful for everyone at the minute. The police were really good though. They looked knackered, I have to say. I asked if they were any closer to finding him but they couldn't give any definite answers.' Mo sips at his tea, his hand still locked with Emily's.

She wants to stay like this, to preserve this moment in time, pretend that the outside world no longer exists. She feels safe here, in her own little sanctuary, just her, Joel and Mo. She wishes time would stand still, that the world would stop rotating and she could stay here forever. Mo is a strong presence, a robust heartening person to have around in times of crisis. It crashes into her mind, the thought that she doesn't want him to leave. She wants him to be here always.

'Move in with me.' The words come out in a rush, a hot desperate flash of passion that leaves her feeling marginally hysterical. Her head spins, her lungs freeze as she waits for him to reply.

He laughs, a low gentle titter that disguises his intent. She looks away, too frightened to see his reaction, too frightened to hear his refusal. There is a moment's silence, an extended period of complete nothingness that scratches at her nerve endings, tearing at her emotions.

'Well,' he says, clearing his throat and removing his hand.

She doesn't want to hear the rest. This is a direct refusal that is coming. She acted on impulse, speaking with her heart and not her head and now she feels silly and childish, like an infant reaching out to the nearest adult for solace and support in an emergency.

'That was unexpected,' Mo continues, his voice gaining momentum. 'Are you sure? I mean, I snore and fart really loudly and I like to have a good scratch of my balls every morning when I wake up but aside from that, I'm a real catch.'

Emily turns, catches his eye, sees the twinkle there, the humour that keeps her afloat, and wants to cry. 'So,' she says, her voice quivering, 'is that a yes?'

He stands, walks around to where she is sitting and bends down to kiss the top of her head. 'If you'll have me?'

Joel bounces around the kitchen. She hadn't planned on telling him but he walked in as they were discussing it and his smile told her everything she needed to know – that this is the right thing to do. She and Mo are an item now. A proper couple, and it feels good. After so long alone, she has a partner, a man who cares about her the way she always dreamed somebody would, and now they have just taken the step that she never thought possible.

'So, do I have a dad now?' Joel shouts as he fist bumps Mo and hops from foot to foot, excitement oozing out of him.

'Well, you already have a dad,' Mo murmurs as he surreptitiously glances at Emily. 'But I'd love to be your best mate?'

'I'm going to start calling you Dad now,' Joel shouts, oblivious to Mo's words.

'Go on.' Emily nudges Mo's arm, knocking him off balance. 'Make his day and let him call you Dad.'

He staggers, hysterical laughter gripping him, as he snatches at Emily's arm to steady himself. 'Okay, okay. Dad it is!'

Mo grabs Joel and lifts him in the air, spinning him, tilting him every which way, Joel screaming with excitement until Emily intervenes, convinced that he is about to throw up over the table. The boys collapse in a giggling feverish heap on the kitchen floor, laughing and panting for breath.

This, Emily thinks, *is how family life should be. This is what is missing from Sarah's life and this is precisely why she is such a miserable specimen, determined to ruin what others have. It is jealousy that fuels her words and thoughts. Jealousy and a deep-rooted need to destroy the lives of those around her to elevate her own pitiful existence.*

'You and me have an appointment later, up in the bedroom.' Mo whispers as she stands up. He places his hand over Emily's backside and gives it a firm squeeze.

32

LYNDA

His face is starting to slip from the TV screens, his disappearance becoming less and less worthy of the primetime news slot. Other items have begun to creep in, taking precedence over his story. Lynda shifts in her seat, feeling distinctly uncomfortable about the whole thing.

She imagines social media will still be awash with gossip and tales of what has happened to him. Not that she would know, having made a conscious decision to steer clear of all that palaver for many years now. Why on earth would she want to converse with strangers online? She can barely stand the sight of them in real life. She isn't about to start arguing with idiots on the internet, keyboard warriors who think they know it all when they know absolutely nothing about anything. If they did, they wouldn't be sitting staring at a computer screen for hours at a time. They would be out there, doing something positive, putting their purported knowledge to good use. There's an army of bored armchair psychologists and scientists out there cluttering up the internet and she is relieved that she has chosen to avoid them.

She stands, turns off the television and stares out over the patch of green. Tonight, she is attending the choir with Moira, trying to act as if everything is normal when it is anything but. The world is spinning wildly off its axis and she is powerless to stop it.

Slipping her arm through her jacket, Lynda stops, pats at her collarbone, dismayed to feel that her locket is missing. She is bare without it, bereft even. She hasn't left the house without wearing it for so many years now that it has become a part of her. Knowing she is already late doesn't stop her. She has to find it. It's a crucial part of her life, integral to who she is.

She mounts the stairs, rummages through her jewellery box, panic welling up in her chest. It isn't there. Her locket isn't there. *Where the hell is it?* It is only ever around her neck or in her trinket box and now it isn't in either of those places. She cannot bear the thought of it lying somewhere, discarded, possibly even broken. It's all she has of him. The only tangible reminder that he ever existed, her boy. A small amount of rage rips through her. It could be anywhere, anywhere at all – at work, in a car park, discarded by a roadside somewhere, trodden on and ruined by a hundred passers-by. A hand punches its way through her ribcage, grabs at her heart and squeezes it so tightly that she fears she may pass out.

Her feet thunder back downstairs, her head pounding with the effort. She needs to see Moira; tell her she cannot possibly go to choir tonight. She has to find that necklace. It's all that matters. *He* is all that matters.

Spring seems to have deserted them completely as she steps outside and faces the brisk breeze. Birds circle overhead, the distant echo of their cawing sending a chill down her spine. Dusk begins to settle, the sun making its sluggish descent behind a gathering of clouds the colour of gunmetal, a crescent of amber that slips behind a swathe of grey. Shadows creep closer, climbing inside her head, taunting and teasing her. She feels heavy, her limbs slow and listless. She is glad the TV has lessened its coverage of Leo. It darkened her mood, having to watch it over and over, to read about it in every newspaper, being surrounded by pictures of him, his smiling face, photographs of him sitting in his school uniform, rosy cheeked with a grin a mile wide, completely unaware of what awaited him, oblivious to how cruel the world can be, even to small children. Pictures of him reminded her so much of her own lad, the baby they took from her. She has no idea how her boy looked when he was Leo's age, but there is something about Leo's features that struck a chord with her; the colour of his eyes, the skin tone. They all look so familiar to her as if he were her own son.

More memories cloud her brain, images of her mother, wrestling the baby from her arms. How could she? How could they? The ones who allowed it, facilitated it. They all collaborated, took her child away from her without her permission. Fury builds once again, blooming inside her chest, a furnace that burns without mercy.

She reaches Moira's house, her feet crunching on the gravel as she marches up to the door and bangs on it. When no answer is forthcoming, she tries the handle, twisting at it roughly, only for the door to be suddenly opened by a shocked Moira. 'Lynda? What on earth is the matter?'

She can't find her voice nor the words to speak, to tell her friend that tonight is cancelled, that she is too distressed, too bloody worked up and worn out to go anywhere, that it feels as if life is grinding her into the ground. And all because of that boy, him disappearing and raking up unwanted memories. It has dug into her bones, filled her brain with poison and left her wondering what life is really about.

'I'm not feeling too well. I'm not up to going tonight.' Lynda glances at Moira, sees her dishevelled state and stops. 'Mind you, you don't look too hot yourself. If you don't mind me saying so, you look like you've been dragged through a hedge backwards.'

Moira winces, shakes her head. 'I don't think I've quite shaken that bug. Thought I was better then started feeling ill again earlier today. Not sure I'll be going either.'

'Right, well, I'll not get too close if it's all the same with you.' Lynda turns to walk away, stops and starts to speak, her words, thoughts, energy all oozing out of her, leaving her empty – her body a void as they trail away from her up into the ether. She shakes her head, suddenly too weary to say anything at all.

'Lynda? Everything okay?' Moira clutches the door frame, her knuckles taut, her skin bone white.

'What? Oh, yes. I'm fine, I suppose. Just feeling out of sorts.'

'Well, you know where I am if you need me,' Moira says softly, her voice gentle and soothing, her head tilted to one side, her expression one of sympathy.

Lynda would like to reach out, to hug her, just to experience that feeling once more, that comforting warmth that comes from knowing somebody else is there to shoulder the burden of her worries. Instead she moves away, thanking Moira, wishing this moment in time would disappear. She would like to fast forward it to a brighter day. A day when the sun shines high in the sky. A day when she no longer spends each second, hour after hour, pining after her boy.

He is waiting for her when she arrives home, up from his place in the basement where he spends most of his time.

'Hello there. It's good to see you.' She scoops him up in her arms, strokes his silky black fur, nuzzles her face into his soft, thick neck. 'Have you missed me? I've missed you. No going out for me tonight. We're going to have an evening snuggled up on the couch.' She lays him down on the sofa while she shrugs off her jacket. 'I need to give you a name, don't I?' Lynda narrows her eyes, assessing him, delighted that this creature decided to slink its way into her home and stay for good. Many times, she tried to put him back outside and many times he crept back in. *Some things*, thinks Lynda, *are just meant to be.*

'How about Sooty?' She wrinkles up her nose, shakes her head dismissively. 'Maybe not. How about Rufus?'

He paws the air and lets out a deep satisfied purr.

'You like that?' she says with a small laugh. 'Rufus it is, then. Make yourself at home, Rufus, why don't you?'

She sits down, thinks about her necklace and the lock of baby hair that is enclosed within it. That locket contains the last thing she has of her son. Apart from a blur of painful memories, that is all she has to remind her. One fine piece of hair, carefully snipped from his tiny head. There was one nurse, one shocked youthful looking nurse who did something for her. Something for which she will be eternally grateful.

'Here you go,' she had said as she crept back into the room where Lynda had lain, distraught, inconsolable, blood still seeping out from between her legs. 'Please don't tell anybody. I could get into trouble if they ever found out.'

A tiny white envelope was placed in her palm, the young nurse glancing behind her before closing Lynda's fingers over it. 'It's for you. From your baby. Something to remember him by.'

And then she was gone. Lynda never got to thank her, didn't even find out her name. She was a saint walking amongst a crowd of demons.

With hands that were shaking so violently she feared she would drop it, Lynda had opened the envelope, peered inside and felt the bitter sting of tears bite at her as she saw a tiny lock of fair hair sitting deep inside the fold of paper. That was all she had left of her baby. All she still has.

Had.

A sob catches in her throat. And now it's gone. Her necklace that contained his DNA has gone. She has been careless and stupid and has not got the first clue as to where it could be.

'It's a good job I've got you, isn't it eh, Rufus?' She feels the tears build, a bulge of fluid behind her eyelids that spills out and runs down her face. *Sometimes, it's better to let it happen,* she thinks, *rather than bottle it up. Better to let it out and feel the immense relief of an outburst and a clear head afterwards.* Once this has passed, she will go on a hunt for the last remaining piece of her boy and she will not stop until she finds it. He's here somewhere. She can sense it. She can almost feel him, her baby, her only child. The cavernous ache that cuts deep in her abdomen is a transient thing. It won't last. She will get him back.

'This too will pass,' she murmurs as she holds the cat close to her body. 'This too will pass.'

33

EMILY

She slept like a baby after yesterday's high. Euphoria had flooded through her, giving her flagging confidence and low mood a much-needed boost. Every time she thought of Mo, about him moving in, the two of them being recognised as a proper couple, adrenalin surged through her system, firing up her senses and nerve endings. Her skin still tingles at the thought of it.

'Are you sure?' Emily is staring at Mo, her spoon poised halfway to her mouth, cereal heaped on it, milk dripping over the edge and splashing into the bowl beneath.

'Just been on the news. Didn't say what it was they'd found, just that the police are treating it as a possible piece of evidence. It was found close to the school, apparently, jammed in a grate next to the gutter.' Mo sits down, picks up a piece of toast and chews it idly. 'Could belong to any of the parents that pick up the kids of course, or even any of the staff but the police said they're treating it with the utmost seriousness. It's quite a distinctive piece of jewellery they said.'

Emily heaves a sigh, places the spoon back in the bowl, looks at her watch and feels her pulse race. 'Shit! I'm going to be late.' She stands up, the chair scraping over the tiled floor.

'I'll take Joel,' Mo says, nodding at her to sit back down. 'I'm not starting until 9.30. My usual school pick-up has been cancelled. Kids are off sick.'

'Really? That would be great. I think he's still up there with only one sock on even though I woke him almost an hour ago.'

'You get yourself ready. I'll sort the laddo.' Mo grabs his toast, jams it in his mouth, stands up and pats her on the shoulder. 'Finish your breakfast. It's all in hand.'

Emily shakes her head, laughs and reaches up to touch Mo's face. 'You look really sexy when you've got crumbs stuck in your beard. Such a hottie.'

'That's because I am.' He leans down, plants a kiss on her cheek and laughs. 'Now finish your breakfast and get your filthy hands off me, you wicked woman.'

She watches Mo's retreating figure, guilt scratching at her. She shouldn't feel this blissfully happy when Leo is still missing. She banishes all thoughts of what could have happened to him out of her mind. It's too distressing to contemplate and if it's too distressing for her, then how must his poor mother be feeling? Emily can't imagine losing Joel. It would end her. Even having Mo in her life couldn't make up for it. Everything would be pointless without her boy.

The spoon clatters against the bowl as she finishes her breakfast and places the dishes in the sink. She stands, staring at the pile of crockery, wondering what sort of jewellery it is that they've found, wishing Mo hadn't mentioned it to her. He inadvertently burst her small bubble of happiness by telling her about it, reminding her that there is a world of misery out there beyond her own four walls. At least he's here, helping out, making her feel that there is some good out there. It's too easy to get bogged down by it all. And what do they mean by distinctive? Why release such details if they're not going to tell the public exactly what it is that they've found? It's like some kind of warped guessing game, everyone making wild assumptions. This is the problem with a lack of information – when people are kept in the dark, they make up their own version of events. Whispers and rumours only worsen the situation.

The police need to release more details, thinks Emily as she washes the pots, wipes down the table and straightens up the chairs. She places a bowl of cereal on the table for Joel and fills up a tumbler with fresh juice, a tension of opposites sitting within her. Mo's offer is welcome but what if he doesn't wait until Joel is safely inside the school gates? She takes a deep breath and tells herself to stop it. They're a family now. They have to trust each other. Besides, he is used to taking children to school. He does it every day, picking up kids who have special needs, and pupils who are in care, taking them to schools all over the county in his taxi, making sure they arrive safely.

Dear God, Emily thinks dolefully, *this is what uncertainty does to people: it turns them against one another, running threads of suspicion and anxiety through every relationship.* She needs to shift her focus away from the negativity and pour herself into being positive and hopeful. If only the police would find this boy; if only it hadn't happened so close to home, then her levels of worry and apprehension wouldn't be through the roof.

She heads into the living room, stopping suddenly, jagged chunks of air catching in her chest, compressing and making it difficult for her to breathe. Sarah is outside, walking past the house, her head dipped, hands slung deep into her pockets. Emily freezes, unable to release the air that is trapped in her lungs, compressed into a tight bubble. She wants to forget about what happened, to erase those words from her memory, those vicious words that alluded to Mo being something and somebody that he isn't. Her eyes follow Sarah's movements as she continues walking, heading beyond the green and under the sycamore tree before rounding the bend and disappearing out of sight.

Emily lets it out, the tight juddering breath she has been holding in, then sits down to regain her composure. She runs her fingers through her hair, notices how cold they suddenly feel, how they are trembling uncontrollably. She thinks how terrible it is that a neighbour's appearance can do this to her, and despairs at how far they have fallen in the past few days.

Behind her she hears Joel come bouncing down the stairs with Mo in close pursuit, their laughter booming in her ears. Her chest swells with relief and pride. He is a good one. The best. Part of her wants to go out there and apologise to Sarah for slapping her, and part of her wants to hit her again for being so bloody ignorant, for having such a blinkered view of the world and assuming that all people are the same and thinking that an ethnic group is wholly defined by its wickedest members. Perhaps one day in the near future, she will approach Sarah, speak with her, maybe even make an apology if she sees that Sarah has changed her viewpoint, but until that time, she will keep her distance, let things settle and allow frayed tempers to heal. She could make the situation worse by attempting to talk to her at this moment in time. Everything is still too raw. Having Mo here has lessened the hurt but it's still there, festering and clouding her judgement.

She snatches up her bag, meets Joel in the hallway as she reaches for her coat. 'Be good for Mo! And don't forget your reading book.'

'I won't,' he says breezily. 'And it's not Mo anymore. I'm going to call him Dad, remember?'

She glances at Mo and rolls her eyes, a smirk twitching at her mouth. 'Okay, whatever you say, boss.' She leans down, kisses his cheek and ruffles his hair. 'See you tonight. I'll be picking you up. Wait at the gate for me.'

'Don't worry.' Joel stares up at her and smiles. 'I won't get murdered or kidnapped.'

Ice prickles her skin. She has no idea how to respond. Anything she says will possibly exacerbate the situation. She has no need to worry or wonder how to deal with it. Mo, as always, steps in, saving the day with his wise words and funny quirky little ways.

'I might just do it if you don't get a move on, buddy. I'll whisk you away in my taxi to a gigantic football pitch and your mum will have to come and rescue me from all your bad tackles.'

Joel chuckles, wraps his arms around Mo's waist. 'I wouldn't come back!' He glances at Emily, stops and smiles. 'Well, maybe I would after a bit. Like when I get hungry or I need help with my homework.'

'Go on, you!' she says, a huge weight lifting off her shoulders. 'Get yourself sorted and I'll see you later, you great big numpty.' Her knees crumple ever so slightly as Mo blows her a kiss and winks at her. She heads outside, worry free, Mo's face imprinted in her mind, the day ahead suddenly brighter than it has been in a long long while.

34

SARAH

The prolonged silence is almost too much to bear. Worse than hearing his voice. Worse than the dark thoughts that are currently running through her head. It begins to dawn on her that this could be it. This moment in time could spell the beginning of the end. The end of them and the end of her life as she knows it.

'Malcolm, please answer me. Did you do it?'

She can hear his breathing, low and ragged, can practically feel the heat of his skin and the pulsing and throbbing of his heart as he clears his throat and attempts to speak, to explain his way out of this awful bloody mess. Part of her doesn't want to hear it. She doesn't want the humiliation of having to listen to his feeble words and vain efforts that he will put forward to protect his image, denying all knowledge of this sorry situation. It's sordid and sleazy and she wishes she could just distance herself from it, be married to somebody else, somebody more trustworthy. Somebody loving and decent.

'It isn't what you think, Sarah. There are always two sides to every story. You just need to listen.'

Her blood begins to boil, fizzing and bubbling in her veins making her dizzy and nauseous. *How dare he? How fucking dare he speak to her like this, making her feel as if this is somehow her fault for not being attentive enough?* 'Listen?' she manages to rasp, her throat sore and constricted. 'I just need to listen?' She can hardly breathe. Her ribcage feels as if it is being pushed and flattened into her abdomen, squashing her internal organs into a bloody pulpy mess. Her pulse flutters in her neck like a small winged insect trying to free itself. The room around her begins to spin, the walls slanting and moving, the floor opening up under her feet. 'Don't you dare speak to me like that, Malcolm. Don't you dare turn this around and try to shift the blame onto me.'

She blinks repeatedly, steadying her nerves. A streak of courage starts to take shape in her gut, swirling and shifting, filling her with a new-found confidence that has so far been lacking in her life with Malcolm. For all she has the capacity to stand up to others, when it comes to dealing with her husband, she has remained meek and mild for too long. And look where it has got her. She tried to keep her marriage together, always did her best to turn a blind eye to his many wrongdoings and be the best she can be to keep him sweet, but not anymore. This is where it all stops.

'I have the letter in front of me. I've got all the details and yet you're still trying to shift the blame elsewhere!'

'Sarah,' he says, his voice rising, a noticeable tremble beginning to grip him as he speaks. 'You know what I meant. Now is not the time to start getting all arsey and self-righteous. A little support from you at a time like this wouldn't go amiss.'

Her eyes protrude. The floor shifts under her feet. She wonders if she is going to be sick, right here, right now, all over her recently fitted beige carpet. Did she just hear that correctly? Did she?

Her head swims. She has to grasp the back of the chair to stay upright. Even now, after all he has done – and she isn't going to even allow him the benefit of the doubt, because she knows deep down that he is guilty – he is still being the dominant, selfish pig that he has always been. It's just that she has been too stupid to see it, too frightened of being abandoned and rejected, left on her own. But not now. She has grown teeth, seen her husband for what he really is – a lecherous self-centred bastard. Her only regret is that it has taken her so long to recognise it, to be brave enough to see through his façade and become a person in her own right. A person who refuses to take any more shit from this shallow selfish man.

'Support?' she splutters. 'You're asking me for support?' She moves about, crouches down to stem the rising tide of panic and anger that is running wild in her gut, releasing a sudden rush of adrenalin into her bloodstream. 'I think that's a little rich coming from you, don't you think? I have a letter here stating you are about to be sacked and possibly even taken to court for sexual harassment of not just one woman, Malcolm, but four! You expect me to support you through your grotesque campaign of groping and assaulting women in your office? Are you insane?' She swallows hard, a small amount of vomit burning at her gullet. 'You see, I've suddenly realised something. This was never an equal partnership, you and me. I never had a say in anything. It was always about you, you and your needs. You and your grasping selfish ways. I never figured in any of it!'

She looks around at the immaculate living room, the sweeping views, the expensive ornaments and furniture. 'I get it now. You thought that if you kept me happy with a nice house, it would be enough to allow you to do whatever you wanted to do. And of course, when you came home from your stints of "working away", you would arrive back to freshly laundered clothes, a dutiful wife and a lovely clean house.' She hisses the words down the phone, her jaw and teeth aching from the effort of clamping them so tightly. 'You never actually wanted a wife, Malcolm. All you ever wanted was a housekeeper, somebody who would tend to your every need, be at your beck and call. Somebody who would press your shirts and trousers, pick up your jackets from the dry cleaners, cook your meals and keep a perfect house for you. It's not as if you even needed me for sex as you are quite clearly getting that from elsewhere, or at least trying to!' Her voice is a roar now. She no longer cares what he thinks of her. There is no going back, no retracting those words, not that she wants to. This has been a long time coming. 'But then, these women turned you down and you couldn't handle it. Your ego simply wouldn't allow you to consider the fact that they weren't attracted to you, so you took your chances and decided you would have them anyway, groping your way into their lives, thinking that would somehow make them change their minds.'

He responds quickly, his voice now raised in volume to match hers, his anger billowing through the phone in waves. 'Jesus Christ, Sarah. I'm your husband! How can you say such a thing? *I'm your fucking husband.*'

'No,' she replies huskily, the surge of energy retreating as rapidly as it appeared, leaving her feeling utterly drained. 'You're not my husband. You were never the husband I wanted you to be and never will be. You are now nobody to me. I don't know you and I'm not sure I ever did. You're not a decent husband, Malcolm. You're not even a half decent person. We both know what you are, don't we?' She gasps for breath before enunciating the next few words as slowly and clearly as she can, making sure he can hear them. 'You're a sexual deviant. A complete monster.'

She doesn't wait for his reply. The click of the phone as she ends the call, booms in her ears. She stares down at the handset for a couple of seconds, her brain struggling to cope with what has just happened, then as if it is red hot lava, she throws the phone across the room, watching mesmerised as it lands with a clatter, bits of broken plastic exploding out of it like shrapnel.

The carpeted floor is soft as she slumps down onto it, her body quivering and shaking. It's over; her marriage, her life as she knows it. It's all a thing of the past now. She read that letter, saw those terrible accusations. So many of them. All those women, and her husband the perpetrator, the one who has all but ruined their lives. Being associated with him makes her feel dirty, as if she committed those lewd acts herself. That was why he came home. He received the first letter that day and returned the following morning to collect his things after being suspended from his post indefinitely, pending an inquiry.

Dear God. She rests her head in her hands. *How has it come to this?* More to the point, how did she not see it? Underneath it all, she has always known he was capable of such a thing but has convinced herself that it was just a bit of harmless fun, that the twinkle in his eye was simply no more than him being flirtatious. And now here they are, living apart – him holed up in a hotel somewhere and her, sitting here in her living room, cold, worried, frightened but above all else, angry. She is angry that she has been too dim to see beyond his lies, too accepting of his behaviour just so she could keep him and not have to endure a nasty divorce. Funnily enough, a divorce no longer scares her. She is ready for it, will do what she can to come out of it unscathed and stronger. No longer the biddable browbeaten wife, she is armed and ready to do battle.

Cleaning an already spotless house does little to alleviate her misery. What it does is make her realise how pointless her existence has become. She lives an insular life, surrounded by the same four walls with nobody to call upon in times of stress.

He has done this, insisting time and time again that she is better off at home after losing her job, telling her there was no rush to apply for other positions, that they could manage on his salary. She has been reduced to a lonely dogsbody, somebody who will jump to attention the minute he walks through the door because she has nothing else in her life, her existence vacuous and pointless, relying on Malcolm as her only source of company and entertainment. This was what he wanted all along. Those four women aren't the only victims. They have all fallen prey to his philandering thoughtless ways. Even his own wife.

She stands up, realising that sitting there in a heap will solve nothing. It means he has won and she will not let that happen. Now is the time to fight back. Anger pushes her on, so much of it surging and pulsing through her, she feels faint with it. She needs to do something, anything, to rid herself of this force within. Cleaning is the thing that steadies her, her only source of comfort. She pulls out the sofa in the kitchen-diner and vacuums behind it, hitting the skirting boards with so much force, she fully expects the machine to grind to a juddering halt. So what if it does? Nothing matters anymore – this house, all the things in it – they are all just bits of furniture, fixtures and fittings that represent a life she no longer wants or desires. She is ready for a new one. Has been for a long while now, if she is being honest. This regime she has of cleaning and keeping everything neat and tidy was, and still is, the only thing that holds her together.

She reaches down to unplug the vacuum and that's when she sees it, the glint of metal that catches her eye. Tucked down at the edge of the carpet beneath the coffee table is a piece of jewellery, a necklace of some sort, scrunched and heaped into a tiny silver pile. Crouching down, she kneels forward and scoops it up, holding it in her hand as she stands back up again. With her little finger, she untangles the delicate chain and holds it aloft, the sun catching it as it twirls around like a tiny carousel, oscillating between her pale fingers. She narrows her eyes and studies the tiny locket, wondering if opening it will identify the owner. It can only belong to one of three people – Moira, Emily or Lynda. Nobody else has visited in months, possibly even longer.

Her stomach plummets at the thought of facing Emily and Lynda after her previous encounters. The ferocity and violence of each meeting makes her feel sick and she isn't sure she is up to it. Not after this morning's phone call to Malcolm. Not after the sleepless nights she has had of late. Her body is running on empty, nothing in reserve, her mind as fragile as bone china. There is another way however, she thinks, of finding out who this piece of jewellery belongs to. An easier way. One that doesn't involve another possible confrontation. She is all out of energy when it comes to dealing with people right now, and can feel herself rapidly slipping into self-preservation mode.

Without putting anything away, she takes the locket, slips into her shoes and jacket and heads outside, praying that she will not bump into any of her neighbours. Even a friendly face would feel like an intrusion. Returning this necklace is her only aim. Malcolm has stripped away everything that she is, every single dimension and facet of her personality and she needs time to build up a new layer, to strengthen herself and become immune to any further blows.

Keeping up a healthy pace, she passes Emily's house, dipping her head and lowering her shoulders, her heart flipping about her chest until she moves past and nears the village green. She cuts across the grass, crouching beneath the lower branches of the sycamore tree. In the distance she can see Moira's house. Even if the necklace doesn't belong to her, she can get it to Lynda or Emily. That is infinitely preferable to having to call around to either of their houses to do it herself. Moira is the in-between person, the mediator who can bridge the gap and return this necklace to its rightful owner. Moira is a kind lady, thoughtful and generous of spirit. Clutching the locket, Sarah strides up to her front door, buoyed up at the thought of seeing Moira's friendly face. She will do the right thing by her. Sarah is sure of it.

35

TRENT

It's been a difficult couple of days. Timmy's anger hasn't dissipated. If anything, it has grown stronger. I fear I am going to have to resort to giving him more sedatives again to calm him down. He is leaving me with no option. I am running short of supplies and was hoping to keep them for emergency measures, but then, if this particular bout of anger doesn't count as an emergency, then what does?

I have to control his rage and get him back to his usual pliable self. Then he will realise that being here is the right thing for him. At the moment his judgement is skewed, his perceptions blurred by his lack of self-control. We have had little or no interaction. It simply isn't possible. The last time I tried to socialise with him he ran at me, screaming and hollering, hammering his little fists into my chest, trying to pull at my hair, so I had to quickly extricate myself and retreat, leaving his food at the door for him.

And that's another thing. He has stopped eating, refusing whatever I place in front of him. The boy is already slim. In no time at all he will be reduced to skin and bone, a skeleton of a lad with no energy to do anything at all. He is existing on sips of water and juice and the occasional bite of cold toast. Things have to change. He has to change. If we are to continue living together under the same roof, he needs to adapt to my way of doing things, and the sooner he does that, the better.

I stand outside his door, dread welling up inside of me. This is a new sensation and an unwelcome one. I hoped for fondness, happiness, perhaps even love when he came to live with me, but not this – this level of hatred and resentment that is being directed towards me. I know that this is a new situation for him, but he has had plenty of time to settle down and get used to it. I suppose I should be relieved and proud that he is bright enough to rebel and not be a complacent victim, ready to accept whatever is thrown his way, but I also want my little boy back, the sweet-natured bright-eyed child that came into my home last week, bringing with him the promise of a family reunited. That's the Timmy I want. Not this wild-eyed feral boy who has taken it upon himself to lash out and abuse me.

Using my hip, I push open the door and step inside, determined to be cheerful and approachable when I am around him, hoping it will rub off, that he will absorb some of my positivity and that his anger and despair will diminish, gradually giving way to acceptance and perhaps even love.

He is perched on the edge of the small sofa, his body angled away from me, his face turned towards the wall. I sigh, a wave of gloom already settling under my skin. This is going to be harder than I thought. 'I've got your breakfast, Timmy.' I want to take back my words as soon as I've said them. Using his name enrages him all the more. He seems determined to be known as Leo and flies into a fit of pique if I mention his real name.

'I don't want it and I've told you before, I'm not called Timmy!' He spins around to look at me, his hair ruffled, his clothes dishevelled. He has slept in them again. I can see his pyjamas still folded neatly over the arm of the chair. 'Don't call me that name! I hope you get arrested soon. I hope you die. I hate you!'

If I was more of a threat, he wouldn't be doing or saying any of this. He would be too frightened. I hit him in panic and have backed off since but I cannot see any other way out of this. I need a compliant Timmy, not this savage uncontrollable boy that refuses to do what I say. For the past few days, I have done what I can to help him, begging with him to eat, pleading with him to be well-behaved and biddable, but I can see now that it hasn't done any good. I am going to have to up my game.

Striding over to the drum kit, I pick up a set of sticks and hold them tightly, my hand quivering slightly at the thought of what I am about to say and do. I never thought this day would come, hoped it wouldn't, but here I am, using a weapon to threaten my own child. 'Stop it. If you speak to me like that again, I am going to have to punish you.' I hold the drumsticks aloft, my face stern, my voice low and menacing.

'No, you won't,' he says. 'You won't do that because you're a big fat coward! You're nothing but a big fat fucking lying coward!'

I swing my arm up and bring the sticks down against the back of his legs. It isn't hard. I know that. I am not a violent person by nature but this boy needs to understand that I am in charge, that I am the boss in this house and he will do as I say, when I say. He responds by running over to the other side of the room, his face reddening. His eyes are wild with shock, but even now he is fighting back the tears.

'And when I tell the police how you hit me, you'll get an even longer prison sentence!' The tears are rolling now, pouring down his face and dripping off his chin. I really can't bear it. This is not me, it's not who I am but I don't know what else to do. Is it too much to ask that he behaves himself and does as I ask? I have fed him, given him a lovely room to stay in, let him have full use of an array of expensive instruments and he repays me by being obstreperous and downright rude. He is ruining what we have here. He has a chance to be happy and settled and look what he has done. Just look at us, at what we have become.

'You've got to stop this behaviour. It's rude and uncalled for. You want for nothing here and yet you keep on being badly behaved and extraordinarily rude. Please stop it or I will have to do it again.' I raise the sticks and walk towards him, every inch of me wishing there was another way. He cowers in the corner, the scowl on his face still present but slowly being obliterated by a look of fear as I bring the sticks down onto the wooden table with a crash, just to show him how harsh I can be. Just to show him who is boss.

He quickly rights himself from his stance of fear, pushing back his shoulders and jutting his chin out at me. Lord, this boy is strong willed. I almost laugh as I observe his rake-thin body and legs like pieces of cotton. He is as weak as a wilting flower and definitely no match for me. His mouth, however, is proving to be harder to deal with than I initially expected. Gone is the weak-willed, polite little boy I first became acquainted with. He has been replaced by somebody far stronger, somebody with a will of iron who has emerged under duress and not somebody I ever expected to see. He's brave, I'll give him that. But he's also bright. It won't be long before he realises that this fight he is putting up is a lost cause. He is going nowhere. I won't let him. Timmy is here to stay.

36

LYNDA

It's quiet in the village as she steps out of the door and heads to her car. A day at work is very possibly what she needs to put some distance between her and her dark thoughts. A solitary life is a double-edged sword, allowing her mind to wander to the furthest recesses of her brain and unearth memories that are best kept buried whilst also giving her the freedom to be alone and apart from the people who irritate her when she is feeling down and depressed. She hopes that last night she turned a corner, putting an end to the desperate recollections of her baby boy that plague her so often of late. She went to bed convinced that her locket will turn up somewhere in her cottage. It's what she is telling herself to stop hopelessness from setting in completely. She will search the staffroom today, ask the cleaners if they have found it, trawl through the drawers of her desk – do whatever is required to find it.

'Morning.'

The voice causes her to jump. Despite stilling her fears, telling herself that her nerves are settled and everything is under control, she is still susceptible to waves of shock at the slightest little thing. She turns to see Emily waving at her from over the other side of the road. Lynda stands stock still, thinking, wondering how to react. Emily isn't so bad. She's harmless enough, unlike that dreadful bovine creature Sarah, who has as much charisma and charm as a bath flannel.

She raises her arm and waves back, giving a weak non-committal smile and is both dismayed and startled to see Emily cross the road towards her. Waving and making pleasantries from a distance she is prepared for; having a full-blown conversation in proximity is another matter entirely. She doesn't feel up to it; her well of polite conversation and meaningless soundbites is all but dried up.

'Hi, Lynda. I just wanted a quick word, if that's okay?'

She nods, unable to do anything else. Has Emily found her locket? She shrugs the thought away. Of course she hasn't found it. What a ridiculous notion. Had she located it she would have no idea who it belonged to. Why on earth would she assume it belongs to Lynda?

'Absolutely. Fire away.' She stands, her hand raised to her forehead, shielding her eyes from the glare of the early morning sun.

Emily stares down at her feet, a flush creeping up her neck. Lynda waits, wondering what it is that is so urgent, so difficult to say that this woman is standing here, tongue-tied, red faced and unable to speak.

'Sorry,' she says at last. 'It's just that, well, Mo has moved in with me. I'm not sure why I'm telling you this really, other than the fact that Sarah made some comments the other day about Mo and me and our relationship, and I guess I'm feeling a little bit sensitive about it.'

Lynda waits, unsure what it is that Emily is saying to her. It's none of her business who she chooses to allow in her home on a permanent basis. She nods, feeling marginally embarrassed by this pointless conversation. 'I hope you'll both be happy together. I'm sure he's a very nice chap.'

'Thank you. Anyway, best be off. Got a busy day ahead.'

'Yes. Same here,' Lynda finds herself saying. 'Pity we both have to go to work on such a lovely day, isn't it? Looks like spring has finally decided to show its face.'

'No plans for retirement yet?' Emily asks, her colour returning to normal as she stares at Lynda, waiting for a response.

'Ah, that old chestnut.' She shrugs and smiles. 'Only a year to go and then I'll be free as a bird.'

'Will you miss teaching?'

'Another challenging question. Yes and no.' Lynda thinks about all the pupils she has taught over the years, blocking Ashton from her mind, focusing on the less trying times, the better happier times when she didn't leave work feeling as if the weight of the world was perched squarely on her shoulders. 'I guess I'll miss some of the contact with the kids. I'm not particularly close to any of my colleagues and as for the demands of the curriculum and the bureaucracy, well all I can say is, I won't lose a wink of sleep over any of it.'

Emily smiles, her eyes glistening. *She is a pretty thing*, thinks Lynda. Funny how she has never noticed this before, always too busy with other matters to even think about it, to take notice of the noticeable, things and people, the ones who really matter and are important.

'You'll have more time to do the things you enjoy, maybe even develop some new hobbies. Don't you go to the choir with Moira?'

'I do indeed, although we haven't been for a while.' Guilt pricks at her. Moira hasn't been well lately and Lynda doesn't think she has been a particularly helpful or sympathetic friend, too wrapped up in her own problems to help out or show any true compassion. Tonight, she will call round to Moira's house, perhaps take some flowers. They can chat, have that long overdue coffee they have spoken about. Maybe even have some cake. She smiles at the thought of it, a small fluttering taking hold in her chest. They can have a good old gossip about anything and everything, perhaps even get around to dissecting that day at Sarah's house.

'I like Moira,' Emily murmurs. 'She has a strange but gentle way about her.'

'Oh, she has her ways for sure.' Lynda laughs, thinking about her friend's purple trousers and green striped shirt that she favours wearing to almost every occasion. And then there's her hair – wild and wiry like an abandoned bird's nest. 'I'm sure once I have more time, Moira and I will get out and about, do things together. We can wind our way through the country lanes like a pair of ageing miscreants in that sports car of hers.'

'Moira has a sports car?' Emily sucks in her breath and splutters, laughing and holding her chest. 'Really? She is the last person on earth I would have guessed owned a sports car!'

Lynda nods and shakes her head, chuckling quietly. 'I know. You can't imagine it, can you? Dotty eccentric little Moira with a two-seater open-top car. A red one at that. She is a complete enigma. Just when you think you've got to know her, you strip back another layer to find something else entirely lurking underneath. Anyway,' Lynda says briskly, feeling more buoyant than she has in quite some time, 'best be off. Those teenagers won't teach themselves.'

Emily steps forward, as if to say or do something, and falters, her self-reserve appearing to stop her. 'We must have another get-together soon – you, me and Moira, I mean.' A scarlet web creeps up Emily's chest, spreading over her throat and settling on her pale cheeks.

'That sounds like a perfectly good idea to me,' Lynda replies, trying to keep her voice low, gentle even. This slip of a thing is obviously trying to dance around the issue of Sarah's bad manners and tactlessness. 'Perhaps this weekend we can have coffee at mine. You can meet my new housemate, Rufus. He clawed at my door until I let him in and now, he refuses to leave. He's practically part of the furniture.'

Lynda is aware that there is a family out there, mourning the loss of their beloved cat. At least she can say she tried to get him to go home, did her best to do the right thing by them, but Rufus simply refused to leave. And at least she can say that he is being cared for and loved unconditionally. He is safe where he is, with her in her home.

Emily's face breaks into a smile, relief obvious in her features, the way she grins, the lightness in her tone. 'That sounds lovely! I look forward to it.'

They say their farewells and part, slipping into their respective vehicles and starting the engines. Lynda watches as Emily heads out of Middleham, her small car leaving a trail of grey smoke behind. *Maybe*, thinks Lynda cheerfully, *life isn't so bad after all.*

37

SARAH

She knocks again and waits, the sound of her own breathing reverberating around her head. Birds circle in an empty sky, their cries filtering overhead. In the distance, farm machinery rumbles into life. She steps closer, tries to listen for any sounds within but is met with silence. On impulse she tries the handle and lets out a low gasp as it turns and the door opens with ease.

Guilt pricks at her as she nudges it further and steps inside. She refuses to go down the route of thinking how dangerous it is to leave a door unlocked. She has enough drama and worry in her own life. She has no need to go rummaging around in somebody else's, telling them what is and isn't right or good for them, trying to influence their decisions. Her big mouth has got her into enough trouble already lately. From here on in, she will remain silent, let other people be whatever they want to be. *We are all capable of making our own decisions and living with the consequences*, thinks Sarah as she pads her way through the long hallway towards a closed door that she surmises will lead into the living room. This is a big house, not particularly modern or well furnished, and large and gloomy. The high ceilings and artexed walls are painted a murky shade of grey giving the whole place a sombre feel, eerie even. Shadows skulk in corners, dark spectres that sway and move making her skin prickle and shrivel.

'Hello?'

The handle is cold, as if it has never been touched. She turns it and opens the door into a long sparsely furnished living room. In the far corner is an old green leather sofa piled high with cushions of varying sizes and colours. A small television sits in an alcove and a low wooden coffee table is set in the middle of the room. Underneath on a shelf are piles and piles of magazines and newspapers that are sprawled all over the surface. An old net curtain covers the French windows, part of it hanging loosely from the rail. Sarah can see the garden, the large expanse of neatly trimmed lawn and well-tended flowerbeds that are just coming into bloom.

She turns, half expecting to see Moira standing behind her. It's nobody. Just shifting shadows and a strong sense of foreboding that she can't seem to shake. What if Moira has collapsed somewhere in the house? Should she start looking around for her, checking in every room? The thought of it makes her uneasy, knotting her stomach and causing her head to pound. This is a big house, a dark, and dare she say it, unwelcoming old house. The thought of moving through it, finding something unpleasant causes her insides to shift.

'Moira?' Her voice bounces through the room. She swallows, saliva sticking in her throat. She splutters, covers her mouth with her hand and straightens up, tensing her muscles in readiness.

Something isn't right. This whole situation is skewed, not normal. Moira wouldn't disappear like this, leaving her door unlocked for anybody to enter. She is eccentric certainly, but not stupid. So where the hell is she?

Fearing the worst, Sarah paces around the room, unsure what to do next. She stands for a few seconds, her heart stampeding around her chest. The kitchen. That's the obvious place to look. She can start there and then take a look in all the other rooms.

A breeze at her neck causes her to turn around. Her blood bounces in her veins as she sees Moira standing there, ghostlike, silhouetted in the door frame, her hair springing out at peculiar angles like wire springs that have broken free from an old mattress.

'What do you want?' There is a grimness to her tone, a sharp-edged timbre that sends a finger of ice down Sarah's spine. Hairs stand up on her arms. A hand squeezes at her throat. She shivers and backs away, stumbling over an old discarded shoe.

'I just wanted to see if you were okay. I knocked but there was no answer.' She is gabbling, her voice slow and distant. Her jaw begins to quiver. She needs to calm down or risk coming across as unhinged. *This is Moira. Lovely dear old Moira.* And yet, there is something about her stern glare, her pasty appearance. Something that is causing Sarah's knees to buckle and her heart to bounce around her chest.

'So you just came in?'

'I'm sorry. I was worried something had happened to you. And I brought this in case it was yours.' She holds out the silver locket, draping it over her splayed fingers, letting it swing there, chinks of light catching it as it dances back and forth like a tiny pendulum. 'I found it in my house and was wondering if you had lost it last week, or if you recognised it?'

She steps closer, hoping to appease Moira, to let her see that she is sorry for intruding on her personal space. Why is it that she always seems to say and do the wrong thing? No matter how hard she tries to be a good person, she always emerges as the bad guy, the tactless one whose loose tongue gets her into no end of trouble.

'It's not mine. I think it belongs to Lynda.' Her tone is flat, devoid of emotion. 'I lost an earring. Not a locket.'

Something squirms in Sarah's stomach as Moira takes a step towards her. 'Here,' she says flatly, the palm of her hand turned upwards. 'One like this. You haven't found an earring like this, have you? If you have, it belongs to me.'

A tiny silver treble clef earring glints in the narrow streams of sunlight. Dust motes envelop it, swirling and floating. Sarah casts her eyes over it, looks back to Moira's face, fear tugging at her as she sees the dead look in her eyes, a bottomless chasm of darkness.

'No, sorry. I've not seen it.' She swallows, doing her best to lighten the mood. 'I can help you look for it, if you like?'

'No, it's fine.' Moira steps away, her eyes sweeping around the room. 'It'll turn up I suppose.' She glances back over to Sarah. 'What else do you want?'

The fluttering and squirming in her stomach increases a hundredfold, a coiled snake slithering about, its venom oozing out into her guts. 'Nothing. I just came about this necklace.'

A flash of something, a bright colour in an otherwise dull room, catches Sarah's eye. She tries to surreptitiously move closer to it, sidestepping the coffee table, almost stumbling over the random shoe in a bid to see the item. She can feel Moira's penetrative gaze, is almost able to feel the heat of her anger as she reaches out and sweeps the item of clothing up off the radiator. It's a sweater. A child's school sweater with a distinct emblem on it. Sarah sees the name for just a second before it is snatched out of her hand by a furious Moira.

'Atenby Primary School?' Sarah feels her anxiety levels ratchet up another notch. 'Why have you got a sweater from Atenby Primary School here at your house?'

It's a blur, what happens next. She is caught on the back foot, her mind still trying to fathom it, knowing deep down what the answer is whilst not wanting it to be true. Moira runs at her, arms outstretched, eyes ablaze, mouth stretched wide in fury.

Sarah feels herself being pushed to the floor; Moira's strength is worryingly deceptive for such a fragile looking creature. She has no time to react, to put up any sort of defence. Her head is thrown backwards, hitting the ground with such force that her vision blurs. She lets out a deep rattling gasp. Stars burst behind her eyes. Pain snakes itself around the base of her skull, rising and popping, leaving her dizzy and disorientated. She tries to rouse herself, to clamber back up, but Moira launches herself at her, sitting astride Sarah's chest, pinioning her to the floor. The blows are ferocious, one after another after another until Sarah feels sure her face is about to explode. She bucks about, pushing and shoving, trying to throw Moira off her but is weakening from the violence being meted out, her energy draining away bit by bit. With one last surge, one final huge push, she lets out a roar of protest and twists to one side, freeing herself and managing to topple Moira onto the ground with a thump.

Her breathing is erratic, her own loud gasps echoing in her ears. She has only a second to gather her thoughts, to prepare for her next move before Moira is up and back on her feet, kicking against Sarah's ribs. She coughs and raises herself onto all fours, panting and gasping before pulling herself up using the arm of the sofa and launching herself at her tiny opponent using all of her body, throwing as much weight as she can into the push, hoping it will be enough to knock her off balance and send her reeling to the floor. It works, but Moira is fast, retaliating with everything she's got – nails, teeth, feet. She claws, kicks, spits, writhing about like a wildcat, her eyes bulging with rage. The measure and fierceness of her backlash is staggering, sending Sarah reeling.

'You!' she manages to splutter, 'are sick! You are a sick, sick woman.' Sarah feels saliva and bile build in her throat, coating her mouth. Strings of pink drool hang from her mouth as she leans forward, coughing and spitting, the metallic taste of blood glazing her tongue, resting in the recesses of her gums.

She scrabbles away, cat-like, fear and fury driving her on. Moira follows but Sarah is fast. She grabs at the coffee table, upturning it, magazines and newspapers spilling out over the floor. The corner of the table hits Moira, catching her unawares. She stops, stunned, but not for long. A manic grin is plastered over her face as she runs full pelt across the room, snatching up a vase, clutching it tight and raising it high above her head.

Sarah ducks, raises her fists, lets out a scream to stop her, to halt this madwoman who has an inner strength that belies her diminutive frame. Moira keeps running. They collide, their bodies crashing together, bone and flesh enmeshed as one as they tumble to the floor once more. Sarah feels her head hit something, extricates her hand to cover the pain and sees blood oozing through her fingers. Moira leans back, gasping, smirking, the jagged remains of the vase still in her hand, thick red fluid smeared over the broken edges.

The room gyrates, a vibrating carousel that spins and tips. Sarah's eyes blur. She tries to focus, tries to plead with her attacker, to beg her for help, but words are hard to form, her thoughts muddled and chaotic. She swallows, gags on more blood that rises up her throat, then slumps back, her cries for help distant and ethereal, a ghostly sound that is disembodied and unrecognisable as her own voice. 'Please,' she croaks. 'Please, Moira. Help me. I'm dying.'

Everything shrinks, her vision attenuating. She is unable to stop it. Her eyes are heavy. The room continues to spin and kaleidoscope, everything slowly decreasing before disappearing altogether.

38

MOIRA

And now it's all slipping away – my dreams, my life, everything I have ever wanted – she has stumbled in here, uninvited and ripped everything away from me. How dare she? Who the hell does she think she is? I stand up, woozy with exhaustion, and stare down at her supine figure. There's no way out of this now. She has set something in motion with her interfering ways, a process that cannot be undone or stopped and now I have to finish it.

I peer down, wondering if she is dead. Her body is still, no apparent movement, her chest rigid. Timmy's defiance was more than enough for me to have to deal with and now I have this, her lifeless figure lying here on my living room floor. She has thrust this upon me, this unwanted scenario, leaving me with no other option than to dispose of her, and quickly. She only has herself to blame for this sorry little mess. She owns this situation. It is all her doing.

The room is in disarray, the coffee table upturned, papers and magazines strewn all around. I hastily drag it all to the side of the room, clearing a space for what I'm about to do next. Grabbing at her wrists, I drag her backwards, her clothing resisting the movement, friction making this task harder than it should be. Her jacket is bunched up under her back, her blouse pulled up over her chest. I stop, remove the jacket and pull down her blouse, tucking it into the waistband of her jeans. A small groan makes me stop, a breath catching in my throat as I stare at her. I had hoped she was dead. My intention wasn't to kill her but it would make this thing I'm about to do a whole lot easier. I'm not sure I have the stomach nor the energy required to finish her off. My head buzzes. I wipe at my forehead, trying to work out what to do next. My knees feel weak as I watch pools of blood spill out of the back of her head. Perhaps nature will take its course, do what needs to be done and help me out of this situation. Perhaps her blood loss will be more than her body can stand. I sincerely hope so. I'm not up to this. It isn't what I set out to do. Killing people wasn't part of my plan. She just got in the way. None of this is my fault.

Taking an old handkerchief from my pocket, I wrap it around her eyes, knotting it tightly at the back, diverting my gaze away from the large gash at the base of her skull and the tide of deep red blood that is seeping out of it. Another moan rises up from her belly, her lips parting as she lets out a low cry. I need to find something else to tie around her mouth to shut her up. I look around and see nothing. She lets out another noise, a sickening gurgling sound that makes me retch, the sound of somebody drowning, gasping for oxygen as they choke on their own bodily fluids. My heart bashes around my chest. I need something and quickly. Time is against me.

Grabbing at an old cushion, I remove the cover and grasp it between both hands, steeling myself as I pull and rip it apart into two long pieces. I feel her body move at my feet, the weight of her form shifting against my toes. It's a tiny infinitesimal movement but enough to send a shudder of disgust rippling through me. I nudge her away with my foot and then give her a sharp kick to her face to stop the moans and groans bubbling out of her throat. I can't listen to her. Her predicament, her presence in this room sickens me, filling me with revulsion. I just need her to stop, to let me concentrate. The feel of her soft flesh next to my foot doesn't exactly thrill me but neither does it make me horrified. This is just something I have to do to get her to be quiet. It's a necessary evil.

The material in my hands is coarse, perfect for the job. Stretching it out, I bend down and wrap it around her mouth, pushing it deep inside her lips then pulling it around the back of her head. My hands become slick and stained red. I swallow, suppressing a wave of vomit that rises as the warmth of her blood spreads over my fingers, coating my skin. I feel her damaged flesh shift under the pressure of the gag. I tie and knot it as tightly as I can, ignoring her stifled howls of protest, her slightly twitching body that is increasing in strength. I need to hurry, to get her out of here before she fully regains consciousness. A limp possibly dying body is more manageable than a fit one that has the ability to fight back. She is heavy in this state but nothing I cannot cope with.

With the gag firmly in place, I once again grab at her wrists and haul her out of the room, ignoring her clothing that is askew, ignoring her moans and writhing that is gaining in momentum. I am focused solely on removing her from my living room and getting to a place that is secure. It's not ideal, what I'm about to do, but needs must until I have time to think of a better plan, a more appropriate one.

Hauling her down the few steps to the music room is something I had not anticipated and it is more difficult than I hoped it would be. Her spine catches on each step, clattering and bumping over them. Her head twists from side to side, her mind becoming more cognisant as she gradually comes to.

By the time I make it to the bottom, sweat is coursing down

my back and my arms and shoulders are aching, every muscle and sinew screeching at me to stop. I stand outside the door, trying to catch my breath, aware that every second that passes is working against me, giving her a chance to gather her strength and fight back. I have neither the time nor the energy to tie her wrists together let alone her ankles. I need to get rid of her while I still have some strength and she is still semi-conscious. At least she has no idea where she is. Not that it matters. Once she is locked inside this room, she has no chance of escape. Nobody will know that she is here. They can't hear her or find her. They can stay in here together until they decide to co-operate and until I decide what to do with the pair of them.

My breathing escalates – I can taste it, hot and sour – as I slip the key out of my pocket and unlock the door. I twist the handle and open it a crack, a line of light appearing on the shadowed wall beside me. I give it another slight push with my elbow, both hands firmly grasped around Sarah's wrists. Using my body, I edge my way in, my legs apart as I pull her slowly waking form along the floor. From the other side, I hear a shriek, then a small roar of defiance at my appearance. Something catches me, something substantial that hits the side of my body. Then a loud crash as the offending object crashes to the floor.

I stare at my music stool as it rolls around at my feet, the leather seat damaged where it hit the door frame. Timmy is standing there, eyes blazing, his mouth wide with shock when he spots Sarah's body. This is not how I wanted things to be but it is what it is. I can't change or undo any of it. We will all just have to make the best of it. He is going to have to get used to sharing his space with her and be less aggressive towards me. I don't have enough time or patience for any of his nonsense.

'Stop that right now, Timmy! If anything happens to me, you'll end up locked in this room forever. Nobody will know where you are and you will starve to death.'

He strides towards me, his mouth quivering, more tears streaming down his face. I don't have time to summon up any pity for him. I need to get her in here and lock this door to stop either of them from escaping. Using what little strength I have left, I pull her inside and slam the door, leaning back on it to catch my breath before swiftly turning and locking it behind me.

'You're a murderer.' His voice is a boom.

I shake my head and ignore him, focusing on dragging Sarah over to the corner of the room. He follows me, striding quickly, his hands tucked behind his back.

'You don't frighten me, you know! I'm not scared of you. I was once picked on by a boy two years older than me at school and I hit him.'

My laughter fills the room. I can't help it. For all I am worn out, dripping with sweat and trembling from the effort of silencing this useless creature at my feet, I can't seem to stop. He hasn't realised. This poor child still has no idea that his fight against me is pointless. I'm not going to give up. Does he really think he can beat me, after all we've been through? After all the things I've done to him, does he honestly and truly expect me to cave in and let him go?

'Timmy, you know this is useless. You don't have to be frightened of me anyway. As long as you're a well-behaved pleasant boy and you do exactly as you're told, nothing bad is ever going to happen to you. Anything that I do to you, I do for your own good.'

He bares his teeth, snarling at me like a hungry wolf. I stop laughing and stare down at Sarah, unable and, quite frankly, unwilling to tend to her wounds. She asked for this, brought it on herself with her rude conduct and unwanted actions, poking around in other people's business, coming uninvited into my house. I bring back my foot and give her another hard kick in her ribs, all the time watching Timmy for a reaction. He doesn't disappoint. His face freezes, flushing with colour before it all leaches out again, leaving him a sickly shade of yellow. His body recoils, bending double as he scurries over to the corner of the room, a small moan leaving his slack jaw. He thinks he's brave. He thinks he is match for me. He isn't. He doesn't know me properly yet. Not the real me, the stern me that refuses to be beaten. Just like Sarah, he is going to learn the hard way that I am a force to be reckoned with, somebody who is determined to win.

I back out of the room, leaving them both in there. I need some time to think, to work out what I'm going to do with her. I slam the door and lock it, giving it a couple of hard tugs just to be sure, then head back up the steps and back into the safety of the house.

39

SARAH

Every inch of her, every centimetre of her bruised flesh and aching bones, is in pain. Even breathing is difficult. A pocket of oxygen rattles somewhere deep in her abdomen, groaning and creaking in her lungs. She feels as if she is drowning. Her head is muddled, her thoughts disorganised and jumbled. She can't remember where she is, how she got here even. Everything is blurred. She stops moving, trying to gather her strength while she lies perfectly still. Is she dying? She feels sure she is. The surface beneath her is cold and hard, the air around her still and stuffy. Fabric covers her eyes and mouth. With quivering hands, she reaches up and removes both pieces of coarsely tied material and blinks. She opens her mouth to speak but nothing comes out. Her throat is swollen, her mouth dry and gritty. She coughs, feeling something move against her tongue.

Raising herself up with her arms, she spits on the floor, feeling a lump escape out from between her pursed lips. It lands inches away from her, a small white mound. She squints, blinking again with swollen eyes then runs her tongue around the inside of her mouth, feeling for the gap where her tooth should be. It's one of her bottom teeth, a molar. Not one of her front teeth, thank God. She suddenly feels grateful for any small mercy thrown her way.

Her arms give way under her weight, fatigue and pain forcing her back down to the floor. She lies still for a few seconds to catch her breath. There is a heaviness to this room, as if she is existing in a vacuum. The pulsing of her heart, the squirming and squelching sounds of her stomach all boom in her head, amplified a thousand times over.

Then she hears it, above the sound of her own blood as it is carried through her veins, above the sound of her lungs forcing oxygen in and out of her body, a small murmur, a voice, thin and reedy coming from somewhere close by.

She blinks, tries to clear her throat, to allow herself some thinking time. Is she in hospital? No. She's on the floor, that much she does know. Her breathing is ragged, uneven and rapid.

And then in a flash, the memories come flooding back, tipping her off balance, exacerbating her pain, causing her to retch. She turns to one side, her gag reflex kicking in, Moira's face filling her mind – her twisted features, her unhinged expression. And the violence. Those blows to her body, rapid, relentless. Tears spill out, streaming down her face. She sobs, sniffs them back, tries to compose herself but it's impossible.

'Are you all right?' the voice says.

She turns, senses somebody close by, can hear the low shuffle of movement as they edge nearer. Thin warm air wafts around her face. She looks up to see a boy standing over her, his face looming closer as he squats next to her, his hand resting on her forehead. The feel of his cool soft skin makes her cry out again. She reaches up, covers his hand with hers, places it on her sodden cheek and shuts her eyes against another rush of pain that ricochets up and down her torso.

'She kidnapped me,' he says.

Sarah opens her eyes and stares at him through a veil of tears. She wants to apologise, to let him know that she has thought of him often, tried to help in the search for him, but the words stick in her throat, glued into place with fear and dread. Instead, she holds on to his hand, reaches out to touch his face and is relieved when he lets her. His skin is soft, his eyes huge and dark in contrast to his pale skin.

'Just a minute,' he says, as he moves away and returns, carrying something. It's a towel. He bends and dabs at Sarah's face, wiping away the blood and tears.

'Thank you,' she whispers. 'Thank you, Leo.'

He stops, her words making him recoil as he stops and steps away. 'How do you know my name? Are you just like her? Are you her friend?' Panic is creeping into his timbre, his voice beginning to break.

She shakes her head and squeezes her eyes closed, trying to muster up the energy to speak. She wishes she had something to help combat this pain. 'It's been on the TV, that you've gone missing. The police are looking for you. Everybody is trying to find you.'

'But I'm here! We need to tell them that I'm here and that I want to go home!' He bursts into tears, his sobs filling the room.

She wants to hold him, to comfort him and let him know that she is here to help but everything feels like too much of an effort. Even breathing hurts. 'We'll get out of here, Leo, you and me. We can do this together. I just need to lie still for a while so I can get better.'

'You're bleeding,' he says through his tears. 'The back of your head is covered in blood and your face is red and sore. You look really ill.'

She doesn't reply, can't bring herself to tell this little boy that she feels really ill, as if her life is being sucked away from her with every breath that exits her body. She has to be strong for him, get them both out of this place. She isn't prepared to die here, in this house, in this room and she isn't about to leave Leo in the clutches of this madwoman. She will do whatever it takes to escape. She just needs a little while to gather her strength, to learn how to deal with this pain. 'I just need to wait a short while, Leo, until I feel a bit better, and then you and I are going to get out of here.'

'Have you got a mobile on you? Mum always takes hers everywhere in case her car breaks down.' The obvious eagerness in his voice almost breaks her. 'My dad is out of work and she doesn't have enough money to buy a new car so she says that paying for a phone is worth it. My uncle is a mechanic and he said if anything happens to it, she has to call him and he'll tow it in and fix it for her.'

Guilt swamps her. Sarah lies still, fighting back more tears. Bitter tears of regret at this poor boy's plight. Tears of regret at how she judged his mother. She bites at her lip, trying to wish away the pain in her ribs, praying it will pass. She counts the seconds, breathing hard, telling herself that there will be an end to this, a positive outcome. Death won't take her. She won't let it. She's a fighter. The last few days have proven that she is stronger, more resilient than she ever imagined.

'No. My phone is at home. It's broken anyway. Sorry. So stupid of me,' she gasps breathlessly.

'Don't be sorry,' he says, reaching out to her again and stroking her hair softly. 'I'm going to help you get better and then we can escape together.'

The tenderness, the innocence in his voice almost kills her. She has got to do this, to summon up enough strength to move and get out of here. Her ribs are broken, she is sure of it. Every movement is agony. She has to find a way of blocking it out though, of bypassing the pain or she will be of no use to anybody.

'Here,' Leo says as he bends again and places the towel against her head. 'This might help stop the bleeding.'

She presses it against her skull, feeling a moment's reprieve from the agony as the soft fabric touches her skin.

'We'll have to get you better before Trent comes back in.'

Her neck slowly twists around, her eyes bulging at the mention of that name. 'Who?'

'Trent,' he says, his voice now a trembling chirrup. 'That's her name. She told me. She said to call her Trent.'

The pain beneath her ribcage, in her head, behind her eyes, increases tenfold. Trent? What on earth is going on here? Why would Moira say such a thing? Is she somehow trying to implicate Sarah and her husband in all of this? She lets out a shuddering breath, too tired to try to work it out. Getting better, being strong enough to get out of this hellhole is all she has to focus on for now. The details can wait until later. Let the police and forensic investigators and the psychologists work out Moira's plans and excuses and reasons for this unholy mess.

'Okay, well the thing is, Leo, she told you a bit of a lie. Her real name is Moira.'

'You know her?' He jumps back away from her. 'You said you weren't her friend!'

'I'm not her friend. I'm her neighbour. I called by to see if she was okay and when I saw your school jumper, she attacked me. I promise you, I didn't know you were here. Nobody knows you're here but I'm going to help you.' Her voice begins to lose impetus, her breathing suddenly horribly laboured. She stops, gulps and wipes away more tears. 'Do you think she would have done this to me, tried to kill me if I was her friend?' Sarah's eyes ache as she watches his face for a reaction, willing him to believe her. They have to stick together. They only have each other.

He shakes his head, tears dripping down his pallid little face. 'She's a bad person. A really nasty person. At first, she pretended to be my friend saying my mum had sent her to pick me up from school, but then after a while, I realised she was lying and told her so. That's when she started to be horrible, hitting me and shouting at me. She keeps on calling me Timmy. I don't like her. At first, after she hit me, I was scared of her, but then I started to get angry and shouted at her that she was a liar.'

More tears flow, both of them crying and smiling, holding one another's hands. *He's a feisty one*, thinks Sarah. This will help. If he has spirit, he could help her get out of here. It's not a definite plan, but it's a possibility. She's badly injured, in a lot of pain, but two of them has to be better against her than one. Moira is small, birdlike.

A tiny bud of hope shoots up, fresh and new, something she can hold on to. If the bleeding stops and she can overcome the pain to at least stagger to her feet, they could overpower Moira, drag her to the floor, hit her with something – anything – and then get out of this godforsaken house.

'And I've got a key.'

Her blood stills in her veins. Every sound in the room is accentuated, rolling around her head, tumbling into her skull like crashing cymbals.

'A key?'

'Yes, I took it a few days ago and she shouted at me and then forgot to ask for it back.'

Sarah swallows, hardly daring to ask. 'Is it for this door?'

Disappointment settles on her like a deadweight as he shakes his head dolefully, crushing her into the ground. 'No, it's for the door that leads out into the garden. But if we can get out of this room, we can escape through the back garden! She told me that a young girl next door was dying and that I had to keep the noise down but she's lying. She only said it to stop me from making any noise and letting people know I was here.'

Sarah can hardly believe what she is hearing. Lie after lie

after lie just to keep this boy here, held captive, away from his mother while the entire country searches for him. What sort of a psychopath is she? What in God's name are they dealing with here?

At that moment, she hears the distant scrape of a key being turned. Not now. Please God, give them some time to prepare themselves and formulate a plan. At least give her some time to regain her strength and conquer this pain. But before she can think anymore, the door is opened and a silhouette fills the room, spreading across the floor like the shadow of death.

40

MOIRA

I've got the advantage here. She is injured, incapacitated and bleeding heavily. He is a child. I've got a weapon. I can do this. I can win, and the sooner it's over with, the better. I need to stop her talking to him, telling him things I don't want him to hear. He is my boy and I am the one who decides what he is and isn't allowed to know. I control everything about him. Every little thing. And this is what rankles me. Why is he so reluctant to start showing me some respect? I've earned it. This is my house and my rules. I have looked after him, provided him with a comfortable place to stay, kept him fed and watered. The time has come for him to start repaying me. Is it too much to ask for a little love and veneration in return for what I have done for him?

The hammer is concealed behind my back, my fist grasping it tightly. I push the door to with my foot, my body turned to one side as I clutch at the wooden handle. This isn't going to be easy. Timmy is going to see things no child should ever have to see. I can't help that. Her appearance in my house isn't my doing or my fault. She can't seem to help herself, this one; with her wandering eyes and loose tongue, she has managed to slither

her way into my life and now I have to get rid of her. None of this is my choice. I didn't ask for it but now I have to end it.

Timmy is kneeling by her limp body as I step inside. Already, I am white hot with fury, a ball of anger burning brightly within me. Who the hell does she think she is, coming here and inducing his pity? He is my boy. Mine and mine alone. My initial thought is to go right over there and bash her brains out, finish what I started earlier, but then I think of Timmy and how he will react, so step carefully into the room instead, doing my best to conceal my fury, to keep it under wraps until he is safely locked away in the bedroom. I don't want him to have to witness this. I don't really want to do it, but needs must. She has dented our plan, intruded on our lives, and now it is time to rectify that aberration.

I can sense their fear as I close the door with a click and pace closer to them. The air is heavy with it, the hot sizzle of anxiety and trepidation hanging over us all. The weight of the hammer behind my back feels reassuringly heavy, the solidity and heft of it causing me to shiver. Violence is always the last resort but if I am going to do this thing, I need it to be efficient and swift.

'Go into the bedroom, Timmy.' My voice is clear, calm. It resonates around the room with a crispness that almost makes me shudder with delight. I feel supremely confident. This is going to be easier than I thought. My authoritative tone surprises even me.

There is a momentary lull before his reply breaks the silence, making me stop and suck in my breath.

'No! I'm not moving and if you try to make me, I'll hit you with this.'

He is brandishing a metal object. It glints under the yellow glare of the overhead strip light. I step closer, unmoved by his threat, and can see that it's a leg that has broken off an old drumming stool that I kept stashed away in the corner. Bless this child. Bless his willingness to do the right thing. One day, he will realise. He will see that sometimes we have to go against the grain and do what is best for us, not what is best for the world at large. This is about our survival – Timmy and me. We need to get through this difficult period of our lives so we can remain together.

'Timmy, my love. That is a lightweight piece of metal. Please put it down. It's useless and won't help you in any way whatsoever.' I can't help but laugh at the sorry sight before me – him standing with a chair leg, and her, that stupid docile woman laid at his feet, her face half bashed in, blood still oozing out of her head. It's comical. The fact that she is half dead is going to make this thing so much easier. 'Now do as I say, back away from her and go in the bedroom. I'm not going to ask you again. Remember last time when you made me hit you because you wouldn't do as I asked?' I produce the hammer from behind my back and hold it aloft, making sure he can see it properly, assess its potential and realise just how much damage it can do.

I stand, waiting for his face to change, to see the look of terror in his eyes, but of course I've misjudged him. This lad is made of sterner stuff. He remains impassive. Any alarm he is feeling is well concealed, hidden behind his steely gaze and inflexible stance. Part of me is proud of him for having a backbone, for being principled and courageous, but then the other part of me is infuriated at him for making this so much harder than it needs to be.

My approach is silent as I shuffle along in tiny barely imperceptible increments, my legs splayed apart in readiness for what I'm about to do. The hammer feels wieldy in my hand, the weight of the metal head causing my fingers to quiver. I lower it slightly, my sluggish deliberate speed impeding my strength.

'Get in the bedroom and close the door, Timmy. Now is not the time for games or disobedience. Just do as I say.'

Even if he refuses, dragging him aside and throwing him in there will take no effort at all. He is as light as air. He may well have a will of iron but in comparison, his body is soft and slender.

Still he refuses to follow my instructions. I shuffle even closer, aware that Sarah is beginning to twitch and move. It's slight and no match for my strength but it's more than I would like to see. I want her motionless, close to death.

I almost reach them and stretch out my free arm to scoop up Timmy with the intention of carrying him off into the bedroom when I feel myself being forced backwards, the weight of his tiny torso pushing at my midriff sending me reeling onto the floor. Shockwaves pulse through me as I lose my grip and the hammer falls out of my hands dropping somewhere behind me. I try to scramble to my feet but I am being held fast by something or somebody. I look up to see Timmy standing over me and Sarah, that deceptive dim-witted woman, holding on to my ankles. I let out a roar of protest, hoping it will scare him, knock him off kilter, but he continues standing there, the hammer clasped between his bony little fingers, his eyes twinkling with delight and a small amount of menace.

'Timmy, put it down. You know you're not strong enough to do this. You know it!'

He grins at me and I am suddenly overcome with a wave of anger so strong, so uncontrollable that I lose all reason. Bucking about ferociously, I manage to free myself of Sarah's grasp, her fingers falling away from my feet. I jump up and throw myself at Timmy but he is already on the move, running towards the door, his small legs carrying him away at a pace that makes me think I could never outrun him. He may be weak and lean but he is also young and fit. Doing my damnedest, I follow him but not before turning around and delivering a hard kick into Sarah's stomach. I want to make absolutely certain she makes no attempt to follow me. Once I reach Timmy, I'll come back for her, finish what I started. This thing isn't over. Far from it. It's just the beginning.

41

SARAH

She curls up into a tight ball, pain pinballing around her stomach, shooting up into her chest, exploding into her nerve endings. Everything is falling away from her, unravelling fast. No way to get it back. And now Moira has gone, intent on catching Leo and bringing him back here. She will kill them both, of that Sarah is certain.

Seconds turn into minutes as she counts, waiting for the excruciating ripples of pain to subside. Time loses all meaning, every second a minute, every minute an hour. It stretches out in front of her, endless, ethereal; the usual intangibility of time now taking on a torturous form with which to taunt her.

After what feels like a lifetime, the sickly twang of pain turns to something less nauseating, something that is marginally bearable. Sarah tries to visualise it, giving it a solid form in her head. She pictures it as a deadweight, a heavy rock that is being slowly rolled away, freeing her crushed body, allowing her to breathe properly. Her lungs pump wildly, inflating and deflating until she feels she has enough oxygen in her bloodstream to move, to swing her body to one side and climb up onto all fours where she stays, gasping for more breath, doing her utmost to embrace the waves of agony that are rolling through her. She can do this. She feels certain she has it in her to get out of this room and help that boy. If she can learn to embrace the hurt, use it to fuel her anger, pushing adrenalin into her system, she may just be in with a chance, albeit a slim one, but a chance all the same. Her body may be battered and broken but her mind is sharper than it has ever been; no longer dulled by domesticity and needless drama, she is at last thinking clearly.

A noise fills the room, gruff and guttural. She stops and waits, wild eyed and terrified before realising it is coming from within, her own visceral reaction to the slightest movement, her body reacting adversely to what she is about to do. It doesn't matter. She is going to continue, refusing to give in. She thinks of Leo and that woman. And the hammer. Her head begins to vibrate, her muscles twitch. Bile rises up from her belly. If Moira manages to retrieve it from him, then God only knows what she is capable of. And for what? Why the fuck is she doing this? What the hell is going on inside her warped demented mind?

No. She can't just stay here. She has to get out there, help him, do whatever she can to get him back home to his mother.

With one final momentous effort, she pushes herself upright, the pain almost making her topple over. She clutches on to the wall to steady herself. The room swims. A pain screeches over her skull, stopping behind her eyes. She counts again, first to ten, then continuing to twenty. Just long enough to focus her attention, to prepare her body and regroup her mind.

Somewhere beyond the confines of the room she hears shouting and then a crash. It catapults her into motion, her legs forcing her on, her brain struggling to keep up.

The door is open. She slams through it, bouncing against the frame as she hits it sideways. A burning pain shoots up her shoulder. She is impervious to it, has suffered far worse in the past hour. She keeps on running – down the hallway, through each room, searching for Leo, shouting his name over and over only to be met with a wall of silence.

Outside. She needs to get out of this house, out into the village and alert people, get them to help Leo and call the police. With liquid legs, her arms pumping furiously at her sides, she turns and heads back into the hallway, the front door a welcoming sight. It has to be unlocked. *Please let it be unlocked.* She all but barges into it, twisting at the handle, grappling with it, and crying out into the eerie silence when the door refuses to budge.

She turns, tears streaming. There has to be another way out of here. And then she remembers what Leo told her about the key that he has. She can't remember which door it fitted. He wouldn't have had the time to escape out of here and lock it behind him, surely? With her body now ahead of her brain, she finds herself charging through the kitchen towards the back of the house.

A cool breeze awaits her, the back door swinging open, a trail of something dark and sticky covering the wooden floor. Her heart leaps up her throat. She visualises Leo, injured somewhere close by, bruised and bleeding, crying for his mother, then thinks back to the resilience he displayed when faced with Moira's threats.

Let him be okay. Dear God, please let him be alive.

Part of her thinks that Moira is fond of the boy, wants to keep him alive, then another part of her remembers with sickening clarity the look on her face in that room, the dead-eyed expression that indicated she had lost all reason and logic as well as all compassion.

And then from outside comes a noise – a scream and the sound of people scuffling, fabric ripping, voices shouting, sounds disappearing as they are carried away by the breeze.

Sarah creeps through the door to the side of the house,

afraid of what she may find there. The trail of blood thins out, turning into a small streak, cotton-like, strands of it dotted about over the back lawn.

Her eyes dart about, sneaking glances around every corner of the garden, scouting for them, trying to detect any movement. Her skin prickles. They are out here somewhere. This is the source of the noise – those shouts and screams – they came from this point, this place. Leo is here in this garden with her. She can sense it, every inch of her skin crawling with revulsion, her mind heightened to the fact that danger is close by.

She spots it after sweeping her eyes along the perimeter of the garden – a hole in the hedgerow. Leaves are scattered on the lawn, over the border, across the recent buds that have emerged from the cold post-winter loam. Creamy yellow primroses and snowdrops with their sad drooping heads are crushed and broken where feet have stampeded across the soil. Foliage from the hedge has been roughly torn apart to reveal an opening through which daylight can be seen. Sarah's breath catches in her throat. Her chest balloons. The hole is small, perhaps too small for her to fit through but she is determined to give it a try. Leo is out there somewhere with that deranged woman and she needs to find him otherwise all of this – her injuries, his attempted escape – will all have been for nothing.

She isn't prepared to accept that scenario. Her own death and Leo being forced back into this house of horrors isn't something she is going to let happen. She will fight it with every breath in her body. Not that she has much fight left. Sarah suspects that her head is still bleeding and that she has several broken ribs. God knows what sort of internal damage she has suffered, but still, she'll do what she can because something deep inside is pushing her on. She is overcome with a need to save Leo, to see him reunited with his mother. She isn't frightened – tender and aching, yes, her body as fragile as it has ever been, but not fearful. Definitely not fearful. She is angry. It burns within her, that rage, white hot flames flickering and blistering her insides.

Her legs are weak as she hobbles over to the gap. Dropping to her knees, she presses her body down onto the ground, her sweater riding up, her belly touching the cold wet earth. She peers through the hole to the garden next door and is greeted with an expanse of green. Her vision blurs, a veil of moisture clinging to her eyelids and lashes while she scans the area for an exit point.

It's there. At the side of the house, a wrought-iron gate that is swinging in the breeze, the squeak of its hinges drowning out the beat of her own heart that is thrashing around like a dying fish inside her, slapping and bashing against her breastbone.

Her backside sticks, becoming snarled in the thorny branches, ripping at her clothes and holding her back. She squirms and rotates her body, freeing herself of the gnarled bits of wood that are hindering her progress. They snap and she springs free, her body slithering forward, the strong scent of the soft dewy earth filling her nostrils as she lands face down in the mud. And the pain, dear God, the eye-watering levels of pain that rip through her, slicing her in two.

All she has to do is make it to that gate and get back into the village. They can't be far. She lifts her head, wipes at her eyes and nose with her sleeve and staggers to her feet, the ground soft and spongy underfoot. It makes the short journey that much harder, keeping her balance on a damp surface that has all the texture of elastic. Patches of sodden moss and concealed rabbit holes cause her to trip and fall on numerous occasions. She stares up at the house. It looks old and neglected. She tries to remember who lives here but it escapes her. No time to ponder over such things anyway.

She passes the window, hammers on it with her fists, then

slips and slides her way over to the patio area, through the open gate, a scribble of inky black metal that towers above her, and down the side of the house that will lead her back into the heart of the village.

Something stops her, a slimy sensation on the ground beneath her feet making her shudder. More blood. A stream of it trickling down the pathway, a small vermillion river, incongruous against the grey concrete. The images that tap at her brain, she pushes away; images of Moira carrying Leo's limp lifeless body back into the house, his head cracked open, his eyes staring up, seeing nothing but endless darkness. She can't let that happen. It isn't the case anyway. She doesn't know how she knows that – she just does. They're out there somewhere. Still alive.

The roar of a passing car catches her attention. It's the whine of a reversing vehicle, shattering the usual calm and quiet of Middleham village.

Ignoring the howl of pain that rips her in half, using it to focus her mind, she staggers down the path, clutching at her sides, trying to work her way through the stabbing sensation that accompanies every single step. She emerges into the light and into the road, blinking.

42

MOIRA

He is fast, I'll give him that but he's young and immature, lacking in the ingenuity and acumen needed to outwit me. This is just a blip. He heads through the house, always ten steps ahead of me, and enters the kitchen where he stands, trying to unlock the door. This gives me an advantage. I reach him just as he grapples with the handle and make a grab at him but he turns and slings the hammer in my direction, a wild hit that catches me on my arm. I lose my balance and fall, my head catching the corner of the kitchen counter.

Thick oily fluid blurs my vision, falling from my head and dripping onto the floor. A gasp escapes unchecked. Then fury rears its head, dark and dense. I won't allow this. He is not going to get away from me. I lost him once, it's not going to happen again. By the time I stagger to my feet he has made it out into the garden and is attempting to shimmy his way through the hedgerow to next door's patch of lawn after checking my eight-foot gate which is double locked with a padlock.

Dizziness hampers my progress but I shake it off, determined to get to him, determined to reclaim my boy. My Timmy. I drop to the floor and manage to grab at his lower half, pulling at his legs. He squirms and cries out. I shuffle through the branches, ignoring the stings of the nettles and the sharp snag of thorns that prick at my skin. His lithe snake-like body slips through the tangle of shrubbery but I too am small and surprisingly supple and manage to hold on to him, grabbing at his arm, reaching for his hand. Grabbing for his fingers and unfurling them from his hold on the hammer. But then he is up on his feet and I am forced to follow him. However, I now have that prized possession; the weapon. I am back in charge. I conceal it under my sweater, aware always of its presence, its weight, the protection it will afford me should I need to use it.

I reach Timmy as he makes it down the side of the house and heads out through the front garden. I grab at his upper arm, pulling him close to me and hiss in his ear, 'Don't you dare say a word, do you hear me?' I turn, press him even closer to me and brandish the hammer, holding it close to his face, trying to cover his body with mine to screen the object from view. 'I can't make any promises that I won't kill you. You know I'll do it if I have to, don't you?' I make sure my voice is threatening, my face furled in anger, my eyes full of fire and menace. We are already on the pavement in full view of the locals. God knows who has seen us, who we may or may not bump into.

He shrinks beside me, nodding furiously, his eyes brimming with tears. I keep my grip on his arm, intent on going back inside away from the curtain twitchers, but then hear something behind us. Shit. It's too late now. We've been spotted. I've got to think on my feet, do something to get us out of this perilous situation. A thought forms in my brain. It's not ideal but given the circumstances, it's the best I can come up with.

I am in no doubt that we cut a sorry sight, the pair of us, as we stumble down the road, our shadowy outlines incongruous and distressing against the backdrop of the sinking sun; one small silhouette, one larger person, bent almost double, clutching hands as we attempt to break into a run, only to falter and fall by the roadside, landing in an ungainly heap together. Timmy's cries fill the air, drowning out the birdsong from the treetops and nearby hedgerows.

The car approaches, getting nearer to where we lie, the roar of its engine too close for comfort. It rounds the bend, metal and sunlight colliding in a sudden eye-watering flash. We stand up, cry out, wave our arms about in a frantic show of desperation. Timmy tries to run, then stumbles and falls, as I hold him close, the hammer pressing against his chest, reminding him to stay quiet, to be amenable and compliant and do exactly as I say. The vehicle drives past us, and I almost turn and walk away, dragging him with me, but then it slows down, grinding to a sudden halt, the gravelly sound of rubber against tarmac pounding in my ears. Timmy stands up, screams for help, sobs loudly as the car begins to reverse, the high-pitched whine of the engine a screech in my ears.

'Do exactly as I say or I will kill both you and this driver,' I bellow at him, my face only inches away from his.

He nods, tears dripping, snot cascading out of his nose in great wet bubbles.

The driver's door opens, a man steps out, his expression pained and bewildered, turning soon to panic as he stares first at Timmy then back at me, huddled at his side, doing my best to appear helpless and desperate.

'Please,' I whimper as I hold on to my head. Blood continues to ooze through my fingers. 'Please help us. You have to do something.' I clutch at the hammer behind my back, biding my time, glancing at the car, thinking how unfortunate it will be to ruin the interior when it gets splattered with this man's blood and brain matter.

Timmy begins to cry again; an ear-splitting howl that could shatter glass. I tighten my grip on his arm, pretending to comfort him, giving him a dark threatening stare but am suddenly unsteady on my feet, the wound on my head still throbbing.

'I'll help you,' the man says as he opens the passenger door and pushes Timmy inside. Before I have time to protest, the man grabs my arm, knocking me off balance and forces me against the back door of the car. 'I know who you are. I fucking know you and I know what you did.'

In a flurry of terror and blind panic, I cry out before being bundled into the back seat. I hear the sharp slam of the door and the click of the lock, realisation dawning that we are both trapped. It doesn't matter. This helps my plan. Let him think I am helpless. I play along, pulling at the handle, crying out for help, clawing at the seat as the driver climbs back in and starts the engine, pulling off at speed.

Timmy starts to speak, to tell his story to this stranger. I lean forward, catch his eye, tap the hammer in my upturned palm and give him a wink.

It works. He is suddenly silent, slumping down in his seat, his limbs frozen, his face ashen.

'You,' the driver says, staring through the rear-view mirror as he glares at me. 'It's you. Don't move or speak.' His voice is low, authoritative. It doesn't faze me but once again, I play his little game, pretend to be the victim as I object, my shouts reverberating around the confined space.

He takes me by surprise, that much I will admit, as a hand connects with my flesh, taking my breath away as the driver swings around, fist clenched and smashes it into my face, silencing me in seconds before turning back to grip the steering wheel. 'I said, don't speak, okay? Don't say a single word. I know exactly who you are. I've heard about this on the television, read about it. You're a fucking psychopath. People like you should be hanged. You're nothing but scum.'

Pretending to be dazed, I slump back into the seat, more

blood pumping through my fingers, saturating my clothes; sticky warm blood oozing in great waves, coating my skin, clothes, the upholstery of the vehicle.

'I hope they arrest you,' the driver says, the words loaded with venom as he spits them out and stares in the rear-view mirror, 'and throw away the fucking key.'

'She's going to kill us both!' Timmy pulls at the door handle in a vain bid to escape, then shrinks down into the well beneath his feet as I bring the hammer up above my head.

The thud shakes the entire car, darkness enveloping us as a shadow appears out of nowhere and lands on the windscreen. Outside there is a scream, a hollow gurgling sound and then nothing. Rubber screeches against tarmac, the car swerving to a sudden halt. The hammer falls out of my hands. I have no idea where it lands. Confusion reigns. The shadow is still splayed across the windscreen. And then there is a moan, a thin desperate cry for help coming from somewhere within the vehicle.

I scramble forwards and see it – the blood seeping out of Timmy's head, the hammer resting awkwardly on his lap, the look of terror in his eyes as he twists in his seat to look at me.

'No! Dear God, no!' I barely recognise my own voice, its strangulated frantic tone, the grating pitch. They were empty threats to make him comply. I didn't want this. I never wanted him to get hurt.

The driver is already out of the car, tending to whoever or whatever is draped there, over the bonnet. This is my chance, my only way out of this. I clamber into the passenger seat, grapple with the door and drag Timmy out, refusing to look at his face, at that wound. At what I did. This is all wrong. Everything is shifting away from me. I need to get it back.

'Don't you fucking move!' Beside me stands the driver of the vehicle. Next to him, laid on the floor is Sarah, her mouth moving, no noise emerging.

I see an opportunity, take my chance. 'She's the one you should be accusing! I found this boy in her house. She kidnapped him and God knows what else she did to him while he was there.'

Timmy starts to protest, his voice reedy and waif-like. I shove him behind me, pressing him close to me to muffle his voice, his head pushed into my back.

'Look what she did! She's a maniac. What sort of sane person would throw themselves in front of a moving vehicle? She did it to try and get the boy back.'

The driver stares first at me then back at Sarah. He is panting now, his eyes wide as his head swivels back and forth between me and her. I can see the doubt creeping in, the uncertainty as his eyes flicker, his skin turns pale, his posture becoming less rigid while his brain tries to register what the hell is going on here.

'I rescued him from her house. She is completely unhinged.'

All the while I take steps backwards, Timmy still pressed close to me. If I can get back in that vehicle, get away from here, just me and my boy, everything will be fine. We can leave this place, drive far away from here and leave it all behind us. I glance at the car, wondering if the keys are still in the ignition, trying to think of somewhere we could go, a secret place where nobody will ever find us.

'She's lying!'

He breaks free. A momentary lapse of concentration, that was all it was – a second of overthinking and Timmy is away from me and running towards the man who is standing aghast, his jaw slack and eyes liquid and full of confusion as he tries to work out his next move.

I don't have time for this. It is against me, seconds and

minutes slipping away. Every moment that passes is a step closer to Timmy persuading this man, giving him time to work out what is really going on here. I need to move and I need to do it now. At the minute the village is quiet, all the locals still at work, but soon they will return and they will see this spectacle and then I will have lost. That can't happen.

I run to the car, wrestle with the driver's door, knowing what I have to do next. I can't get Timmy. He's too close to the driver. But he's not so close to Sarah, to her lifeless body that is lying next to the front wheel. I have another way out of this, another plan to get him back.

As hoped, the driver has left the keys dangling there. Relief and opportunity bloom within me. If I can do this next part with enough accuracy, then Timmy is mine for the taking.

The engine kicks into life. I rev it up, reverse slightly and wait, assessing the distance, the level of precision needed to do this. My heart begins to thump, my nerves screaming at me to get a move on and get it over with. I can't hit Timmy. He is my life, everything I have ever wanted. My reason for living. I have to get this right. I need to hone every skill that I have and hit her straight on. She is one less person to deal with, one less interfering do-gooder that I shan't miss. Once she is out of the way, I can concentrate on getting Timmy away from this man. I should have ignored his car, gone back to my house and taken my chances with Sarah. I could have got away with it if she hadn't been such a stupid bitch and thrown herself into the road.

Pressing my foot to the floor and keeping my eyes fixed firmly on her body, I feel the propulsion of the moving vehicle, its weight and intensity as I am slung forwards at a rapid pace. I am rocked by the thud and crunch, hitting something ahead of me. There is a sudden spinning sensation as the vehicle veers out of control. An involuntary growl pushes out of my throat when I see it. A split second, that's all it is; her body to one side, untouched, still twitching, still moving, but no sign of the driver and no Timmy. Fire burns in my head, flickering down over my flesh; flames biting at every inch of my skin. Dear God, what have I done? What the hell have I done?

The dark limbs of the tree spin before me, a knotty tangle of claws reaching out, grasping and covetous. Then the dark rough bark of the huge trunk in my peripheral vision, growing closer. Time loses all meaning. I am suspended in a void. I feel a solid painful thud, the crunch of my own bones hitting plastic and metal. Then nothing.

43

LYNDA

She squeezes Emily's hand, the enormity of the situation still sinking in. Even now, after almost two weeks, it all seems terribly surreal. Their once peaceful existence has been shattered, torn asunder and thrown into the four winds by recent events.

Bubbling clouds scud across a salmon sky, dark and ominous, obliterating the sun. A spot of rain hits the ground, splashing at Lynda's feet. She steps back, away from the crowds, keeping her head low for fear of photographers taking snapshots at such a horribly inappropriate time. They were asked to stay away by family and the police but already she has spotted somebody lurking near the hedgerow that surrounds the churchyard; a man with a camera slung around his neck and a disingenuous look on his face. His eyes dart around as he watches and waits, hoping to catch a glimpse of the coffin as it pulls up by the roadside. Some people have no shame. *Still*, thinks Lynda, *it's what the public want to see and read, what they demand. Reporters only report what people want to hear.*

'It's here.' Emily's voice is brittle, tinged with apprehension.

Lynda turns to see the hearse pull up; a sleek back car

adorned with white flowers atop an oak casket. A bubble of air catches in her throat. She swallows, rubs at her eyes and takes a deep breath. Emily is young, easily dented. Lynda has to help her through this. She has found this whole thing incredibly difficult to deal with. Perhaps it should be Lynda who is struggling through this time, and yet it isn't. Moira was her friend. She thought she knew her. She didn't. It has taught her that none of us really knows anybody as well as we think we do. Folk have hidden depths. In Moira's case her secrets were so well tucked away, hidden so many fathoms down, that Lynda could never have guessed at what was going on in her mind. She has seen much in her life and thinks that perhaps her many experiences has armed her with a tough veneer, helping her to cope in this crisis but never in a million years could she have guessed at the intricacies of Moira's life, the dark secrets that she kept from everybody, including her purported best friend.

Since this terrible gruesome event, she has also sought help for her own feelings about the loss of her child, the baby boy she was forced to give away. An appointment has been made to see a counsellor which is a huge step for her, unaccustomed as she is to opening up and speaking about her innermost feelings and emotions. She will do her best to co-operate, to talk when she feels comfortable and alleviate the load that has been sitting with her for so long now that she is almost certain she will float away into the ether once it is lifted, her body and mind free of the burden that has been pressing down on her for all of her adult life.

She feels Emily sway, her body crumpling slightly as the coffin is lifted out and placed on the shoulders of the waiting men. At the far side of the crowd, Lynda spots Celine, Leo's mother. She catches her eye, gives her a small smile and feels a lump rise in her throat. A tear escapes out of her eye and rolls down her cheek. Lynda lifts her hand and waves at Celine who returns the small gesture. A certain amount of pride swells in her chest. They are here, united by grief, by what they have been through. A group of people ready to pay their respects to a perfect stranger who gave his life to save those around him. A man who gave his life to save Leo Fairland and to save Sarah.

Maxine, Ewan's wife, steps out of one of the cars, her head dipped, her eyes concealed behind a pair of dark glasses. Lynda's knees begin to give way as she watches this lady attempt to stand upright and hold herself in a dignified manner A heavy presence on Lynda's arm hoists her back up. Emily moves closer, holding her tightly, gripping her hand as the coffin is carried into the church, the mourners following in a slow-moving huddle. So much hurt, so many victims. They all fell prey to Moira's dreadful actions, to a plan she set in motion to steal what she felt sure was hers and hers alone.

Even now, she believes that Leo is her son, the baby she claims to have lost. Lynda doesn't know her at all and if she is being perfectly honest, never did. It was all a façade, an act. The real Moira is the one they see now, the twisted damaged Moira who has ruined so many lives. The twisted damaged Moira who killed this man, made his wife a widow, left his children fatherless. And despite being her friend for almost a decade, Lynda knows she can never forgive her. They are strangers now, people who just happened to live close to one another.

The service is a sombre affair but thankfully swift. Everybody leaves, Lynda and Emily filtering away leaving the throng of mourners far behind as they make their way back to Emily's car.

'I wonder how she is today,' Lynda says as they slide into their seats.

'Hopefully better than yesterday,' Emily replies, putting the car into gear and heading out onto the main road. 'She still looked like she'd been kicked by a horse when I visited. I can't believe how long it's taking for that bruising to go down.'

'Yes. She does look pretty dreadful. Still,' Lynda murmurs, staring out of the window at the thinning crowds, 'at least she's alive. If Moira had had her way, Sarah wouldn't be here now. That man,' she says, rubbing at her eyes and shaking her head. 'That poor man. Wrong place, wrong time. He could have driven past. He could have ignored it but he didn't. He did the right thing and look where that got him. Sometimes, there really isn't any justice in this world.'

Emily moves her hand away from the gearstick, squeezes Lynda's cold fingers and gives her a smile. There was a time, not so long ago, when such a tactile move wouldn't have been possible between these two, but things have changed, the landscape of their existence transformed beyond recognition.

'I think,' Emily says softly as she manoeuvres her way through a street of parked cars, slaloming her way through deftly and emerging out the other side onto a wider road, 'that sometimes we have to accept what has happened and move on otherwise we'll be forever caught in a trap of our own making. Our minds will get stuck in a groove. As long as we learn from our experiences then it's no bad thing to try and forget this time in our lives and push forward.'

Lynda clutches at her locket, the one that Sarah managed to keep safe throughout the attack, and nods her head, thinking how wise her friend is for somebody so young. Joel and Mo are lucky to have this astute, intelligent creature in their lives.

'Coffee at mine?' Lynda says as they push through the traffic and head back to Middleham. 'You can meet Rufus. He's kept me sane for the past month, helped me see through the fog that almost swallowed me whole.'

'Coffee sounds perfect,' Emily replies. 'As long as there's cake on offer as well.'

44

He opens the note, his fingers trembling. He doesn't like unexpected occurrences. Not in his life. Not after what he did. Gaynor has slipped away after handing it to him, as if she knows its contents, realising that they could possibly be private and personal.

His heart pounds as he lifts out the slip of paper. Who would send him a note at the community centre? After the recent bout of graffiti his senses are heightened, his nerve endings blazing beneath his skin. For all of his adult life he has made sure that every aspect of his life is carefully planned and executed. No surprises, pleasant or otherwise, just precision and predictability. It's easier that way. He won't get caught out and always knows what his next move is going to be.

The words blur on the page, swaying and dancing before his eyes as he scans the writing then starts again, this time reading it carefully, letting every word settle comfortably under his skin.

He tries to say the words out loud to himself, just to be sure that he isn't hallucinating, that this letter is real, something tangible and true and not a figment of his imagination.

Dear Andrew,

I hope you don't mind me calling you that. Don't worry, from this point on, you will be known to me as Ashton but I couldn't continue without letting you know that it is me, Lynda Croft. I saw that you recognised me and I think you realised that I, too, recognised you. Things have happened lately that have made me reassess everything I thought I knew about what I have experienced and I felt that I had to write to you as you were and still are, a part of my life.

I would like to continue to attend your classes and will be bringing a couple of new friends with me if that's acceptable? Moira, the lady who came with me last time I was there, will no longer be attending but that is a story for another time.

Our days together at that school often seem like such a long time ago but then there are times when it feels like only yesterday. I am not going to go into details or rake over ancient history but I just want you to know that I never wanted to speak against you. You were a child and I cared for you. Still do. We may not be friends but we have a shared history, a kind of bond, and I feel duty-bound to tell you this, to clear both my conscience and the air. It will make it easier for us in the future if I say these things. No more furtive glances across the room. No more secrets.

I apologise for what I was forced to do and say in that courtroom and I want you to know that I understand about your upbringing and how it affected you deeply, more than most will ever know. I'm not a particularly demonstrative person but I do understand people and I want to say sorry for everything you have been through.

I fear that the graffiti may have been the result of my loose tongue whilst in company with somebody I thought was a friend. She is no longer in my life and no longer a threat to your anonymity, but once again, that is a story for another time.

Please take this letter in the manner in which it is intended – with sincerity and friendship.

Thank you for reading it, Ashton. Onward and upwards.

Regards,

Lynda

He focuses on his breathing, blinking repeatedly to clear his misted vision. Can it be that this thing, this secret that he has carried around for so long, may at long last become something he can put behind him? Is it truly possible that he is now allowed to continue with the upward curve of his life without any hindrances or obstacles being thrown his way?

His fingers grip the paper as he thinks about that other boy. He no longer has any contact with him but his mother has kept her ear to the ground over the intervening years and has heard that he now lives in London, has a good job with a finance company and is married. That feels good, knowing that he has managed to live his life positively and not been damaged by what Ashton did.

And now with Lynda offering the hand of friendship, the sun has finally begun to peek through the clouds of his overcast world. This is more than he could have ever hoped for. It's a better outcome than he ever dreamed possible.

He places the paper back in the envelope as Gaynor reappears, poking her head around the office doorway, a grin fixed on her face. 'All set for tonight, then?'

'All set,' Ashton whispers, his voice cracking with emotion, his heart soaring up into the heavens.

45

SARAH

The pain is easing, thank God. She watches the birds out of her window, thinking how wonderful it will feel to be out there with them as soon as she is able. The doctors have said she just needs rest and time. Her broken body will heal, her mind, however, may take a little longer.

There are days when it all feels surreal and dreamlike, as if it happened to somebody else, and then there are times when it hits her like a truck, slamming into her brain over and over, how close she came to death, the blows that were repeatedly meted out by Moira. Kicks and punches to her face, her ribs, every part of her body. She has never known such pain. But as for fear – that didn't register. She knows that she is no hero, not the hero the newspapers have made her out to be, but terror didn't have time to muscle its way into her brain. All she could focus on was saving Leo and her own survival.

What the incident did was prove to her that her sense of self-preservation is strong, that she is far more resilient than she ever knew. She isn't the weak feckless individual she thought herself to be. She is stronger than that, has some fight in her. Enough to save Leo and enough to save herself.

But not enough to save her marriage. That is one part of her life she is prepared to let go. It isn't worth saving. All those years, all that effort she put into it, and for what? To discover that her husband is a serial philanderer and sex pest, moving through people's lives, tearing them to shreds and leaving them utterly devastated before moving on to his next conquest. She was wrong for so many years, believing she needed Malcolm by her side, that she couldn't function without him. It was a line he fed her, a subtle barely discernible narrative that she was drip-fed over so many years that she began to believe it – the idea that she was better off being home to cater to him, that his working away provided her with more than she could ever need. He was wrong. She was naïve. But not anymore. Being close to death has given her a new lease of life. For so long she simply existed. It's now time to start living.

Malcolm has moved out of the house with a view to selling it. That is something she definitely wants to do. Too many memories here. Too much bitterness. It's too big for her anyway. This place was always about status and being recognised as successful. None of that matters to her now. That was a different Sarah. She has broken out of her chrysalis and is seeing the world through fresh informed eyes. She will find a smaller house similar to Emily's. It will be good for her. She can make it her own, put her own special touches to it. It will give her something to look forward to.

Emily and Lynda have been unbelievably supportive, the pair of them her main reason for getting out of bed every morning. After the incident, after finding out about Malcolm and what he did, things seemed bleak, but their presence in her life has been uplifting, reminding her of what is important and what is superfluous to requirements and best forgotten.

They brought her home from hospital, have helped

administer her medication, but more importantly than that, they have helped her to smile again, to leave behind that nasty trail of bitterness that used to trail in her wake. She is alive again after so many years of being half dead.

And it feels wonderful.

46

MOIRA

They've been questioning me relentlessly, trying to work out what makes me tick, why I did what I did. I don't slot neatly into their boxes, you see, their profile of how a kidnapper should be. I'm a reserved middle-aged woman living in a large house in a small village. I have no criminal record. I've never even been stopped for speeding. They have nothing on me, nothing at all. I'm their enigma, their human paradox, the one they cannot fathom. I have plumbed to new depths and they do not like it. Women in my demographic don't do such things.

They keep asking me why I did what I did. I have told them time and time again what happened but they don't seem to believe me. It looks like I'm going to be here for some time which I suppose is a good thing. I need as much time as possible to adapt to my surroundings, to come to terms with my life from this point on.

They claim they have access to my medical records and have sent in psychologists to assess me, to get me to say things that will prove to them that I am mad, losing the plot, teetering on the brink of insanity, call it what you will. But so far, they have found nothing to back up their flimsy claims that I am mentally unstable.

That's because I'm not.

Sometimes, people get to a point in their life when they simply refuse to endure any more of the misery that is heaped upon them by others. I am at that point. I reached it quite a few years ago but managed to maintain an aura of calm, always emanating a peaceable and tranquil air when I was in company. I've had years of heartbreak, you see. Years and years and years of it, and at some point, even the strongest of branches snap. I bent with the wind for most of my life until eventually I broke, did some things, and now there is no going back. I have reached the point of no return.

I know that they don't believe my story, or actually care enough to listen as deeply as they should, but that is their problem and has nothing to do with me. If they had taken the time to understand what I was saying, they would realise that I didn't do these things alone. My crime is a shared one. Nothing in life ever happens in isolation. For each action, there is an equal and opposite reaction. That's indisputable. It's part of Newton's Third Law of Motion. Things happened to me that set off a chain reaction. I am not saying that I am not responsible for what I did, I'm simply stating that I wasn't alone in this sad and desperate journey. Others around me are just as culpable. They too need to look at their actions, to take a long hard look at how they pushed me, used me, hung me out to dry like a piece of old rag. They are just as much to blame and have helped make me what I am today.

Timmy was my baby, my child. The only child I ever had. After Jack died, I was very much alone. We may not have had the best of marriages but it wasn't until after he passed away that I realised how difficult it was, being on my own, battling the feelings of isolation and solitude that ate away at me day after day after day. I had never known loneliness before. I had always spent my life being surrounded by other people, going out to work every day, teaching other people's children. It hit me hard. Being alone wasn't how I expected it to be. Far from it. I only knew a handful of people in Middleham at the time. There was no Lynda to help me out. I had nobody.

And then one day, I spoke to someone, a person who showed me kindness, stopped to chat, told me I needn't be by myself and that he would always be around for me. Things escalated, probably went further than they should have. I ended up seeing Malcolm as often as I could. He would spend days at my house under the pretence of working away. His wife had no idea. Poor little Sarah, only yards away while I had her husband all to myself for days at a time. We lived in our own little enclave, spending our time locked together in secretive bliss.

And then it happened. I didn't plan it. I was forty-five years old at the time. It was my first baby. Jack and I hadn't thought about having children. We didn't avoid having any, it just never happened for us. Malcolm's reaction was less than positive when I told him. He said I had done it on purpose, had tried to deliberately trap him. We fought. He said things that were deliberately designed to hurt me, so I hit him, slapping him across the face. I think perhaps I even threw things at him. It's all such a blur now.

We parted, him saying that if I told his wife about our affair, he would simply deny it, write me off as an eccentric old woman. I had no intention of telling Sarah about our time together. After the way he reacted, I no longer cared about Malcolm. All I wanted was my baby. Alas, it was not to be.

I gave birth to Timmy after keeping my pregnancy secret from the outside world. We lived at home, just the two of us, happy together in our own company for a while. Nobody needed to know about him. He was mine and mine alone. My beautiful delightful boy. We needed nobody else.

And then one day I got up, and he was gone; no Timmy, just a pale face and a limp body. No breath left in him. I told nobody. Why would they need to know? Timmy was all I had ever needed and he had known nobody but me. We had our own special relationship. He was my guilty secret, my reason for living after Jack had gone and Malcolm had abandoned me so I decided to keep him with me. Sending him away with a team of strangers was unthinkable. I set about finding a place for him in the garden, the same garden where he played recently after he came back to me. I always knew I would find him, that he wouldn't stay dead for forever. He was my little gift from heaven. The boy I lost, returned to me when I least expected it.

I've tried telling the police this but they stare at me vacant-eyed, a glazed expression on their faces. How can I possibly expect them to understand the depth of the relationship Timmy and I had? These people are plain-minded, unused to delving into the intricacies of the human psyche. They want black and white answers to questions that are peppered with colour. Soon I will stop talking to them. They don't deserve my time or patience. I have been through enough already. Do I not deserve some lenience at this troubling time?

They have told me that they've scanned the garden, dug it up and torn it apart and found no evidence of a child's body. They think that I'm lying, that I made it all up, fabricated the pregnancy and spun a lie so big, so outlandishly absurd to cover myself and garner pity and sympathy that it is an insult to my intelligence. Why would I do such a thing? It's preposterous. Timmy is there. I know he is. He just doesn't want to be found.

Yesterday, the leading detective mentioned Jack, asking me questions about our marriage, probing me about whether or not we were happy. I told him that we were as happy as any average couple. The detective denied my words, told me that Jack, in the run up to his death, had sought advice from a solicitor about getting a divorce. The detective said we were on the verge of splitting up. I told him he was deluded and that he knew nothing about Jack and me. I know what they're hinting at. It's only a matter of time before they come right out and say it.

They think I pushed him off that ladder. They are trying to blame me for his death. It's absolute nonsense. They are grasping at straws. What do they know anyway? They're police officers, more used to stopping people for speeding and dealing with minor shoplifting offences in a small village than solving a murder. And they are not, by any stretch of the imagination, marriage guidance counsellors. It's a desperate ploy to pin something else on me. They are trying to add more deaths to the list. I won't co-operate with them. It is my right to remain silent and if they keep on taking the line that I killed my own husband, then I will stop speaking altogether.

I didn't mean to kill him really, that man. He just got in the way. He was trying to stop me getting to Timmy. He shouldn't have done that. He had no right and now he has paid a hefty price.

Having Timmy back with me for the short amount of time that I did renewed my sense of purpose. It wasn't easy. I'm not going to pretend that it all went really smoothly because it didn't. I could have planned it better, been a nicer parent to him. He pined after his other mother, the one who stole him from me. She made it difficult for him to settle at his new home. But what joy I got in that short space of time, knowing he was under the same roof as me, even if he was difficult and unruly towards the end.

And how fortuitous that Lynda mentioned the reappearance of Andrew Gilkes in her life. It gave me the opportunity to divert the attention over to him and push the finger of suspicion in his direction. I didn't need to do too much to set the ball rolling. That's the thing with social media and online interaction, it gave me the freedom to stir up a hornet's nest of worry, hatred and anxiety. I created an anonymous account and set about dropping in comments on a Facebook local community page about a convicted paedophile being back in town, letting it slip where he worked and what he was up to. I didn't have to mention any names. Keyboard warriors and trolls don't need to know the finer details. All they need is a grain of information, truthful or not, to set them going, to unleash their inner bile and hatred.

I didn't wish him any harm; it just helped to deflect any attention away from me, shift everyone's radar elsewhere. I hoped he wouldn't get hurt but wasn't entirely certain that some random stranger wouldn't take it upon themselves to dole out their own form of vigilante justice. It was a chance I took and it worked out well in the end. Somebody taking it upon themselves to daub a building was perfect, better than I could have expected. There are so many uninformed people out there who feel they are championing somebody's cause, taking it upon themselves to be the defender of all that is just and right. It is actually rather frightening. And of course, I may well see the colour of their anger once my story hits the papers. That's because they don't understand my position and could never truly comprehend why I did what I did and nor do I expect them to. They have their lives and I have mine.

I sometimes wonder what would have happened had I not driven past the school that day. Life is full of what ifs and maybes, isn't it? We could go round and round in circles questioning our choices, driving ourselves mad with the many possible permutations and trajectories our lives could take. However, I did drive past and although I am not a religious woman, I like to think it was some kind of divine intervention that brought me and Timmy together. I firmly believe that our paths in life are set, everything we do preordained, each of us travelling on a route from which we cannot deviate.

There is no point in looking back. It's a waste of time. I must now look to the future, uncertain as it is, and try to be positive. I hope whoever has Timmy is caring for him. I've asked the police to pass on my love to him and to tell him that I never meant him any harm. All I wanted to do was love him in the best way I knew how.

Lynda hasn't been in touch and I don't expect she will. We live separate lives now. Whether or not she is able to understand my motives and forgive me is another matter entirely. I like to think she will see things through my eyes but am not holding out too much hope. I have to accept that I am here indefinitely, or at least until they decide what to do with me. Is there hope for a woman like me who doesn't slot neatly into the usual category of kidnapper and murderer? Is there a place for a woman like me who has been used and rejected, lived a life of suppression until she finally snaps and does something terrible and unforgivable? I do hope so. I really do, or all of this will have been for nothing. I like to think that something good will come out of this period of my life, otherwise what is the point?

Soon they will come for me, take me out of this dark little cell and question me some more. I am all out of answers. I have nothing left to give. In the meantime I will sit here and devote my time and thoughts to Timmy, hoping he is being loved and cared for, hoping that he remembers me the way I want to be remembered – as a thoughtful loving mother who never stood a chance in a callous uncaring world.

A spider skitters across the floor, stopping at my feet. It doesn't scare me, this tiny worthless creature. I bring up my foot to stamp on it but then think better of it and instead pick it up and place it near the bars on the window in the hope it finds its way to freedom, because after all, we all need as much help as we can get in this busy unsettling world.

I watch as it slinks between the cracks and disappears out of sight, then smile. It makes me feel good knowing I helped somebody or something in some small way because let's face it, I'm a middle-aged, middle-class woman, not a monster.

EPILOGUE

The sun makes a rare appearance as they shake out the picnic blanket and lay it on the ground. Celine watches her boy as he kicks the football about in the distance. She is tempted to follow him, to monitor his every move and keep him so close to her that he can barely breathe, but knows that it simply is not possible if they are to pick up the pieces of their life and continue on their journey together as a normal family. She is treating Leo's disappearance as a learning curve, something they can all use to better themselves.

Jason opens the picnic hamper and pours out two cups of coffee, handing her one with a small amount of diffidence. They are trying harder with their marriage. Jason is back in work and although it doesn't sit easily with her, they have made some money by selling their story to the highest bidder.

At least this way, she can give up work and make sure Leo is never left alone again. It all makes perfect sense to her and besides, she feels that they have earned it for all the suffering and heartbreak they have endured. The media painted her as a terrible mother, somebody who valued her job and money above her own child, leaving him on his own outside the school, night after night after night. If only they had known about the eye-watering debts they had accrued while Jason was out of work and how she was working around the clock to try and pay them off. If only they had seen the levels of depression into which her husband had slunk, how he became a shadow of his former self, his expression pained and haunted, his body thin and wiry. Most days, he was barely able to get out of bed. At one point, he moved out of their family home and went to live with his parents on the west coast in a bid to get himself together. But that's all behind them now and the money they received has helped ease the pain that the media and the keyboard warriors put her through. She feels vindicated. She has her family back together and although Leo still suffers nightmares, he is definitely somewhere close to being the boy he used to be before it all happened and that is all she wants; her boy back to his usual buoyant self, her family unit together once more.

Birds take flight from a nearby field, scattering up into the cobalt sky in one swift hazy movement, their small bodies peppered against the landscape, their cries filtering through the cloudless swathe of blue.

'Leo! Come and get a sandwich.'

He comes running, the football firmly lodged under his arm, his grin making her chest swell with love and contentment. The thought that he survived what he did and made an escape will never leave her, the memory and sense of pride she felt and still feels, forever staying in her consciousness. Her boy, the real hero. Once Sarah is well enough, they will visit her, say thank you properly. Perhaps even take some flowers and arrange a lunch in a nice restaurant. It's the least they can do. Without her, Leo would still be stuck in that awful house with that deranged woman. The thought that he survived what he did and made an escape will never leave her, the memory and sense of pride she felt and still feels, forever staying in her consciousness. The scar on his head from the attack is still visible but in time will fade. No lasting damage fortunately. Her boy, the real hero.

Jason leans across, takes her hand and squeezes it, dragging her back to the present. Enough of raking over old ground, torturing herself with what could have been. She leans forward, plants a kiss on his forehead, thinks how lucky she is for this moment in time, how fortunate she is to be experiencing this day in all its grandeur and beauty. They are here, her husband and her boy, and that, she thinks, is all she needs.

The breezes settles, the sun resting gently on the back of her neck as she pulls Leo close to her, closes her eyes and embraces the moment.

THE END

ACKNOWLEDGEMENTS

Writing this book was a bit of a milestone. Just over four years ago, I received an email from Betsy Reavley at Bloodhound Books offering me a contract to publish my first book, *Undercurrent*. Four years later and here I am writing the acknowledgements for my 10th novel. What a rollercoaster of a ride it has been with many ups and downs and a steep learning curve thrown in for good measure.

As always, there are so many people to thank that I worry about missing many of them out, but here goes. Firstly, another big thank you to Fred Freeman and Betsy Reavley for publishing my writing. Without your assistance I would still be stuck at home, wondering when somebody is going to finally take on my endeavours and publish them. Thank you to Clare Law, my editor, for making the whole thing such a painless and dare I say it, enjoyable process! Your words and guidance are always wise and well received. Thank you to Tara Lyons and the rest of the team at Bloodhound Books for your help and assistance. You guys are the greatest.

I am also lucky enough to have the best ARC readers in the

world. To each and every one of you, a huge thank you. Here's to another ten novels!

Online book clubs provide writers who work in isolation with such a massive network of support. I cannot imagine how lonely it must have been in times gone by when writers had to sit in a room and type away without touching base with readers and other authors, so in no particular order I would like to say a huge thank you to: Book Mark, Fiction Book Club, Crime Fiction Addict, The Paperback Writers, UK Crime Book Club, Meet the Authors, Skye's Mum and Books, A Love of Books, Book on the Positive Side, North East Authors and Readers, The Fiction Café Book Club, Crime Book Club, Reading Between the Lines and Psychological Suspense Authors' Association. Apologies if I have missed anybody out. There is so much support out there that it is amazing.

My family have provided me with a massive amount of help over the years. Thank you to each and every one of you. I couldn't have done it without you.

Finally, my thanks go to you, the reader, for taking the time to buy and read my book. With so much choice out there, I am honoured that you chose me. Reviews are always welcome!

Should you feel like chatting or getting in touch, please feel free to contact me at:

www.facebook.com/thewriterjude
www.twitter.com/thewriterjude
judebaker41@gmail.com

Made in the USA
Middletown, DE
25 January 2021